MAFIO$O

PART FOUR

Melodrama Publishing
www.MelodramaPublishing.com

FOLLOW
NISA SANTIAGO

FACEBOOK.COM/NISASANTIAGO

INSTAGRAM.COM/NISA_SANTIAGO

TWITTER.COM/NISA_SANTIAGO

Order online at
bn.com, amazon.com, and
MelodramaPublishing.com

This is a work of fiction. All of the characters, organizations, and events portrayed in this novel are either products of the author's imagination or are used fictitiously.

Mafioso - Part Four. Copyright © 2018 by Melodrama Publishing. All rights reserved. No part of this book may be used or reproduced in any manner whatsoever without written permission except in the case of brief quotations embodied in critical articles or reviews. For information, address info@melodramabooks.com.

www.melodramapublishing.com

Library of Congress Control Number: 2017909508
ISBN-13: 978-1620780831

First Edition: July 2018

Printed in Canada

MAFIO$O

PART FOUR

NISA SANTIAGO

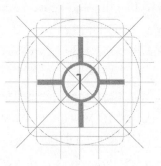

NewYork-Presbyterian Hospital was one of the best in the city. It was affiliated with two Ivy League medical schools and was one of the world's busiest hospitals. And tonight, Presbyterian became a whole lot busier. The admission of two men created commotion in the lobby, the emergency room, and the exterior of the building. The presence of the FBI loitering about made folks' heads swivel back and forth, and the gossip started. Who were the agents here for? Who was hurt and why? Was it the mafia? A drug kingpin? A killer? Questions circulated through the hospital as things looked like they were spinning out of control with visitors, agents, and doctors.

Bugsy was the first to arrive at the hospital. He raced to Presbyterian with his carload of goons, including Choppa, to visit his father. The news of his father being shot multiple times was terrifying, and the presence of law enforcement was worrisome. But despite the discomfort Bugsy felt, he knew Scott needed him.

Maxine was there to meet him, and she was frantic with grief. She had been crying since the incident. "They're not telling me anything, and they won't let me see him. All they would say was that he was in surgery," she told Bugsy.

"What they got on him?"

Maxine shook her head. "Drugs, I guess. It all happened so fast, Bugsy. Scott thought it was a hit, and before I could fully process the scene, he was shot. They treated us like shit and kept screaming that he was a drug kingpin and he was going away for life."

"Don't worry," Bugsy said to the teary-eyed Maxine. "I'll handle things from here."

Agents were everywhere, implementing their strict protocol within the limits of the hospital. The victim was under arrest and a drug kingpin—allegedly. Maxine figured Bugsy could use his position and influence to find out what was happening. He was Scott's son; she was only his girlfriend.

Bugsy walked over to the nurses station to get an update.

"Patient's name?"

"West."

"He just got here. They're prepping him for surgery."

"He's already *in* surgery. We're waiting for an update from his surgeon."

"Sir," she snapped. "I know you people are used to—"

"You people?" Bugsy was losing his patience with this stuck up, presumptuous bitch.

She continued. "I said, Meyer West just got here. Now sit down and wait for an update."

"Meyer?"

"One more word and I'm going to call security."

Bugsy was one second from smashing her face through the Plexiglas. However, he had more tact than that. He needed answers, so he worked his charm and said calmly, "Did you say 'Meyer West', ma'am? I am asking about my father, Scott. Meyer is my twin brother."

His humbled tone and respect made her feel important. She looked down at her computer screen, feverishly tapped her fingers on the keyboard, and then replied, "Meyer West just came in with multiple gunshot wounds. Scott West arrived less than an hour ago and you are right, he's in surgery. No update yet."

Hearing that his twin was shot up too nearly knocked Bugsy off his feet. What the fuck was going on?

At that moment, Lucky arrived with her goons. She went straight to Bugsy, and he filled her in. The news also devastated her. Not only was her father shot, but Meyer too. To Bugsy and Lucky, the fact that both of them were gunned down on the same night wasn't a coincidence. Someone was gunning for their family again—and Scott was being set up.

"I can't lose either of them," Bugsy said. "We need answers on Meyer."

Lucky hugged her older brother tightly and frowned at Maxine sitting across the room. *Why is that bitch there?* But it wasn't about Maxine at the moment. She was worried about her family.

The agents looked their way, and Lucky felt her stomach do a flip-flop. Would they arrest her right there? What did they have on her father?

The siblings watched the FBI make their presence known; their radios crackled boisterously in the room. Their flight jackets and bulletproof vests were embroidered with "FBI," and they flaunted their holstered guns and badges. There were over a dozen of them crowded from the lobby to the emergency room. They were there to intimidate and investigate.

Everyone was baffled. What case did they have against Scott? Who was snitching? They didn't know. No one in their organization had been arrested lately. Bugsy kept tabs on everything and everyone, and he had eyes and ears inside the local police department. But this was federal, and these alphabet boys were more tight-lipped about indictments.

Three agents patrolled outside the hospital, watching the comings and goings of men known to be part of Scott's organization, snapping pictures, taking down license plate numbers, and seeing who was a new face and who wasn't. And they weren't being subtle about it either. They were bold in the faces of the gangsters and killers.

From Bugsy's understanding, his father had been arrested for drug distribution. But until his arraignment, no one knew what the specific charges were. The only thing they knew was that Scott was still in surgery and law enforcement was monitoring his condition.

"Where's our mother?" Lucky asked.

"I don't know. I've been calling her," said Bugsy.

Layla's absence added to their uneasiness. Where was she? Bugsy and Lucky had been frantically calling her phone and leaving messages, but they hadn't gotten in touch with her yet.

Bugsy and Lucky went off to a nearby corner to talk in private. They whispered carefully to each other about family business. There were too many folks around to speak openly. Lucky felt that her brother knew a lot more than he was saying. He was the brains of the family.

"You didn't see this coming?" she asked Bugsy quietly.

"No," he muttered to her. "I can't be everywhere at the same time."

"And Meyer . . . what is going on?"

Both of them were desperate for answers, but they were among a sea of people—more observers than influencers. Their brawn and brains were weakened by the presence of the FBI. They were the West's kryptonite. And they were under attack.

From across the room, Maxine watched Bugsy and Lucky converse. She overheard Lucky inquiring about Layla. They needed to know. Their mother had been raided too. She dried her eyes, took a deep breath, and proceeded toward the siblings.

When she reached arm's length of them, Lucky pivoted and scowled at her. "Get the fuck away from us, bitch! We don't want you here!"

The harsh words stopped Maxine in her tracks. She and Lucky locked eyes briefly—the tension between them was thicker than a brick wall. Clearly, the immature child hadn't heard about her momma's beat down. Maxine was about to put them paws on her, but one look at the federal agents and she quickly came to her senses. *Another time*, she thought. She was going to tell them about Layla, but fuck it.

Lucky convinced herself that if they weren't in the hospital surrounded by folks and police, she would have cut Maxine's throat. She despised Maxine and made it known repeatedly.

Bugsy slightly touched Maxine's arm to try and comfort her.

"I'll be with you in a moment," he said to her followed by a quick smile.

Maxine nodded and walked away. Lucky glared at her brother and hated that he was so neutral with Maxine. What about Layla?

"Why is she here?" Lucky griped.

"She was with our father when it happened," he said.

"I want her gone, Bugsy. You know when Ma gets here she is going to fuckin' flip."

"Lucky, chill. We got too much going on for you to be worried about Maxine," he said coolly.

Bugsy's ringing cell phone interrupted their chat. He answered, while Lucky stood by in silence. She was trying to keep it together, but it was difficult. The FBI was all in their shit, her father and brother were probably dying, Maxine was there while her mother was MIA, and she couldn't do anything about any of it.

Bugsy ended his call and looked at his sister.

"What is it?" she said.

"That was a source of mine, and he tells me that Luna shot Meyer," he said.

Lucky's jaw dropped. "Luna? How the fuck is that possible when he's dead?"

"I don't know. Meyer's apartment building is all over the news saying it's the scene of an attempted murder-suicide. Luna was identified as the shooter," said Bugsy.

Bugsy felt like he'd started reading a mystery novel in the middle. Meyer supposedly killed Luna, so how could Luna have shot him? He couldn't have come back from the dead. Bugsy was angry at Meyer. How did he become so sloppy? How did it all fall apart? If Meyer didn't die from the gunshots, Bugsy was going to kill him for not killing Luna when he had the chance. Meyer had lied to everyone. Why? Bugsy was stumped.

***

Maxine sat alone on the opposite side of the hospital lobby, sunken into the dark blue armed chair. She couldn't get rid of the picture of Scott's bullet-riddled body from her mind. Witnessing it all—her man arrested and lying in his own blood, the loud voices, the disarray—was traumatizing.

She felt like an outsider even though she was Scott's fiancée. It felt like the room was getting smaller and the walls were collapsing around her. She was having a hard time catching her breath, though she was seated and still.

Security was clumped together with everyone in the reception area, trying to keep harmony in such a tense environment. The room was full of henchmen, both Scott's and Layla's. There were over a dozen men from Scott's organization—hardened gangsters and killers lingering amongst the sick in the atrium, and many of them were intimidating the civilians with their presence alone. The hospital staff tucked them away from the rest of the patients and families so that they could keep order. There was too much happening in one night. The FBI and a notorious drug organization under the same roof—it was a melting pot of disaster.

Maxine's paranoia was amplified. Between the FBI kicking in the door, Scott's condition, and Wacka's blackmail, she wasn't able to think clearly. She was stuck between a rock and a hard place. Wherever she turned and whatever she tried to do, there were obstacles. Although Bugsy was extremely nice to her—and she thought he treated her like a stepmom— he hadn't stood up to Lucky for her. And Lucky wasn't going to go away so easily. She was a sharp thorn in Maxine's side, and her prick felt like it was festering.

Maxine's dilemma was clear-cut. Should Scott die, so would her power and ties with his family and the organization. She was just gaining traction with Scott, and he was just about to add her name to some of his legit business dealings. Now, if he died, she would have nothing except the pricey ring on her finger. Lucky and Meyer would see to that. With most of her nest-egg from her parents' home depleted by Wacka's blackmail and Wacka still harassing her for five million dollars, her future was looking bleak.

Layla sat in a small, drab room in the federal building in New York City. She was exhausted, alone, and terrified, and everything from her hair to her clothing was in disarray.

A few hours earlier, federal agents had busted in and raided her home, and she gave them a run for their money. She hid inside her panic room and refused to open the door. It took the agents nearly an hour to break into the tightly secured room with battering rams and explosives. When they finally put their hands on Layla, they were far from nice. Two federal agents took it upon themselves to rough her up for the hassle she put them through. But Layla fought back, punching one agent in the nose. They'd barged into her home, and she wasn't going down without a fight. After they finally had her subdued, they read her rights and cuffed her.

She released a deep sigh and shifted in the metal chair behind the metal table. On the opposite side of the table was another chair for the interrogating agent when he came into the room. There was nothing for her to do but sit and wait, and she only had her thoughts and her mistakes to occupy her time.

Layla knew that the FBI only moved in on you if they had a solid indictment—hard evidence. She thought about Maxine. Could Maxine have ratted on their organization? But that bitch didn't know anything, did she?

Sitting in that windowless room for hours had her mind going berserk. She replayed everything, trying to deduce where she had messed up or gotten sloppy. How did she get into this predicament?

Finally, the door opened and Layla turned to observe three suited agents coolly walk into the room. They looked at her straight-faced. Two of the agents remained standing nearby, leaning against the wall and watching her closely. The primary agent on her case took a seat opposite her.

She locked eyes with the tall, pasty agent with exceptionally broad shoulders sitting across from her. He was lean with a muscular physique under the suit, clean shaven with piercing blue eyes that looked predatory, and he had an aura of confidence about him. He reeked of law enforcement. Had it been an amateur in the room with him, he would have come off as intimidating. But Layla was no amateur, and his daunting stare didn't faze her.

"You've been a very busy woman, Layla West," he started off.

She remained quiet. She had nothing to say to them, and she had nothing inside her apartment—no drugs, just a registered gun and some cash. And did they have a search warrant? She didn't remember them producing a warrant to raid her place.

"That agent you hit, you broke his nose," he said.

"I wish I would have broken his fuckin' face," she quipped.

The agent didn't laugh. "You are a feisty bitch, I'll give you that. But you fucked up. You do the crime, you do the time. But if you play ball with us, we could work something out."

Her mouth stayed shut and her eyes continued to glare into his.

"Your options are few, Layla. As we speak, your husband is in surgery fighting for his life. He shot first and my men shot back. So far it's touch-and-go with him. And your son, he too is in surgery, shot multiple times, but that was a separate incident from your husband. So you have a son and a husband in the hospital, and you sit here in jail," he said to her. "It's all falling apart for you, Layla."

She remained silent. Was he lying? There was no way—he had to be lying. Which son? Layla refused to show him any emotion, although she felt sick to her stomach.

The agent said, "Help us help you. We want your connect, Angel. And we want your husband. You're a heavyweight in this city, I see, but you're nothing compared to your husband and Angel."

"I'm no fuckin' snitch," she growled at him.

"No, you're a coward who lets innocent people take the weight for you. Isn't that right? Isn't that what happened to naive Maxine Henderson?"

"I don't know what you're talking about."

"Come on, Layla, admit it. You play tough, but you can't survive hard jail time. Right now your mind is telling you that you will find a way out—a loophole or some sucker to fall on the sword for you, and I am telling you that you don't have nine lives. You get one chance to cooperate with me. One. If not, I go to trial with what I got, and I promise you that I'll get a conviction."

"With what evidence?"

"So you admit that there is evidence to find?"

He momentarily confused Layla. "I did not!"

"With your indictments, you're looking at life, easy."

"I want to speak to my attorney. I'm done wit' y'all."

He shook his head. She was being stubborn, but they were always stubborn. When the arrest was still fresh, they always felt there was a chance for freedom without snitching on their cohorts.

"If you roll the dice against us, Layla, I can guarantee that you will not win. I'm giving you a chance to help yourself."

"Like I said, I'm done wit' y'all. I want my attorney present. Fuck you!" she cursed at him.

Her insult didn't faze him. He sat across from her nonchalant. He didn't care if she cooperated now or later. He still was going to win. She would be charged with the RICO act and her case would be brought forward to the grand jury. They had an ace up their sleeve that they felt would lead to guilty verdicts and lengthy imprisonment.

Composedly, he replied, "It's your life—well, what's left of it." He pushed his chair back and stood up.

She'd invoked her right to an attorney. Their interrogation was done. Layla knew the rules.

The three agents filed out of the room, and the door closed behind them. Layla was left alone, taking in everything the agent had said. Scott had been shot, and she had no idea which son had been shot too—Meyer or Bugsy. He purposely left out the name so she could feel helpless and confused. She fucked with them, and now they were going to fuck with her.

Layla had to reach a phone and talk to someone. She needed information. Her heart was in her stomach.

"I want my fuckin' phone call!" she screamed at the walls at the top of her lungs.

They made her wait alone inside the room for another hour until the door opened again. This time it was a booking officer. He was there to transfer her from one law enforcement location to another.

"I want my phone call," said Layla.

"You'll get your call," he replied dryly.

She was handcuffed and escorted out of the area. A half-hour later she was granted one phone call, no exceptions. She wanted to call her counsel, but nowadays who knew anyone's telephone numbers by heart? Layla racked her brain to remember her lawyer's number, but she felt fucked. She had to call her daughter from the unknown number and she wasn't surprised when Lucky didn't answer her cell.

She left a frantic message on her daughter's voicemail.

"Lucky, I've been arrested on some trumped up federal charges. I need you to get in contact with my attorney immediately. And what's this I hear about your father and your brother shot? Which brother is in the hospital? Please, get in contact with my attorney and tell him my situation. I need to see you ASAP!"

Her call ended. She huffed. She wanted out. Layla strongly felt that she didn't belong in lockup with the other criminals. That's what the underlings were for. But she was handcuffed with the other detainees and carted off to Lower Manhattan for arraignment.

The sun was bright in the early morning, but the January air was cold. New York-Presbyterian was still crammed with folks and law enforcement. It was just after nine o'clock, and Lucky, Maxine, and Choppa were asleep in the lobby. Their bodies were stiff from being in the uncomfortable and small hospital chairs for hours. Bugsy, however, hadn't slept. He paced around the hospital floor and made phone calls. There was still no word on his father or Meyer, and it had been hours already.

Bugsy had gone up and asked for updates on Scott and Meyer each hour, and it felt like he was being stonewalled. He didn't know if his loved ones were dead or alive. He felt like he could put his fist through a brick wall. If the FBI wasn't on the scene, he would have flipped out and gone ballistic.

He stirred his sister awake. She opened her eyes with a frown. Sleeping in a small, uncomfortable chair wasn't her idea of a good night's sleep.

Lucky looked up at her brother and asked with urgency, "Any word on anyone?"

"Nah, I'm still waiting," he said.

It was ridiculous. They were a powerful family, and it was embarrassing for them to wait like common folks. Lucky leaped up from her seat. It had been long enough. Something had to be done.

"Fuck this shit!" she yelled.

Maxine awoke too. She had a small crick in her neck from sleeping coiled in the chair. It was slightly painful, but she slowly turned her head in the direction of the siblings. Her eyes looked over at Lucky and Bugsy fretting about something. Her heart skipped a beat. Had Scott's condition worsened—or was he dead? She removed herself from the chair and wanted to approach them, but she stood away with caution, knowing how Lucky felt about her. She wasn't in the mood to argue with anyone.

Bugsy looked her way. He showed nothing—his expression was pokerfaced. Seeing no tears and no grief was a good sign.

Bugsy signaled Choppa. Choppa walked toward him and awaited his orders. They were simple.

"Go get everyone some coffee and breakfast," said Bugsy, reaching into his pocket and pulling out a wad of hundreds. He peeled off a C-note and put it into his lieutenant's hands.

As an afterthought, he said, "And when you're done with that, I want you to go find Layla."

Choppa nodded. "I'm on it." He turned and marched off.

Bugsy pivoted and he and Lucky marched toward the nurses station. Maxine was right behind them. She didn't care anymore. She needed to know something. It was her fiancé fighting for his life.

The staff from last night was gone, and a new batch of nurses and orderlies were on duty and spreading the juicy gossip about two notorious patients who came in code blue last night. They were excited to hear the scandalous details of an alleged drug kingpin in their hospital—Scott West and his son. Was it a gang hit? Was it the cartel? There were rumors about Scott West, but none of them were ever confirmed. He pranced around the city a legitimate and shrewd businessman, philanthropist, and a playboy with wealth beyond their dreams.

Bugsy heard them and interrupted their gossip with, "I'm his son, Bugsy West, and I want to know how my father and brother are doing."

The gossip was instantly silenced, but a petite white nurse right away snickered at his name.

"Bugsy—as in Bugsy Siegel?"

Before Bugsy could reply, Lucky shouted, "You find something funny? People are in here dying, and all you care about is the origin of his name? Get off my brother's dick, bitch, and do your job!" The joke was getting old. Lucky was so tired of everyone asking the obvious about their names.

Instantly, the young nurse was intimidated. Lucky approached her, and the look on her face pushed the nurse into a full blown panic.

"I-I-I'm sorry," she tried to apologize.

"You are a sorry-ass, silly bitch!" Lucky continued to rant.

The young, frightened nurse had a coworker, Adriana—an LPN who wasn't as fearful of the petite loudmouth.

"And you're a wannabe—" Adriana did air quotes, "—gangster bitch!"

Lucky's head swiveled and her eyes connected with the young Italian woman. The dark-haired, dark-eyed beauty had an edge. They glared at each other and things quickly got ratchet.

"I will beat fire out of you," Lucky warned. She was about to turn up and no longer cared about the feds.

"Oh, please!" Adriana mocked. "Does that routine really work on people? Am I supposed to fear you because you've misappropriated my culture? Where I come from the real Bugsy and Meyer are our brothers and uncles—not names jacked from a fictional movie."

"Who's the wannabe now? Nurse Jackie in here pretending to be mob affiliated." Lucky shook her head and laughed. "Bitch, have several seats."

Adriana wasn't pretending at all. Her husband ran a faction of the Gambino mob out of Staten Island. Both of her uncles were made men, and her grandfather was one of the forefathers of the Bonanno crime family. Adriana's family was Cosa Nostra; she had generations of mafiosos in her bloodline to prove it.

"I pity you," Adriana admonished. "I'll be quiet now, though. I was taught to not argue with fools."

"Fool?" Lucky was insulted. "Guido."

"Niglet."

"Dead bitch!"

"Dead-eye!"

Lucky lost it. "Say it again! Say it again, bitch!"

Bugsy stood silent with his hands stuffed into his pockets. Lucky had to learn when to be quiet and when to pop off. Now wasn't the time. She and Meyer were hotheads who thought everything could be solved through insults and brute force.

Finally, the supervisors hurried to aid the nurses and called security to defuse the situation. Since last night, everyone had been on edge. Agents quickly intervened and their presence provided quick comfort to the staff. One particular agent, Agent Devonsky, scowled at Bugsy and Lucky. Lucky returned the matching look.

They heard the agent say, "You're next."

Devonsky was itching to put the silver bracelets around Lucky's wrists, and Lucky was ready for a battle with everyone. Her emotions were in overdrive. She was angry, and everyone was to blame.

The surgeon who operated on Scott eventually moved through the double doors and glided their way with his hands in his white lab coat, a stethoscope around his neck, and a look that no one could read. He was tall and aging with salt-and-pepper hair. His brown eyes were tired and bloodshot as if he had been up for days. All eyes were on him. Maxine grew more nervous the closer he approached.

"Are you the family of Scott West?"

Bugsy and Lucky jumped to attention and confirmed that they were.

"I'm Doctor Pym, one of the surgeons. He's successfully pulled through his surgery."

There was a sigh of relief from everyone. Maxine felt herself climbing out of tragedy, but she wasn't out the frying pan yet.

"We were able to remove all but one bullet. The bullet penetrated the chest wall, and it damaged and collapsed his lung. We were able to stop the bleeding in his lungs and we removed one of his lobes. He's awake and resting now."

It was one down and one to go.

"And what about our brother, Meyer?" Lucky asked him.

"He's in critical condition. He suffered massive internal trauma and he lost a lot of blood. He's still in ICU. We're monitoring his condition constantly, but he might not live through the night."

It was devastating news. They couldn't lose Meyer—not another sibling. If there was a time for prayer, it would be now.

Maxine didn't give two fucks about Meyer, but she stood there and listened anyway. There was a part of her that hoped he would die, but she kept that to herself. As long as Scott was alive and awake, she was fine.

Dr. Pym turned and departed from the family. He was exhausted. They were left to contemplate their situation. Bugsy didn't show any emotions. His eyes didn't water, but inside he was grieving about his brother's condition. Lucky, however, was falling apart. If Meyer were to die, it would send her over the edge.

Scott was confined to his hospital bed by two things—handcuffs and his injuries from his gunshot wounds. He felt weak and drained and cut up like Frankenstein. His right arm was cuffed to the hospital bed. He tried to wipe his mouth, and the handcuff clanged against the metal bed rails. It was a surreal situation for him. He was the king of New York, and now he was a weakened, imprisoned man.

He was arraigned from his bedside at eight in the morning, denied bail, and remanded to federal custody as soon as his doctor gave the okay. The surgeons had an ethical duty to inform the family, but the agents had corrupted them with stories of drugs and violent murders. The surgeons didn't want to be involved and went home after Dr. Pym gave the brief update without any additional contact with the infamous crime family.

There were two FBI agents posted at his room watching him closely. They overreacted to everything and everyone in the area. They were there to intimidate people, and it was working. Scott had nothing but contempt for them. They tried to kill him, but he shot first. He would declare that it was self-defense. He wanted to speak to his lawyer. He wanted to fight the feds and he wanted to sue those muthafuckas. It all had come back to him. They'd burst into his home during the night. He didn't remember seeing a warrant. And where were Maxine and his kids? He wanted information and details and he wanted it yesterday! This wasn't going to be the end of him.

***

Choppa arrived and handed out McDonald's breakfast sandwiches and coffee to everyone, including Maxine. With that done, he left to go find Layla. She still wasn't answering her phone, and Bugsy's intuition told him that something was wrong.

With permission, Scott had a right to three visitors for one hour. And every visit would be monitored. Immediately, Lucky tried to block Maxine from visiting her father.

"Where she think she going?" Lucky asked Bugsy as if Maxine wasn't standing right there.

Maxine finally snapped and hollered, "To see my muthafuckin man, little girl! Now stop me!"

Her outburst startled everyone, including the agents on duty.

"Lower your voice!" one agent warned.

"No, I'm tired of this little bitch! She better shut the fuck up if she knows what's good."

Lucky, standing a few feet behind Bugsy, chanted like a child, "Make me shut up, cunt" repeatedly. She was tired of getting screamed on all day and wanted those around to fear her. Why was no one fearing her?

The aggressive agent, Agent Devonsky, was about to regulate the whole situation and toss everyone out. But the quiet agent, who was his superior, subtly shook his head, and Devonsky knew to stand down. Devonsky's superior, Agent Randall, knew that Maxine was the girlfriend who had done jail time for Scott's wife. Scott was shot, pumped up on drugs, and everyone was emotional. If anyone said anything—one small iota of incriminating information that could help with the case—it would all be admissible. They were there to listen more than police.

"She's allowed to visit, ma'am," Agent Devonsky stated.

"But she's not family!" Lucky wasn't letting this go.

"She doesn't have to be!"

Bugsy was relieved that he wasn't put in the position of choosing sides. He knew his father would want to see Maxine, and he also knew that Lucky could be a grudge-holding drama queen just like their mother if he had gone against her.

The sight of Scott hospitalized was a heartbreaking scene for the siblings and Maxine. There he was, confined to his bed with handcuffs and an IV in his arm. The agents stood nearby with their steely gaze. To the family, they were enemy number-one.

Scott was trying to be calm and strong for the family, but he was baffled. He had always been careful. He had the right lawyers and accountants on his side. He rarely met with the cartel, and in the eyes of many, he was a legit businessman worth hundreds of millions.

Bugsy's eyes looked at Scott for answers. "Pop, I'm glad to see you're okay, but we'll talk."

Scott slowly nodded. He understood.

For months Lucky had despised her father, but seeing him in a weakened condition was depressing. She looked at him with mixed feelings. Seeing that he was okay, could she forgive him for everything he had done to her and his family? How many times had she wished he was dead when she was upset with him? Now it looked like her wish had almost come true.

"Get some rest, Daddy. I love you," Lucky said.

Bugsy and Lucky shared a glance. Someone had to tell Scott about Meyer.

"There's something we need to tell you," Bugsy started.

His gloomy look told Scott that it wasn't going to be good news. He studied his son's eyes, and Bugsy looked reluctant to spill the beans.

"What?" Scott whispered in a low and raspy tone.

"It's Meyer. He's in here too . . . in ICU. He's been shot multiple times and they don't know if he's going to survive the night," said Bugsy.

Scott didn't respond right away. The news about Meyer hit him like a ton of bricks had fallen on him. He felt smothered by one tragedy after another. He wanted to hold back the tears, but it was hard to do—another child was knocking at death's door. Yes, he was a dangerous drug kingpin responsible for killing sons, fathers, uncles, and brothers—but he, too, was a father. He and Meyer had not been on good terms lately, but Meyer was still a West. Meyer was still his flesh and blood.

Scott wanted to ask Bugsy so many questions, but their talk had to be limited with agents right there in the room with them. Scott was already under indictment, and Lucky and Bugsy didn't want to fall victim to an arrest too. So far they had their freedom and that was still a mystery to them. Bugsy was Scott's right-hand man, so what did the FBI have on his father that they didn't have on him?

Scott wanted them to visit Meyer and tell him to hold on. He wanted Meyer to see that the family was there for him. He said with his labored breathing, "Tell him he better not fuckin' die on us."

Scott's kids left the room and a tear trickled down his face. Maxine couldn't wait to comfort and console him. As she was about to hug and kiss him, a voice boomed through the room.

"No contact!" The agent glared at them.

Maxine hated that she couldn't touch her man the way she wanted to.

"I love you," she said.

"I love you too," he whispered. Scott's deep, baritone voice was barely audible. The news about his son had sucked his remaining strength. "Did they hurt you? Are you hurt?"

"I'm fine, baby. Don't worry about me." Maxine looked at Scott's condition—shot and chained to a bed—and the tears began flowing uncontrollably. She sobbed. "I thought you were dead."

Scott couldn't physically comfort her, but he tried with his words. He needed to show strength. He needed her to know that he wasn't a defeated man. "Shhhhh . . . no tears. They can't kill me, baby. No one can. I told you that how long ago? Remember?"

Maxine wiped her tears and thought back and then smiled. "I do remember."

"Where were we?"

"It was 1994 and you came to my parents' home driving a black droptop Porsche. You wanted me to listen to a song from Biggie Smalls called "Warning." I remember listening to the lyrics and getting so scared for you"—Maxine chuckled—"I was so naive back then. I thought the song was about you and someone wanted to kill you."

Scott managed a smile. "And what did I tell you?"

"You said no one can kill Scott West. You said that you decide when you die."

"I'm still here, right?"

"You are."

"Now go home and get some rest and try not to worry. This will all be over soon. It's just a formality."

She sighed. She didn't want to go home, but the medication in Scott was making him drowsy and weak. He was becoming no good to her. His eyelids started to slowly close.

Maxine watched him fade away into a deep sleep.

Wacka and Tarsha were blowing through the five hundred thousand dollars fast. In one week they'd purchased a used Lexus for $40K in cash. Wacka decided to put the car in Tarsha's name. He felt it was safer. Subsequently, they spent two grand on recreational weed that would last a few weeks. And there were the shopping sprees. For three days straight, and for hours at a time, Tarsha was popping designer tags. She almost had enough clothes to fill an entire bedroom, and she wasn't done yet. They bought jewelry—his and hers. Wacka sported a big face diamond watch, and Tarsha sported earrings, diamond bracelets, and necklaces. She wanted to look like a millionaire, but, more importantly, she wanted to become one.

Tarsha climbed out of the burgundy Lexus on the shopping strip in Maryland looking high and mighty with her new lace front wig and her flawless make-up. She strutted toward one of her favorite high-end clothing stores with a purse full of cash and a desire to rack up a few items for the winter. She received compliments in her leather knee-high boots, tight blue jeans that accentuated her curves, and her pricy auburn leather jacket. She grinned and walked into the store and her eyes danced around some of the best couture in town. She moved through the store and started picking out a few stylish outfits with the help of a sales representative. Price tags meant nothing to her. If it looked nice and trendy, she was walking out with it. Money wasn't an issue for Tarsha. Blackmailing Maxine was the best thing they could've done. Tarsha felt on top of the world again.

In a short time she placed a mountain of clothing on the checkout counter—shoes included. The sales representative was all smiles. Tarsha was quickly becoming one of her favorite customers. She knew what she wanted and price didn't mean a thing to her.

The total came up to $5,901. Tarsha pulled out a ten-thousand-dollar stack and dropped an even six grand on the cashier.

"You know what? I'm in a really good mood—keep the change. You deserve it," she said.

The young girl beamed. "Ohmygod! Thank you."

"You welcome."

Tarsha paraded outside with a handful of shopping bags on the sunny, but cold day. She placed the bags into the trunk of the Lexus and climbed into the driver's seat. The engine purred when she turned the key, and she glanced at her image in the rearview mirror.

"Damn, you're a pretty bitch," she told herself.

Tarsha pulled up to her Maryland home and parked. She popped the trunk and lugged her purchases inside. She couldn't wait to model her new fits for Wacka.

Their son was with a friend, so the two had the house to themselves. Wacka was seated on the couch, watching TV and minding his business. Tarsha came through the front door all smiles and her hands jumbled with bags. He looked at her straight-faced as she greeted him with a kiss on his cheek and removed the new items from the bags for him to see.

"I see you're having fun," he said.

"I am," she replied happily. "And I can't wait to show you how much."

Their new hustle got her excited. It was making her pussy wet. Wacka looked sexy to her in his long basketball shorts and wifebeater. His handicap was no longer an issue. The money was the turn-on.

She straddled him on the couch, kissed him fervently, and began nibbling on his neck. New clothes, a new car, and lots of money—Tarsha wanted to have sex right away. She fondled him below and he grew hard underneath her. Though he was missing some fingers, his erection was all there.

"Fuck me!" she groaned into his ear.

She pulled down his shorts, undressed from the waist down, straddled him again, and sank his hard dick inside of her. Slowly and passionately, she rode him on the couch. She squealed in delight as he relaxed with his hands on the couch, her pussy sliding up and down on him.

He soon came and she came right behind him—but it was the money that made her come. She wanted more of it.

Moments later, she tried on every outfit and modeled for Wacka. Tarsha looked great in everything. She thought she was Kim Kardashian with her long, black Brazilian wig and expensive garments. She was living the good life and had no intentions of giving it up.

But five hundred thousand dollars didn't last forever, especially with the spending spree they went on. Soon, the honeymoon was over. The couple barely had any gas money. A week later, they woke up broke on a cold January morning. Wacka wanted more sex, but Tarsha wasn't in the mood. She removed herself from their bed with a frown and walked into the bathroom to pee. Wacka lingered in the bed with a morning hard-on. The past week had been good to him; she had been giving him blow jobs in the morning and sex during the day.

Tarsha exited the bathroom in her panties and bra and looked at Wacka with a puckered brow. "Call that bitch again."

"Maxine?"

"Our account is empty and she's the bank. Five hundred grand wasn't shit. I want our millions."

Wacka didn't argue with her. He looked around for his cell phone and found it under the bed. He had Maxine's number on speed dial. He put the phone on speaker and they waited for her to answer. The phone rang and rang and rang before her voicemail picked up.

Wacka left a threatening message. "Look, bitch. Don't ignore me when I'm calling. Dig this, we need that money we talked about, and we need it ASAP. If not, then we talk to your boyfriend and your fairytale life wit' him ain't gonna be a fairytale anymore. You feel me, bitch? You got twenty-four hours to call me back wit' some good news."

He hung up. Tarsha felt good about the message he'd left. It was strong and demanding—no sugarcoating. Damn, it almost made her pussy wet again. Five million dollars—she would take it in the ass for that large amount. She would live like a queen and never be a broke bitch again.

"You did good, baby," she said to him. "That bitch gonna get the hint and call right back."

Wacka wasn't so sure. He had his doubts that Maxine would be able to come up with such a large amount in such a short time. Tarsha had set the amount, but Wacka felt it might be too much to ask for. One or two million was understandable; Maxine probably would have paid it to keep them quiet. But five million? Where would it come from? What drug dealer had that much cash around just to give to their woman?

"Five million is fuckin' crazy," he said.

"You sound like you on the fence about it, nigga," she said. "That bitch is paid, Wacka. I know in my gut she can come up wit' that money. I saw her fuckin' ring and it's worth some stacks, so that bitch better pawn that shit and raise that paper or we gonna set her world on fire and watch it fuckin' burn." It was said with finality.

Tarsha refused to let Maxine win—or better yet, get one over on her. She crawled into bed with Wacka, her stink attitude transitioning into a smile. She straddled him and kissed his lips. Then she said, "With this money, you and I can do whatever we want. Think about it, Wacka. We would never have to worry about money again. We can invest this money into a business and make somethin' out of ourselves. I'm smart, you know. I got a business mind. You pull this off and I'm yours for life." She removed herself from his resting frame and exited the bedroom.

It was a positive thought. However, Wacka was tired of dishing out threats and playing the role of a menace. He didn't tell Tarsha his true feelings because she wouldn't understand. He wanted to rest and recoup. He wanted things to be simple for the moment. He wanted to drive around town in his new Lexus—or even be chauffeured around town—smoke weed, have sex, and just live before he started stalking, threatening, and seeking revenge against Maxine.

Truth be told, he wasn't that broken up over his family's murders any longer. Yes, he wanted to see Maxine dead, but over time it started to become less of a priority. He was tired. He felt defeated, and he'd been through hell and back. His body had taken a lot of abuse from the gunshot wounds and the car crash. How much more could his body take? The street life was taking a toll on him, but Tarsha wanted him back in action. He was her payday.

Meyer's condition was dire. He looked nothing like the notorious killer that he was known to be. He looked like a dying man. Getting through the first twenty-four hours was an uphill battle, and every passing hour looked bleaker. His body was struggling to breathe, so he was hooked up to a respirator. The trauma team had to keep suctioning blood that repeatedly accumulated in his mouth. All sorts of wires for monitors and IV tubes meandered out from his motionless body.

His fragile appearance brought tears to Lucky's eyes. This was a man who walked through the city like he was Superman. Now he looked like he had fought Superman and lost.

Bugsy sat in the chair next to his twin brother's comatose body in the ICU unit. He took his brother's hand into his and said, "Don't you die on us, muthafucka. You're too stubborn for that. This is only a setback, you hear me, bro? This shit is temporary. You gonna pull through and we gonna be all right."

Bugsy held back the tears. There was no time for that. His brother was going to fight. They had a business to run and a city to control.

Lucky decided to change the mood of the room. She wiped her tears and asked, "You know you gotta switch shit up now that Pops is down. Move the coke, relocate the trap—"

Bugsy kicked the shit out of her.

"Owwwwww!" she complained.

Bugsy placed his finger over his lips and gave his sister a stern look. She should know better. He took out his cell phone and turned on his iTunes catalog on shuffle. Kendrick Lamar's "Loyalty" came blaring through. He then leaned in close and whispered, "You know those people could be listening. This whole room could be bugged."

Lucky was feeling some kind of way about the kick. "You're being extra right now. They can't just bug rooms without a court order."

Bugsy was irked that she would even try to justify her stupidity. "Assume that all this shit is tapped, bugged, cloned, with or without an order. Don't talk business freely in your truck, your apartment, the elevator, nowhere. Stop thinking they play fair, because they don't. At the end of the day, those feds are regular people—corruptible. Always remember how they got Gotti when he switched from holding meetings at the Ravenite Social Club to outdoor walk-talks."

"Yeah, those fuckers brought in someone who read lips."

Bugsy nodded confirmation that his dim-witted sister had gotten his message. He took her cell phone and typed a note and then erased it: I AM NOT GOING TO JAIL.

Lucky spoke, "Me neither."

"Don't sleep then. Stay woke and we should be fine. If they had anything on us, we would be knocked already. We're good as long as we don't get sloppy."

A knock on the door halted their pep talk. The room door slowly opened, and Choppa peeked his head into the room. The sight of Meyer was heartbreaking, but he had business with Bugsy. He looked at Bugsy and spoke with his eyes that there was information that he needed to hear. Bugsy stood up and approached his lieutenant.

"What do you have for me?" asked Bugsy.

"I found her. Layla is in federal custody in the city. They raided her home too—last night. They took her down fighting and screaming."

"What?" Lucky had overhead him. She was shocked to hear the news.

"It's fucked up. I don't know her charges, but she asking for her lawyer."

Bugsy took the news straight-faced, but inside his head was swimming with, *What the fuck is going on? What is happening? Who's next?*

Lucky was spent. She didn't want anyone to go to jail—but and however, if anyone had to go then she strongly felt it should be Scott. He had a long run and she wasn't fucking with him anyway. But, Layla? Lucky watched as her father flaunted two mistresses in her face and her mother still held her head up high. Layla was doing big things, holding court with the most thorough gangstas on the east coast. Her mother had just started to come into her own. Layla's reign on top was short lived and Lucky felt terrible. She needed to do something!

"It's gotta be a fuckin' snitch," Lucky said.

Choppa nodded. "She might be right, Bugsy."

Bugsy sighed heavily. "I need to think."

"What else you need me to do?" Choppa asked.

Bugsy pulled Choppa out of the room and whispered in a barely audible tone, "I want you to go out into the streets and let everyone know we're not done—far from it—and you let our strength be heard and shown. The news of my parents and Meyer is going to spread, and muthafuckas are going to think this is their chance to start snarling at us and showing their bite. They try to buck at us, we buck back harder. You understand me, Choppa?"

Choppa nodded. "I'm wit' you a hundred percent, Bugsy. I'm ready to fuck up anyone that disrespects this organization."

Choppa's eyes showed loyalty for the family and he was ready to set the streets on fire for the Wests.

"When you move, move like you're being shadowed. Make those triple right turns and keep your eyes peeled on your rear- and side-view mirrors. When you speak, talk like those people are listening. If a nigga starts talking reckless over the phone, hang up and report back to me what was said. We got a snitch among us, and it's up to me to smoke him out. And kill him."

"Yo, I gotchu. We not going down without a fight."

Bugsy corrected, "We not going down, period."

Choppa left to execute the orders given to him.

Bugsy walked back inside the room and narrowed his eyes on Meyer, knowing that their empire was crumbling. Still, they had to maintain the façade of strength and power when so many pieces had fallen. Their enemies would come after them. Now would be the perfect time. Meyer was out of commission, and Scott and Layla had been indicted. Bugsy had to think four steps ahead of their rivals. He was the last man standing.

***

Choppa climbed into the passenger seat of the Durango and lit a cigarette. The driver, Pluto, handed him his pistol, and he stuffed it into his waistband. There were so many agents loitering around the hospital, watching everyone and taking notes, the hospital started to feel like a federal building. Everyone had to watch what they said and did. Scott's arrest was making headlines, and a goon like Choppa didn't want to be caught up in the shit storm for carrying his gun inside.

He inhaled and exhaled the nicotine smoke and said to Pluto and others in the backseat, "Bugsy wants us to make a strong statement on the streets—let everyone know we ain't fuckin' crumbling. So whoever trying to come against us, we do what we do best."

Pluto said, "I know a muthafucka right now that's trying to jump ship and make his own moves."

"Oh really? Who is this nigga?" Choppa said.

"Spank. Word on the streets is he copped a Dominican connect and he proclaiming to be the next boss. He's undermining the organization and talkin' that shit."

"Spank. Sounds familiar, but I can't place him," Choppa said.

"Yeah, he used to run wit' Meyer's crew a year back. He broke off, left town for a minute, and came back like he a god in these streets. And wit' so much goin' on, niggas been overlooking this muthafucka. But he on the come-up and he talkin' that petty shit 'bout your twins. It ain't nuthin' nice, my nigga."

Choppa had heard enough. He vaguely remembered the man. But he was ready to carry out his first message for Bugsy.

"Let's go handle this nigga. Bugsy wants to send a message, we send a message that this organization is still alive and dangerous, and those niggas that wanna run out or go against us, we cut their fuckin' legs off," Choppa said gruffly.

***

The next day, Choppa eyed Spank's black Jaguar XJ parked in front of the barbershop on the Brooklyn Street from a block away. After doing some research, Choppa found out that Spank was moving five to ten kilos a month and encroaching on territory that didn't belong to him.

It was late in the evening and the sun was setting, the streets were chilly, and a cold wind thrashed up the street and blew straight through the pedestrians walking, almost turning them into walking blocks of ice. The men in the SUV were swathed in their warm winter attire, pistols in hands, and assault rifles fully loaded. They donned ski masks to cloak their identities.

Four men sat in the Durango including Choppa, each armed and dangerous, hotheaded and itching to break bones. Spank was their primary target, and at six-one, high yellow with long cornrows, and wrapped in a long, brown leather shearling jacket, he wasn't hard to miss. The man had a narrow face, broad shoulders, and intense eyes, and he moved with a tiger's stride on the block. He commanded his respect and he wasn't shy to violence. He had his cell phone to his ear conducting business, and he was flanked by one of his soldiers.

"That muthafucka right there thinks he's Nino Brown of Brooklyn," said Pluto.

"Nino Brown, huh?" Choppa chuckled. "Fuck it, we on this nigga right now. Let's go fuck this nigga's world up."

Pluto put the Durango in drive and slowly crept toward their mark. The barbershop was on a one-way street, nestled in the middle of the block, and traffic was at a minimum.

Everyone in the Durango was ready to create a crime scene. They wanted Spank to go down in flames for the streets to see. They wanted it to be ugly and look ugly.

Pluto and Choppa fixed their eyes on Spank. Now he was leaned against the side of his Jaguar still on the phone and looking like the man of the hour while his soldier's head was on a swivel. The stinging cold day was a benefit for the invading killers—fewer people outside meant fewer witnesses to the bloodshed, and the usual beat cops were nowhere around.

"Drive by real slow," Choppa ordered.

Pluto nodded and moved the Durango at a steady pace to avoid attention. Spank's goon remained alert. He was wrapped in a black double goose leather coat with the fur trimmed hood. His hands were in his pockets, and his eyes were squinted for any trouble creeping. There was no telling what he was carrying, but he would be outgunned quickly. Choppa was going to make sure of that.

This was Choppa's world—murder and violence was his forte. It's what he woke up in the morning to be, and that was a cold blooded killer. He and his crew racked up homicides in every borough. But the recent death of his partner, AJ, sent Choppa into a deeper and darker spiral of chaos and not giving a fuck.

A few feet away from the target, and Choppa was ready to spring from the vehicle and attack—so were his armed thugs in the backseat. Choppa's gloved hand was wrapped around a Glock19 loaded with hollow-point bullets. His eyes were fixed on Spank and his goon. Every split second counted. They had to quickly get the drop on them before Spank's goon could pull out his pistol and shoot.

"Fuck it!" Choppa uttered.

Nearly a few feet away, Choppa thrust open the door and sprung from the vehicle with his gun in hand. His bloodthirsty cohorts followed, gripping an Uzi and a 9mm. Spank had his back turned to them, but his soldier immediately saw them coming. He frantically reached under his coat for his gun—but seconds mattered and Choppa had the drop on them.

Boom! Boom! Boom! Boom! Boom!

Five rapid shots went into the soldier, pushing him back and violently spinning him around before he collapsed against the concrete. It was Choppa's kill. Spank swiftly dropped his cell phone, ducked, and ran for cover behind a parked car. The man with the Uzi opened fire wildly but missed. Bullets tore into several vehicles and shattered car windows, the heated gunfire echoing through the streets.

Spank was in a full-blown panic. His man was dead. He searched for his pistol, but it wasn't on him. He was fucked.

It didn't take long for Choppa and the others to find him cowering and hiding between the cars. His eyes were wide with fear. He rose his hands up in a desperate plea for his life and stared at death. "C'mon, man, don't do this! Don't do this, please!"

Choppa simply smirked at him and coldly replied, "Fuck you, nigga!"

Choppa and his gunners opened fire, and Spank's body was riddled with bullets from head to toe. His disfigured body twisted on the street as his blood pooled on the crimson stained asphalt. Folks in the barbershop were left aghast after witnessing the cold-blooded killing of two men. Spank was known, but now he was dead. They saw three masked gunmen flee the area and climb into a Durango. Everything happened so fast.

The Durango took off, and a block away, Choppa and men finally removed their masks and rejoiced in the killings. Message sent. The West organization was still strong on the streets. It was about to get ugly for a lot of people.

I t was hard leaving Scott alone, but Maxine couldn't do much for him. The agents were up his ass and hers, and they were watching everything. She grew uncomfortable after some time there and decided to take Scott's suggestion to go home and get some rest. Her hair was loose and disheveled, her droopy eyelids showed her tiredness, and there were dark circles under her eyes. The past day had been an exhausting, emotional trip.

She descended to the first floor and moved through the lobby to the two men Scott assigned to protect her, Mason and Avery. Upon spotting Maxine, the men stood up abruptly, like Secret Service agents do when the President enters the room. She had become the first lady of the organization.

"Just take me home," Maxine told them.

They nodded.

They exited the atrium and were met with a harsh reminder that it was January in New York. It felt like forever since she had breathed in the cold air.

"I'll get the car," Mason said.

Maxine fastened her long pea coat and stood and waited with Avery serving as her shadow. Before her was a busy metropolis—people going about their business and city traffic that swarmed from north to south and east to west. Maxine wanted to get away from it all. She wanted to coil inside her apartment and hide from everyone and everything.

Scott would live, and she was grateful and relieved. But now she had to worry about the indictments. His freedom was at stake. Scott going to prison would worsen her situation. Just when she had readied herself to receive her reparations, this happens. Maxine had so much unfinished business that all hinged on Scott's freedom, his legal businesses, and drug money. Would she have access to it? Would she be the de facto boss? Would his men take orders from her? She had so many questions and worries knowing that his children would always be her opposition. If he received a lengthy prison sentence, could she do it? Could she travel many miles and visit him daily? Could she support him behind bars when he never supported her? And what about Wacka and his threats? Maxine was having a full-on pity party for herself, and she wasn't the one locked up this time.

Mason finally brought the black Escalade to the front of the hospital and Maxine slid into the backseat while Avery sat up front. The heat was on blast, transitioning the cold air to warmth, while Mason fought against traffic. It took what seemed like forever to get from Presbyterian to home.

Maxine finally arrived home to find the place was a mess—furniture overturned, items smashed—chaotic remnants of the FBI's raid. The front door needed repairing. On top of that, the superintendent handed her a letter of intent from the board of directors for the condominium. They wanted Scott out of the building. Stories of his arrest, the shooting, and his indictment were all over the news. It was a high-profile case. He was an alleged drug kingpin, and everyone wanted to separate themselves from him and his businesses. In their eyes, he was guilty until proven innocent.

She turned on the shower and peeled off the clothing she'd had on for more than a day. The water was searing and Maxine stepped foot into the ornate shower and allowed the water to cascade off her skin. She outstretched her arms, placed her palms against the walls, and positioned her head under the stream of water. She lingered in the shower for almost a half hour, turning it all over in her head and trying not to think about it at the same time. She toweled off, threw a quick glance at herself in the lighted vanity mirror, and went into the bedroom. She was ready to crawl into her plush king size bed and get some needed sleep, but it dawned on her that she hadn't checked her messages. She had a ton of missed calls on her phone and the burner phone that Wacka had given her. And there were dozens of messages on Scott's phone.

She listened to Wacka's threatening voice messages. They were angry and blunt. He felt that she was avoiding him. He wanted *his* five million dollars soon. She still had no idea where she was going to come up with that kind of money. It was asking the impossible of her. There was nearly no more money on her end. The measly thirty thousand in cash that Scott had in the suite had been bagged and tagged by the federal agents. She was fucked. How could it be fixed? Could it be fixed?

There was so much to think about and consider. She lay in her bed and cried her eyes out until she decided to not cry anymore. Her world had shifted in a nanosecond. It felt reminiscent of 1994—déjà vu. But this time it was her man that was facing hard time. Not her. Then it dawned on her; this wasn't her fight.

"I feel so stupid."

Maxine got out of bed and walked around Scott's enormous penthouse and fixed herself a martini. She was being blackmailed, her money was gone, and Scott was in jail. What would she do? What she wasn't going to do was allow life to fuck her over again. Max needed to reemerge and she needed to think street and examine her true feelings. Why was she crying over Scott's trifling ass? Maxine had to admit to herself that she could never fully forgive Scott and that the possibility of him doing life in prison actually tickled her. Tipsy, she laughed out loud. In some ways, this was karma. And if Layla got convicted too, her prayers from so long ago would be answered.

Maxine realized that it was only a matter of time before Scott's assets were frozen. Typical move from the feds when dealing with large sums of drug money. But she also knew the tactic would hardly cripple Scott. If Layla could steal fifty million from him and still be alive, then she knew that there was more where that came from. Sure, his kids would be a problem, but Maxine could handle herself.

If she continued to play her cards right, then Scott would make sure she was always taken care of. Now all she had to do was help guarantee that he spent the rest of his life behind bars.

***

The next morning Max woke up feeling smart. If prison taught her anything, it was to be cunning and to put herself first. She needed cash and not for Wacka's extortion. His threats were on the backburner, for now. Just in case her cushy future with Scott went down the toilet, she wasn't leaving broke. She was first in line at Chase, then Citibank, Bank of America, and a host of others trying to pull out whatever cash balances she could from her credit cards before the feds shut them down. It wasn't a windfall, but she managed to scrape together just over sixty-one thousand. The money was stuffed into her Hermes bag Scott had gotten her. The bag cost over thirty stacks, and she had five of them. Oh, those babies were going up on ebay, letgo—wherever she could find potential buyers.

Max rushed home and walked through her large walk-in closet, which was in shambles, looking for more sellable items. Clothes and shoes were strewn everywhere. Those jealous fucks had purposely trashed the place.

First she went into the kitchen and fixed herself a morning cocktail. The lime tequila hit the spot. Next she grabbed a couple trash bags and began tossing in what she could stand to part with. Red bottoms, YSL, Balmain gowns, Chanel shades—all the trappings of a hustler's wife. When one trash bag turned into four, Max had a better idea, a smarter one. Going online to sell the merchandise would leave a paper trail. She remembered that she had done time with a female from Harlem named Skip. Skip was in her early thirties and had sticky fingers her whole life. By age twelve she was boosting, and by seventeen she was into credit cards. Skip was legendary in her hood and had a long list of clientele who paid top dollar for her merchandise. If you were a dude and you wanted a brown mink coat for your chick, Skip would get it and sell it to you for half the price.

Skip was doing a five year stretch for grand larceny when she met Max. It was her fourth bid. Max hoped that she wasn't incarcerated again. She logged on to the missing person locator website—Facebook—and typed in Skip's government name, Stacey Jackson, and five pages came up. Quickly she found, Stacey "SkipStillGettin$" Jackson, and grinned.

Bingo! It was going down.

The next items up for auction were Scott's guilt gifts—well, that's what Maxine liked to call them. Her expensive jewelry had to go. This morning she thought she would only pawn a piece or two, something she was sure Scott wouldn't miss should he beat the case. But after taking a hard look at how the feds destroyed the apartment, they unwittingly gave her an alibi. Max could sell it all because, as far as Scott knew, some fed stole it during the raid. And the bonus was she would sell Scott's jewelry too. He owned several Rolex watches that he had collected over the years. Plus there were diamond cufflinks with his initials and an array of gold and diamond chains that he never wore. Her payday was going to be big, but she had to do it right. She could take a risk, but she couldn't be reckless. The flipside was that Scott could actually beat his case so she couldn't move like she didn't give a fuck even though she now cared less than that.

Once her plans were put into motion it was time to not live in squalor. Max called up Merry Maids, a handyman, and a locksmith. It was time to take full advantage of her newfound freedom. Within a couple hours the penthouse suite was buzzing with activity. Each person that came through those doors tried to hustle her. She hated when people tried to count her money and decide what she could afford. However, she allowed them to think they were playing her.

"I don't know if I have this lock in my van," the locksmith said and then scratched his head. "How did you say it got broken?"

"I didn't."

"Well, something like this is going to cost you extra. This is a specialty lock and will take time for me to do the install."

"A specialty lock, huh?"

"That's correct. But if you want me to fix it it's gonna cost you a little more than I had originally quoted over the phone."

"How much?"

He stared at the lock for a few more moments. "To fix something like this . . ." His voice trailed off and Max's pressure rose.

"Yes, you're here to fix it, correct?"

The locksmith ignored her sarcasm. He was still thinking. He was thinking a lot of things like what the fuck happened in that apartment? Why was she living in such opulence and not him? How did she get into such a posh building and on the top floor at that? Was she a celebrity? Maybe someone he wasn't familiar with. And finally, would she pay his two months back rent?

"It's going to cost you twenty-five hundred to fix this lock."

"Twenty-five hundred?"

"Yes. And I will give you a year warranty on my work."

Max exhaled false aggravation. "Do you take checks?"

"Yes, of course. I'll get to work."

Max smiled politely and went into Scott's office. The once locked drawer was popped open and she located his business checks. It gave her great pleasure to write out a check to this prick that she was sure would bounce for one of two reasons. She was sure the feds would have Scott's money frozen and although she signed Scott's name—well, he scribbled his signature—she wasn't Scott West.

Merry Maids was the same deal. It took four women six and a half hours to clean up. They were moving slowly in Max's opinion. Too busy being nosy looking through her and Scott's shit. They peeped the bags of clothes she had put to the side. One female kept asking if Max wanted her to unpack the bags and hang up the items.

"Are you moving out?" another asked.

"I paid for maid service, not chitchat," Max snapped. She also watched them like a hawk. Maxine wasn't a fool. She had all her and Scott's jewelry along with her money in her Hermes bag, which she held onto firmly.

The women left with a large check that would also bounce. After they cleared out, Maxine crawled into her king size bed, and that night she slept peacefully.

F itzgerald Spencer had a smooth but demanding voice and was one of the top criminal defense attorneys on the east coast. His specialties were federal cases, dealing with magistrate judges, negotiating bail bonds, and getting his criminal clients acquitted.

Lucky called him after she listened to the message Layla had left on her cell phone telling her that she'd been arrested by the FBI and to contact her attorney right away. Her mother sounded shaken up and a bit frightened.

"I already have my people on her case," he told Lucky.

"Already? How? Did she call you?"

"I saw the arrest on the news. Your parents are high-profile."

"So what are we looking at?" she asked him.

"Listen, come down to my office this afternoon around two and we'll talk further."

"Okay."

When Layla stole the fifty million from Scott and broke off into her own faction with Lucky and Meyer, the first thing she did was hire Fitz and put him on retainer for one million dollars. She figured his services would come in handy one day for her hot-headed son or Lucky, and a million dollars was more than enough if a case ever went to trial.

Layla figured herself to be smart and to think ahead. She'd heard enough stories about drug dealers who became indicted and incarcerated and found themselves in boiling hot water because they didn't have enough cash saved for lawyers, bail, and a trial. It wasn't going to be her story. She understood that her world was a game of chess and you always had to think four or five moves ahead of your opponent.

It was another Antarctic day in New York. Lucky dressed warmly in a short, tan Burberry double-snap quilted coat, a warm sweater, blue jeans, and knee-high boots. She exited her building with her gunmen and climbed into the backseat of a lavish black Escalade and headed toward lower Manhattan. They fought against city traffic and crawled through the west side of the city before the truck came to a stop in front of a towering, modern glass building with a glass-and-bronze entrance.

Lucky exited the vehicle alone and strutted through the vast marble foyer and examined a directory of who's who of NYC law. She ascended to the 14th floor of the building and entered the lush law office suite, where the firm name and logo was displayed in tall bronze letters—*Spencer, Donnelley & Bridges*—and the furniture was sleek and Italian. The young receptionist at the desk was expecting Lucky. She smiled and immediately allowed her through the doors.

Lucky walked into the lawyer's pristine office and was met with the aroma of high-priced leather. Law degrees from Harvard and Yale decorated the walls, along with a bookshelf swollen with law books. Fitz sat in his high back leather chair behind his exquisite wooden executive desk and smiled at Lucky. Behind him was a picturesque view of the city from the floor-to-ceiling windows.

He stood up and greeted Lucky with a firm handshake. His grip was reassuring, and his blue eyes were concentrated on her. Fitzgerald was handsomely dressed in a dark blue tailored three-piece suit. He was tall and attractive with his tanned skin and sandy brown hair, and he looked like he could be a Kennedy. He was cool as a cucumber and self-confident.

His resume of acquittals and favorable plea deals spoke loudly from the streets to the courts.

Lucky sat opposite him in the low ancient leather chair and quickly asked, "So, what are we lookin' at? The FBI's got my mother on lockdown."

Fitz was always a tell-it-like-it-is attorney. His eyes didn't falter.

"Unfortunately, the judge didn't grant her bail. The U.S. Attorney fears she could be a flight risk, and a judge signed off on the feds freezing her accounts. The raid on her home didn't produce any contraband, but the search warrant included paperwork. Hopefully Layla didn't have any incriminating documents lying around."

"She's not a dumb ass. My mother's a seasoned vet in this game."

He shook his head. "You'd be surprised how many clients I've had that have ledgers outlining how many kilos they've sold per week and to whom."

"Not Layla."

"Good. One less thing to defend. The U.S. Attorney is out for blood with Title Three indictments, and has charged her with the RICO act."

"RICO! Do we have a snitch?" she asked.

"The U.S. Attorney has a solid source somewhere, but it's my job to break everything down and blow holes in their case. Don't worry. Your mother is in good hands, and she's my top priority," he assured her.

"For you to be on a million-dollar retainer, she better be."

"Her next arraignment, I'll push for an appeal to overturn her bail ruling. I'll argue that she has ties in the community, is a mother of six, and isn't a flight risk, but this judge, he's definitely not what anyone would consider lenient . . . he's hard on crime."

The news was grim, but Lucky held her head high and was determined to get through this.

Fitz, a partner at the high-end firm, had one of the associate attorneys locate Layla and contact the public defender who represented her arraignment to turn over the file. From now on, everything he had was going into pushing for Layla's freedom.

"I just want her out and I want this to go away," said Lucky.

"It's going to be a battle, Lucky, but from what I am hearing, your mother is not the big fish that they want. They want your father and her cartel connection."

"My mother is no snitch!"

"Which is why we have a lot of work to do."

"We've got a million dollars invested in you, and they say you're the best. Well, I wanna see results."

Fitzgerald simply leaned back in his chair and grinned, flashing his golden boy smile and pearly white teeth. His reputation preceded him. That's why he could charge twelve hundred per billable hour plus expenses. He was young, cocky, and successful in courtrooms.

"Believe me, I'm worth my weight in gold," he replied. "Layla chose wisely. I plan to visit her this evening. The details matter. I'll put you on the list for Friday. We're going to fight this all the way."

Lucky had heard enough. She had confidence in him. She got up from the chair, pivoted from him, and walked out of the office. So many wheels were turning inside her head. Her parents were in deep shit, but her father wasn't her concern. To Lucky, her father was Maxine and Bugsy's issue now. Scott was alive and she was happy, but surviving surgery was the easiest part. Now came the hard part—fighting the federal government.

Outside, she climbed into the Escalade and sat back with a deep sigh.

"Luck, where you wanna go?" Miz, her goon driver asked.

"Just go," she said. "I don't give a fuck where."

***

Lucky sat in the VIP section of the Manhattan nightclub isolated from the partying crowd below. She was dressed in her finest jewelry, tight jeans, and red bottoms, her cleavage showing in the glittery sequin top she wore. She slowly worked on the bottle of Ace of Spades on ice sitting in front of her with her goons around for protection—the appearance of a gangster bitch for all to see.

The room was lit and the crowd was turnt up, yet Lucky sat there almost grieving. She had a lot on her mind, and she wasn't in any rush to go home, to see her father or brother in the hospital, or to see her mother in lockup. It had been a crazy week of FBI, hospitals, lawyers, and just trouble. With Layla temporarily out of commission and Meyer, the muscle, fighting for his life, it was up to her to step up. She figured that she could easily run Layla's organization. To Lucky, she was co-owner of her mother's criminal enterprise. She had put in just as much work as anyone else. She was groomed since she was knee-high to run a drug empire. It was all she knew.

Lucky frowned when the old school sound of Slick Rick blared throughout the club, and the revelers danced old school to "Children's Story." A large crowd broke into the wop and running man and some pivoting on one foot, facing in the other direction, and doing it all over again. The dance floor became a spectacle of animated entertainers and retro moves.

"Let's bounce."

Lucky and her protective entourage exited the club with eyes glued on them. Safely in the backseat, Lucky wondered, *What now?* How would their business continue? Things with Angel were running like clockwork, but with Layla's arrest, would it continue? Or would the cartel see them as a threat and jump ship? They'd come too far to slide backwards and lose everything they'd worked so hard for.

A decision needed to be made, and someone had to take control of the machine before it all fell apart.

9

Tarsha sat on the couch in the dark feeling antsy. The cigarette she smoked was almost down to its filter. It was her umpteenth of the day. With no more money to spend and none coming in, there were a lot more stressful days. Once again, the bills were piling up, the shopping sprees had ended, and they could barely afford to put gas in the Lexus.

Wacka was asleep with their son in the bedroom, and Tarsha wondered how he could rest so easily when they were broke again. It frustrated her. He was supposed to be the man of the house, but he did nothing but sleep, linger around her, and do a half-assed job in extorting Maxine. Yet, he still wanted sex from her. Tarsha wasn't in the mood to fuck him. Money got her pussy wet and made her want to fuck. She was materialistic. Nice things always excited her.

She tapped the ashes onto the floor, not caring about the mess. The thrill was over, but there was no way she was going to allow the good life to slip from her hands—not that easily. It wasn't going to stop, not if she had anything to do with it. She finished off the cigarette and removed herself from the couch. She peered in on Wacka sleeping like a baby with their son. She frowned. She wanted to throw some cold water on him and startle him awake. How dare he take it easy when they were in a serious crisis? If their son wasn't lying next to him, she would have done it.

Tarsha missed that vicious and murderous man he used to be. Before the accident with his fingers, Wacka always turned her on, and she always ate and lived a good life. And he didn't take no for an answer. He took what he wanted when he wanted. The old Wacka would have carried out his threats by now, and Maxine would've felt his wrath. He would have fucked her up really good.

But things done changed.

Tarsha was like a bloodhound with a scent. She was tired of waiting around and being ignored by the bitch when they had the advantage over her. If Maxine wouldn't pick up her phone and reply to their threat, then they needed to go see her in person. But there was one fundamental issue; they had no idea of her whereabouts. The house that Wacka had kidnapped her from had been sold.

But where there was a will, there was a way.

It was the Internet age, and access to any information was only a few clicks away. Tarsha sat down at her laptop and signed on. In the dim room her fingers started rapping the laptop keys and she typed Maxine's name into Google. Nothing came up but some obituary pictures of old ladies who weren't the right Maxine Henderson. She was a ghost online. That bitch didn't even have a Facebook page.

Tarsha sighed. There had to be another way around the dilemma. Then she thought, Maxine might be a ghost online, but most likely her notorious and wealthy boyfriend wasn't. There was probably all kinds of information on him. So she quickly typed "Scott West" into Google, and *Bingo!*

The results on Scott West seemed to be endless. There were several articles about the businessman, and his pictures flooded the Internet. But what immediately captured Tarsha's attention were the recent articles about his arrest and shooting at his Midtown Manhattan address.

The story was headline news. Tarsha read and read and collected everything there was about him. There was a photograph of his multi-million-dollar penthouse suite where the chaos unfolded—and there was another shot of the opulent entrance to the lavish building. There were several pictures of Scott being carried out on a gurney from the building, FBI in tow behind the EMS. Then there was the money shot—a photographer happened to capture a picture of a grief-stricken Maxine in the backdrop. Her head was dropped from the flash and she was captured outside of the building, rushing away from something. Tarsha smiled at the image.

There were other pictures, several of the FBI with their high-powered rifles and their vehicles, and of the area. One of the articles went on to say that Scott was shot by agents during a raid of his place, and he had been rushed to the hospital, where he was recovering from his wounds—NewYork-Presbyterian to be exact. The article was less than a week old.

Is he still there? She wondered. If he was, then Maxine was too.

Tarsha felt great. She had hit pay dirt. She looked around for her cell phone and found it misplaced between the couch cushions. Then she searched for Presbyterian's information, made the call, and waited. A female answered.

"NewYork-Presbyterian."

"Yes, I need a favor. A friend of mine was admitted there a few days ago. His name is Scott West."

"I'm sorry, ma'am, we're not allowed to disclose any information," the woman replied.

"Okay, thank you." She ended the call.

There was no way she was going to get through the hospital's strict protocol and with Scott being detained by the feds, it was impossible to know his situation. She would have to find out the old fashioned way, and that was going in person. That meant they would have to take a road trip to New York City. It was about getting this money.

Tarsha sat back in the chair and lit another cigarette. It was inexplicable the hate and rage she now felt toward Maxine. Sure, there was acrimony over how Wacka got played and now had nubs where he used to have fingers. To Tarsha, that was all Maxine's fault. But this deep, dark feeling that had just come over her was in addition to her previous appetite for revenge.

With Wacka's situation there was anger, but reading the news articles brought forth jealousy, and Tarsha became a whole other beast. They both fucked hustlers, yet Maxine's man was important enough to have the feds kick open his door while Wacka was a state level criminal. Tarsha felt that she was younger and prettier than Maxine. She stood up and looked at her shape in the long, vertical mirror. Tarsha sucked in her fat gut and grabbed a chunk of her wobbly phat ass. *Niggas love this ass*, she thought. *I can get any nigga I want. I could have Scott West if I wanted him.*

Tarsha was salty and delusional, but her mind was made up. Once they drained Maxine for every dime she and Scott had, she was taking the largest cut and leaving Wacka to find a nigga just as rich and powerful as Scott West. It was time for an upgrade.

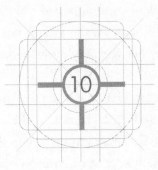

The streets were covered in a thin blanket of snow as an abundance of white flakes fell from an overcast sky and the wind howled like a wolf to the moon. It was a bleak and frigid day. Lower Manhattan looked abandoned and scattered due to the dreary weather. It was becoming a vicious winter.

The black Escalade stopped in front of the Metropolitan Correctional Center building on Park Row. It held male and female prisoners of all security levels, and it was operated by the Federal Bureau of Prisons.

Lucky climbed out from the backseat of the vehicle and shined her fierce look upon the russet colored building. It was where Layla was being detained. Her mother was locked away somewhere in the gloomy twelve stories. The windows were covered by security bars, and it had nearly two dozen closed-circuit security cameras.

Snuggled in her brown mink and riding boots, she trudged toward the front entrance. MCC was a place she hoped to never see as a prisoner in her lifetime. From top to bottom, it was a daunting looking building.

Inside, Lucky battled through the rigorous process for people visiting inmates—thorough security searches, questions, and a lot of waiting.

The visiting room was sprinkled with men and women with their loved ones or waiting for them to enter the room. Lucky sat and waited. She was a bit nervous, but she didn't know why. It was her mother, so what was there to be nervous about?

After ten minutes, there was activity at the prisoner's doorway. Three women were shepherded into the area by a male corrections officer. Layla was in front, as usual—a hint of her power perhaps, but from a distance, she looked like a broken woman behind bars. Lucky spotted her mother and showed no emotions. She simply sat there and waited for Layla to come to her. It was procedure.

Layla walked toward her daughter in the unsightly brown DOC attire. She had been stripped of her glamour and her first-rate clothing. There was no jewelry to boast her wealth, and no red bottoms to feel proud of. Inside MCC, Layla appeared regular like every other inmate, and there was no hint of the lavish life she lived outside.

Layla wore a heavy scowl on her face as she approached Lucky. There were no hugs or kisses exchanged. It wasn't that kind of reunion. Layla sat across from her daughter and locked eyes intensely. She felt angry and she wanted to lash out. She needed to find someone to blame. She had minor bruises from her scuffle with the agents, but they were healing.

"Bitch, you don't know how to answer your fuckin' phone?" They were the first words out of her mouth.

"I had a lot going on, Mother. Meyer's been shot, Scott too and indicted, and you called from an unknown number," Lucky explained.

They were all valid excuses, but Layla didn't care. She shot a hard stare at her daughter. "So it was Meyer, huh? Damn. How's he doin'?"

"He's still alive and in ICU, but it's touch-and-go so far."

Sadness showed on Layla's face. Her son needed her and she couldn't be there for him. She couldn't lose another child, but she was in no position to help him. That was the agonizing part for Layla—not being there for her children and having no control over anything right now. But she felt there was one thing left that she could control—who lived and who died.

Layla snorted. Meyer was her favorite son, and someone put their hands on her children and lived to brag about it.

She whispered, "I want whoever was responsible dead. You hear me? Fuckin' dead."

Lucky shook her head. "See, that's the thing. Dude done died twice."

"Twice?"

"Yeah, Ma. It was Luna. Apparently, Meyer didn't kill him after all. He came back and attempted to murder Meyer and then he killed himself."

"Everything is goin' to shit, and I need to get the fuck outta here."

"I'm doin' my best."

"Are you?"

"Like I said, there's a lot going on, Ma," Lucky repeated.

Layla was restless. She wanted to fuck something up. And with Luna dead by his own hand she couldn't get revenge for her injured son. She wanted out. She wanted to see Meyer. Confinement wasn't for her. Behind bars, everything moved too slowly, life became redundant, and she had no reliable resources. The food was horrible and the cheap fabric was making her skin itch and giving her a rash.

Layla thought for another moment. With Scott jammed up and incapacitated, now was her chance to do what she longed to do. Her sad expression for Meyer transitioned into ice cold and murderous eyes.

She whispered to Lucky, "I want that bitch dead."

"Who now?"

"Bitch, don't play stupid. Maxine. I want her gone. There's no way she's going to gloat over this, seeing me finally locked up while she stays free. I know that bitch is thinkin' this is payback and the end of me—that my karma is coming to bite me on my ass. It's not!"

"Are you crazy? Now's not the time, especially wit' Meyer on life support."

Layla leaned closer with her elbows on the table and replied with a rough whisper, "Yes, it is! I want that bitch fucked up and done with."

"Think, Ma. Yes, we still have the goons on payroll, but there's too much heat crawling up our asses. FBI is everywhere, and you wanna do this? She's not our priority right now!"

"She will always be my priority," Layla growled in a low tone.

The word *no* wasn't an option for her. Her eyes burned into Lucky's skin with her teeth clenched. The audacity of Lucky defying her orders. She was locked up, but she was still in charge.

The subject needed to change, and Lucky said, "I spoke with Fitzgerald. Did he come visit you? Did he tell you about the charges?"

"Yeah, we talked. But it was brief. He said it was too early to get a full scope of the government's case, but most evidence comes out during discovery."

"You think there might be a snitch?"

"Bitch, what I just say? We don't know shit yet!"

Lucky was growing tired of her mother's aggression toward her. She was there to help, but Layla was being an irritable bitch. She wanted to bitch back and shout, but she empathized with her mother. The alphabet boys had her on lockdown, and there was no telling if it would be for life.

Lucky reached over the table and took her mother's hands into hers. They locked eyes. Lucky knew that Layla was hurting deeply inside, despite the hard and angry aura she gave off. She was in a position that no one ever wanted to be in. She wanted her mother to think positive.

"You're goin' to beat this, Ma. The government can't hold you down, and I got a great feeling about this attorney. He's the best," Lucky spoke encouragingly. "You need to stay strong."

Lucky had another question to ask her mother, one that she felt for sure was going to rock the boat between them.

"We have a problem. The feds are freezing your accounts, and that means money is gonna be tight," Lucky started.

"I'm aware of that," Layla replied.

"And there's a second problem—our Miami friend. Where's the hidden money? I need it for the re-up with him next week. We can't lose him, Ma. We worked too hard to get here," Lucky explained coolly.

There was a shipment due the next Tuesday—two hundred kilos at $26,500 a ki, which came to a total of 5.3 million dollars.

Layla looked at Lucky like she was a moron. "Are you out of your damn mind? Do you think I'm stupid?" she barked.

Lucky wasn't following. So Layla continued with, "There will be no business anywhere and no conducting deals with our Miami friend until I'm freed. Besides, our Miami friend won't touch us right now, not with this pending case over my head and the FBI everywhere."

Lucky replied, "So what am I supposed to do until then?"

"Like I said, when I'm out of here, then that's when everything will go back to normal."

It was a selfish statement. Dealers got arrested every day, but the suppliers didn't ever close shop. The cartel was a well oiled machine that never stopped. Life moved on, and money was still out there. But Layla wasn't hearing any of it. Nothing could be said to change her mind.

Lucky was in disbelief. "What am I supposed to do for money, huh? The feds are going to freeze everything. So how am I gonna live and eat, and pay my bills, and pay our men? Meyer's in the hospital and I have nothing right now. I need this money, Ma," Lucky griped in a low and angry tone.

"Right now, the only thing you should be concerned about is my freedom, Lucky. I want out of here. The attorney has been taken care of. And don't ask me where my money is ever again. That's *my* money, not yours or Meyer's! I'll be on my deathbed before I'll give you the privilege to betray me."

Layla felt that her kids would blow through the money in a heartbeat and she would end up broke, jailed, and completely alone. No, the money she'd stolen from Scott was her lifeline—her salvation for rainy days like this one.

The two argued in a low whisper, cursing at each other. Layla wanted to remind Lucky that she was still the boss bitch of the organization. She wasn't about to relinquish control just like that.

Layla still had a bone to pick with a few folks, grudges that she needed to resolve, and a list of demands for Lucky. One, she wanted Maxine dead. Two, she needed to pause her deal with the cartel. Three, she wanted Lucky on top of everything, from her federal case to having all her needs met.

"If you're worried about a place to live, you can move into my place. The lease is paid up for two years. But you and everyone else need to downsize and stay under the radar until I beat these charges and come home to resume my position," said Layla.

Lucky swallowed hard. *This bitch done lost her mind.* Downsize and close up shop, and go into hiding? Lucky was a West, and she felt that one monkey don't stop the show. Lucky was a spoiled brat, and she was used to getting her way, one way or another.

Her visit with her mother ended, and Lucky left with a sour taste in her mouth. Her parents were cut from the same dirty cloth. There was no way she was going to downsize her life and close up shop with the cartel. There was no fucking way she would fold.

Max bought a burner phone from Wal-Mart, set up a fake Facebook profile, and sent Skip a DM, letting her know who she really was. Within minutes she had Skip's digits.

"Yo, bitch, how you be?" Skip asked.

"I be good, fam. And you?"

"Chillin'. Livin'. Eatin'. Fuckin'. Things are good but could always be better. What's up though?"

"I need some help unloading some shit."

"What kind of shit you talking 'bout? You know I only move merchandise. I don't fuck with that powder."

"Nah, we good. I ain't in to all that. I got some high-end shit. You still got your clientele?"

"How high-end? What labels?"

"Christian Louboutins, Balmain, Prada, Chanel—all that good shit."

"Damn bitch, you boosting now wit' your old ass?" Skip joked. "How you got all that?"

"This nigga I used to fuck wit' blessed me. I had to cut his ass off when he got this young bitch pregnant."

"I woulda beat her ass."

"I did beat her ass. And his!" Max lied.

"Max, I know you did. You were always nice wit' ya hands." Skip paused and took a deep pull from her cancer stick. "So, look, come through. But I get twenty percent off the top of whatever we move. You cool wit' that?"

"We peoples. We good."

After Max set up a time to meet with Skip, she changed clothes for a trip to Chelsea Piers fitness center. There she could rent a locker for a year and pay in cash. She needed someplace to hide her money should things go left, and a safety deposit box was too risky. She would basically be handing over her ill gotten gains to the feds. Those boxes were traps for most drug dealers once they got on the government's radar. This locker left no paper trail.

Walking to the gym, she had to hide from Mason and Avery. She saw the truck coming up Park Avenue. No doubt they were coming to check on her. She also kept her eyes peeled just in case the feds were following her.

Dressed in a workout sweat suit and Montclair goose coat and knapsack she headed to the gym. Once her bag was secured, she ran a few miles on the treadmill and then left. She had lots to do, schemes to plan, money to get, and lives to ruin—with so little time.

***

It became her routine—home, and the hospital. It had been a week now since the arrest, and her world felt compartmentalized. She was able to find a few jewelers in the Diamond District to buy the jewelry at fifty cents on the dollar. Max had appraisal papers for all the items, so they knew it wasn't stolen. They just figured she had fallen on hard times. She was clever enough to not go to Scott's jeweler, though he would have bought the jewelry back at eighty cents on the dollar. But he also would have told Scott should they ever speak again, and Max couldn't take that chance for a larger amount of money.

Max sold everything except her engagement ring and her diamond earrings. She netted $990,000. It wasn't bad, but it wasn't great either. She was still behind the eight ball. Had she not paid Wacka, she would also have had legal money safely tucked away in her bank account.

Maxine decided to not keep dwelling over spilled milk. She made the best decision she could with the information she had at that time. Had she known the feds would kick in the door, she would have done lots of things differently.

She hated to visit Scott in the hospital. Maxine's visits with Scott were short and carefully watched. She couldn't speak freely with agents inside the room, so their chitchat was minimal. He was healing from his gunshot wounds, and it wouldn't be long before he was transferred to a federal prison and held there until his trial. It was the inevitable.

Scott could see that something was bothering Maxine, but he figured it was his pending doom with the federal government. He wasn't even remotely correct. She was already over the whole scene. Been there done that. All Maxine wanted was Scott's money and Wacka off her ass. She needed to either pay Wacka or kill him—and neither option was easy.

Lately, Bugsy was seeing to her needs. He had Scott's men chauffer Maxine around to make sure that she was protected. But each time she got into the backseat of the tinted SUV and the doors locked, she worried if they were taking her to an undisclosed location to never be seen again. Maxine's eyes were alert to her whereabouts and the guards' movements. Easily, one could spin around and put a gun to her head, kill her right there in the backseat, and drive her body to an unmarked grave somewhere.

She hadn't forgotten that Bugsy was Layla's son too. Maxine felt he liked her, but blood was thicker than water. She stayed on pins and needles.

There were other issues Maxine had to deal with. She told Scott about the board pushing for his eviction from the building.

"The negative press of your arrest and shooting has a lot of residents feeling uneasy. No one has approached me, but I can feel the shade when I walk into the building. The climate has changed. People glare at me now."

"Fuck 'em. I paid a lot of money to be there and I haven't been convicted of shit. Hold your fuckin' head up high, baby."

Maxine continued to push. "The newspapers have dubbed you a murderous drug kingpin with ties to a notorious Mexican cartel. Maybe it's time that I relocate . . . for my safety."

Scott coughed a little. His body ached and he was uncomfortable listening to Maxine whine about irrelevant shit.

"That building is one of the safest in New York. Please, just be patient and bear with me."

Maxine took his hand into hers and kissed it. "You don't understand because you're in here, in a bubble away from it all. I am going through a lot on my own. I have no money to buy food or essentials. How will I pay the light bill?"

"What are you talking about, Maxine? What about your money from your parents' home?"

She didn't expect that. "I would use that money, but I told you I invested it with a broker. I wanted to be like you and grow my assets."

Scott's mind was sharp as a razorblade. He knew they'd never had that discussion. But her pennies were the last thing on his mind. Suddenly he was aggravated and wanted her to leave. She was supposed to be encouraging him and showing support at this critical time in his life, but it seemed that he was doing all the comforting. Scott understood his situation better than anyone. He knew that it was easier for everyone to disassociate themselves from him. They didn't want that kind of heat and trouble knocking on their front door. He also knew that the arrest was still fresh on everyone's mind, nerves were frayed, and people were paranoid, but in time things would slowly get back to normal.

"Get in contact with my lawyer, Arnold Meade. He'll handle the legal issues. You can trust Arnold. He's been with me for a very long time. I don't want you to worry," he said. "No one is kicking us out of our home. And I will send Bugsy to drop off some cash for our overhead. Everything will be taken care of. I have more than enough to last you three lifetimes."

He could see in her eyes that she was still worried. She managed a weak smile. "Why do I have to be spoon-fed by your son, Scott? I'm a grown woman, your fiancée. When are you going to give me access to your situation?" she said, talking in code. Scott understood that to mean his drug money.

He heaved a long sigh. He couldn't believe they were having this conversation again. He told her what she wanted to hear. "Soon."

Maxine starred deeply into his eyes and knew that he was bullshitting her. "Okay, soon. I guess now is a good time to tell you that the feds stole all our jewelry during the raid."

"What the fuck you say?"

"It's gone, Scott. All your Rolexes, diamonds, and pearls are gone. And with the lock broken on the door most of my expensive clothing, handbags, and shoes are gone too."

Max wanted to irritate him, and she had.

Scott roared at the two agents sitting across the room. "Y'all muthafuckas steal from me? You come in my home and violate my shit!"

"Calm the fuck down! No one stole shit," Agent Devonsky spewed. "If anything is missing, it wasn't our agency."

Scott was seething at the repeated disrespect. "My lawyer will hear about this shit!"

"You're doing life, Scott. Why care about stolen items you'll never get to see again anyway?" Devonsky mocked.

"Fuck you! I'm gonna beat this case. No jury will ever convict Scott West. You'll see."

Devonsky chuckled and walked out the room to get coffee.

Maxine continued her line of questioning. "I can't see you locked away for the rest of your life."

"Didn't you just hear me!"

"Baby, I know what you said. You said those same words to me years ago and look what happened. Don't get mad, but I think if the feds offer a plea deal you should take it. Doing twenty or twenty-five years is better than life. And you know I'll still be here for you when you get out. You're still young, Scott. We could still have a beautiful life together."

Maxine watched as Scott's face went from shock to anger. His eyes turned so dark she could hardly see his pupils. Inwardly, Maxine was cracking up. She had planted a seed. Something for him to consider if the feds ever broached the subject.

"Maxine, I'm going to need you to leave right now before I say or do something that I might regret."

"Baby, I was only–"

"Now!"

"Okay, get some rest, baby. I love you." She kissed Scott on his lips quickly before the agent could shout to her, "No close contact!"

She walked out the room no closer to getting her hands on his money, but she had accomplished something. Maxine wouldn't let up on Scott treating her as an equal when it pertained to his money. And, she wanted to continue to plant the seed in his mind that copping out was better than going to trial.

Quickly, her dark thoughts were halted by the shock of her life. There he was, in a suit and tie under a wool pea coat. He looked like he'd just come from church. It was Wacka, right there in the hallway, locking eyes with her and smirking. She knew he was there to intimidate her. He wanted his money. Maxine stood there frozen, knowing that this Wacka situation had to be handled.

Bugsy sat in the visiting room of the MCC building waiting for Layla. He was dressed in Armani with his cool persona and looked more like a high-powered lawyer than a gangster. He spotted his mother being shepherded into the room by a CO. He kept his eyes on her from the moment she entered the room, walking his way with her contentious frown and ugly brown prison garb. She sat across from him and quickly started with her demands.

"I need you to put your goons on Maxine, ASAP! I want that bitch dead by nightfall. Your damn sister, that little dead-eye bitch, has been ignoring me, talkin' 'bout now is not the time. It's always the right time to see that bitch dead. Especially wit' me in here. I know that bitch is gloating! And don't tell me shit about your father. He can't do shit. How do I know? Because we're in the same situation."

Bugsy listened to her go on and on about being wronged by everyone, griping about Lucky's bullshit, hating Maxine, how trifling his father was, and how much she'd sacrificed. He wondered why he'd come to see her at all. Layla was too consumed with hatred and revenge to even notice he was sitting there. Not once did she ask about Meyer's condition.

Bugsy shook his head at his mother's demands. She was unbelievable. He wanted to laugh, but he didn't want to rile her up even more.

"First off, I don't take orders from you," he said. "I came to visit and talk, not be belittled and bossed. And Maxine is no threat to anyone."

Layla was taken aback by the comment. Her frown tightened and her cheeks got hot with anger. *How dare he?*

Bugsy then continued with, "And your son—you remember him? Meyer? He's still alive, in case you were wondering."

The callous comment set her off. "You muthafucka! You defy your mother like this? I gave birth to you and raised your ungrateful ass. I gave you everything and now you come against me? You rotten-ass nigga! I'm in jail and you allow that bitch to still breathe? Why? If I wasn't in this position, I would slap the shit outta you."

Bugsy had never disrespected Layla the way Meyer and Lucky did. The both of them would have cursed her back, but he continued to sit there coolly and allow the venom to spew from her mouth. His visit with his mother wasn't turning out the way he'd hoped. She was difficult, but she always was a difficult woman—a bitch who was used to getting her way. Jail wasn't going to change that.

Bugsy smiled, which angered her more.

"Why the fuck are you smiling when your mother is in fuckin' jail?" she rebuked. "You find my predicament funny?"

"No! But I love you, Ma," he replied.

He stood up to indicate that their visit was over. She didn't control him, and he hadn't come to argue with her. His kissed his mother on the forehead and left the table.

Layla sat there in silence and in bitterness. She could only watch her son leave the room, knowing she was losing her hold over him and the others. She feared that the longer she was behind bars, the more distant and independent they would become.

Bugsy wasn't killing Maxine. Scott would never sanction it.

***

Bugsy sat in the backseat of the black Range Rover and watched in silence. His goons were seated up front, and they were quiet too. Bugsy just wanted to sit and reminisce—no radio and no conversation. The SUV was parked on the suburban block at night, across the street from a beautiful three-bedroom home with a manicured lawn and a floral arrangement near the front steps. She loved her flowers. Her blue BMW was parked in the driveway, and the lights were on in the living room.

He watched Alicia move around her home. She was still beautiful—breathtaking. She didn't walk but glide, it appeared in Bugsy's eyes. His missed her so much. What he would do to be with Alicia right now. He sat in the dark vehicle stone-faced, but his heart was fluttering with sadness and regret. She was the best thing that ever happened to him, and now she was gone—dismissed from his life because of who he was and what he represented, and who his family was—gangsters. It could never be her world—the drugs, the killings, the authorities kicking in her front door with a warrant at any time. Alicia was the purest thing in Bugsy's life, and he had no right to corrupt her. But he loved her dearly. He was lonely without her, but she was untouchable.

Bugsy watched her petite silhouette move back and forth from the living room window. The good news was, she appeared to be single. She didn't have company and there were no other cars in the driveway. There was a for-sale sign on the front lawn. She was selling the place. He had paid cash for it and it was hers, his gift to her—her name was on the deed. She would be leaving and he didn't know how soon. Maybe she wanted a fresh start somewhere, and the house was only a reminder of their love.

Damn. She deserved to be happy; Bugsy only wished that it could have been with him.

"Let's go," he told Pluto.

Pluto nodded and started up the vehicle. Bugsy took one long and final look at Alicia's home. As if on cue, she appeared in her front window dressed for bed in a long T-shirt and sipping on tea. Bugsy's eyes fixed on her from the tinted windows of the truck and his heart melted with nostalgia. Did she sense that he was nearby? Her eyes gawked at the Range parked across the street, and Bugsy managed to smile.

So beautiful, he said to himself.

Pluto slowly moved the truck away from the curb. Bugsy took his final look at Alicia standing in her window, glowing like the angel she was. He would bother her no more. She was moving on, and so would he.

Maxine stood in the hallway frozen like a human popsicle, her feet rooted to the floor. Wacka looked like a choir boy in his suit and pea coat.

At a snail's pace, he started to walk toward Maxine and locked on to her nervousness. The look on Maxine's face was priceless. She was shitting bricks. He saw that fear inside her, and it exhilarated him. It reconnected him to something dark inside him that he never realized he missed. His ego yearned to be feared.

Coolly, Wacka walked by Maxine and smirked. He didn't say one word to her. He didn't need to. He wanted to generate fear by simply being there, and it was working. He strolled in the hallway like he was looking for a patient's room. In passing Scott's room, he quickly spied inside and observed the armed agents inside and outside the room.

It was definitely true. Scott was in trouble with the feds, and Maxine's safety net was collapsing.

He went to the elevator on the south side of the building and got on with several patients and doctors, and it descended. He exited the hospital lobby and climbed into the front seat of an idling car parked around the corner where Tarsha was waiting.

Wacka smiled and nodded.

"You're on the money, babe," he said. "That bitch saw me, and the look on her face was pure panic." He laughed.

"I knew it," Tarsha said. "We 'bout to get our fuckin' money from that bitch."

"I'm ready."

They were tired of the ignored phone calls and the games. Now it was time to make good on their threats. As they gloated, Wacka's cell phone started to ring. It was Maxine calling. Wacka and Tarsha grinned and Wacka uttered, "Oh, now this bitch wanna fuckin' call back?"

He answered his phone with, "You better be calling me wit' some good news, bitch!"

***

Seeing Wacka walk by and not say a word to her made her furious. He was toying with her. He was making it known to her that she couldn't run or hide anywhere. He was going to be everywhere. It was too close for her comfort. Maxine wondered if he was there to speak with Scott. Was he ready to tell him everything? Was he tired of her jerking him around? But still, it would be suicide on Wacka's end.

Fuck!

She needed to handle Wacka and the situation—either by death or payment somehow. Her time was winding down.

She found some privacy in the nearby stairwell. She turned on the burner phone he'd given her and dialed his number, her hands trembling with nervousness. His phone rang and she waited, not knowing exactly what to say to him.

"You better be calling me wit' some good news, bitch!"

"I'm gonna get you your fuckin' money," she cursed. "But don't you *ever* show up here again!"

"You're fuckin' me around. No more games! I want my payday, now!"

"Real talk, I don't have five million."

"You better shit it out somehow. I'm not fuckin' around anymore."

Wacka didn't want to hear any excuses. He wanted to placate Tarsha and he wanted to be feared again and respected. Maxine continued to tell him that she didn't have that type of money, but they didn't care.

"Bitch, I need something right now. If not, I got a story to tell," he threatened. "Don't fuck wit' me!"

Maxine sighed heavily. Her mind was spinning to find a quick solution. She couldn't afford to have him lingering around the hospital.

"How much you got on you now, bitch?" he asked her.

"I can get my hands on another ninety thousand dollars," she said.

It was a small chunk of money from the sale of the jewelry. It was painful to think that she would have to give it away to a lowlife thug like Wacka. Maxine gritted her teeth at the thought of it. She wanted to smash the phone against the wall. She wanted to scream. She needed to kill this nigga. She took a seat on the stairs and held back the angry tears she felt about to pour out from her eyes.

"I'm tired of your fuckin' peanuts," he said.

"Peanuts? You ain't ever made this kind of money in your life, so spare me the *you get money* act. We both know this is your come-up," she said.

"Bitch, then come up off of it then."

"Wacka, I'm not going to keep being too many of your bitches! You push me too far and we're done! You can go and tell Scott everything. Fuck it, we can go together! Now I said I'm trying to put together some paper for your greedy ass! And for the record, you're a nothing nigga. You're a triggerman who was out of his league. You took on a family that you couldn't beat, and somehow that's my fault? You're weak and stupid, and your family paid the price. Keep fucking with the West family and see if we all don't end up dead."

Maxine had to vent. She could feel that he was too cocky. He continued to hold her secret over her head, and it pissed her off. She gave this wounded goon a half a million dollars, and he wanted more?

She heard the phone being jostled and then, "We want that now," Wacka said.

Of course they did. Maxine could tell that she was on speaker phone. There was an echo and she could hear someone else speaking quietly in the background. It appeared that this individual was telling him what to say. She figured it had to be the same bitch that she crossed paths with at One Police Plaza.

"We know about everything—the famous real estate tycoon wit' his multi-million dollar businesses and a drug kingpin on the side. The nigga is worth hundreds of millions, so five million ain't shit to him. That shit is a drop in the bucket for the dirt we have on you."

"Right now I have ninety large," said Maxine.

"That ninety K may give you an additional week or two . . . maybe."

"What the fuck do you want from me? I'm tryin' to work wit' you, but what you're asking, it's ridiculous."

Her comment angered Wacka. "You had me kill that man's kids! His fuckin' kids! And you calling *this* ridiculous and wanna negotiate wit' *me*? There ain't no fuckin' negotiating! You come off that ninety K, plus our five million."

The harder Maxine tried to deescalate the situation, the worse it got.

She then heard him say, "In fact, meet me right now on the east side of the building and bring me that engagement ring on your finger. We want that."

Maxine was stunned. She couldn't give him her ring.

"I-I can't!" she protested.

"You can and you will. I know that rock is worth a pretty penny, so you dead on that ring."

"Just take the ninety thousand for now."

He was back to calling her outside of her name. "Bitch, you're pissin' me the fuck off! What I tell you? There is no negotiating to this shit. And it won't take me but a minute to go upstairs and leave a simple note for Scott to read. You got that, bitch? Maybe I'll even leave a note for the feds! Yeah, maybe I will! Let them dig into this shit too. I keep telling you I don't have shit to lose! My muthafuckin' moms was murdered right in front my face, bitch! You had my sister chopped up in the shower!"

The tears started to pour from Maxine's eyes as she looked down at the engagement ring Scott had given her. She didn't want to give it up, but what choice did she have? The walls were collapsing in on her, and she couldn't dig herself out of this hole. What was she going to tell Scott when he noticed that her ring was missing? What explanation could there possibly be? And how had she put herself into this situation? It wasn't supposed to happen like this. She wished Miguel was still around. He was her triggerman and he was sprung on her. Miguel would have killed Wacka and his bitch for her. He would have done anything she said.

Despondently, she replied, "I'll be down in five minutes."

"I'm glad you see things my way. And bitch, don't have me waiting long," Wacka said before ending the call.

Maxine felt sick to her stomach. She wanted to throw up. For now, Wacka and his wicked bitch had her dead to rights.

**

"I got this, baby. I'll go meet that bitch," Tarsha said to him. "You did good on the phone. That's the nigga I miss and who I fell in love wit'. I love you."

Wacka smiled. "I love you too."

His adrenaline was pumping and he was so hyped that he didn't feel handicapped. He felt vibrant and alive. The sound of Maxine's voice begging and cracking was a high for him. He had that bitch scared. With another ninety thousand on top of that bitch's engagement ring and five million dollars, he and Tarsha were going to be set for life. And it was the easiest money he'd ever made.

Tarsha kissed her king on the lips and climbed out of the car. She too felt excited and turned on again. She couldn't wait to have Maxine's ring in her possession. She strutted to the hospital in a pair of thigh-high leather boots, tight blue jeans, and her auburn leather jacket. She had grimy written all over her, but her dark shades covered her sinister eyes. She didn't want to create any unwanted attention on herself, so she moved with extra caution, knowing Scott had goons loitering in the area. In her purse, she concealed a .380—just in case it was a setup.

Tarsha went toward the east wing of the hospital. It was a busy area with pedestrians and traffic. The temperature was a modest 40 degrees, one of the better days in late January. Tarsha made it to the east wing lobby and looked around for Maxine. Her head stayed on a swivel and her hand on her purse. She was nervous, but that money made her a vicious bitch.

She spotted Maxine coming toward her. She was mixed in with the lobby mob, and the look in the bitch's eyes could have slaughtered Tarsha right there. Maxine's scowl was boiling with rage, but Tarsha wasn't afraid.

Tarsha felt that if it came to a one-on-one battle, she would wipe the floor with Maxine. She had no idea who Maxine was and what type of life she'd lived for twenty-plus years. She didn't have a clue how deadly Maxine was and how adept she'd become with hand-to-hand combat. Prison taught her a lot.

Tarsha hated that Maxine was on an entirely different level than she was. Scott, though he was jammed up with the feds, was a baller. He made money—so much of it that he could wipe his ass with hundred-dollar-bills for a month. Wacka had to take it from other drug dealers and peddle his drugs on the side. Tarsha's jealousy of Maxine's luxurious lifestyle only amplified her desire to make the bitch pay.

The two females stood in front of each other, and their contempt for one another was evident from their scowls and their threatening body language. Both women were ruthless.

Tarsha started to berate her quietly. "You know what it is, bitch. Come up off that ring if you know what's best for you. That bitch is mine now."

Reluctantly and slowly, Maxine started to slide the large diamond ring off her ring finger. The thought of passing it over to a ghetto bitch like Tarsha was sickening. Her eyes burned into the woman. She wanted to tear Wacka's bitch apart, but she settled for an attitude right now. She grudgingly placed the ring into Tarsha's hand and sucked her teeth with disdain through her pursed lips. The value of that ring was more than everything Tarsha owned put together. Maxine lingered in front of her, spewing hatred with her eyes and sucking her teeth.

Tarsha said, "Bitch, I know you ain't suckin' ya teeth at me. You lucky we in here, cuz I would fuck you up for what you did to my man."

Maxine's eyes cut deep into her and she simply replied, "Enjoy the ring for as long as you can. Wear it in good health."

Maxine's glaring black eyes spoke loudly. Her mouth said nothing else. In fact, her furious glare was so intense that Tarsha grew a little nervous.

Was she threatening them? Tarsha wondered. A slight tremble developed inside of Tarsha for some reason, but she refused to show it. She felt the urge to get away from Maxine as soon as possible. Not another word was said between them. Tarsha started to backpedal away from Maxine, keeping her eyes closely on her. But before Tarsha could turn away, she observed Maxine raise her index finger to her neck and make a slicing-of-the-neck movement.

Tarsha managed to smirk and mouthed, "Yeah right, bitch. Try it."

But inside, she was somewhat shaken up. Maxine was that crazy bitch who had Wacka murder her man's kids. Who knew what else she was capable of?

Layla sat in her cell and waited for her day in court. Fitzgerald Spencer had begun to do a 180. His optimistic promises of acquittals and living happily ever after had been placed on pause after he met with the U.S. Attorney. He was working on her case night and day. She desperately needed to get out. She felt swallowed up in a sea of miserable bitches. Life behind bars was fucked up. The only thing she could do was sit around and read and anticipate visitors.

She was a big deal inside the correctional facility. Her name rang out like church bells on a Sunday morning. Her face was in the news, and her husband was notorious in the city and beyond. The last thing Layla had to worry about was somebody messing with her inside. Her pedigree was recognized by everyone—from the hardest gangsters to the wannabes. The corrections officers treated her fairly, and the inmates stayed out of her way or wanted to connect with her. But Layla was in no mood to socialize with people she felt were beneath her—subordinates in her book. She had enough to deal with. She mostly kept to herself.

Today was another court day—a second chance to appeal her bail ruling. It was early morning and it was her time to transfer from the lockup facility to the federal court across the street. The guard called her name and subsequently came the procedure for inmates' travel to the adjacent building. There was a change of prison dress and a thorough pat-down in all the awkward places.

Layla was presented to federal marshals in the basement of the building. She was shackled at the ankles, chained at the waist, and cuffed at the hands as she marched through a tunnel nearly forty feet below the city street. Security was extremely tight, and cameras were everywhere. During this movement through the corridor with electronic doors at each end remotely controlled by watchful officers, no one would lay eyes on Layla but the marshals and people in the surveillance stations.

Finally, they reached the north end of the tunnel and waited for the prisoner elevator. Inside, there was a locked cage for the prisoner to ride up to the courthouse cells. Layla was quiet and brooding. Her fate with the judge was only moments away. It was hard for her to stay calm, but she didn't have a choice. She hoped Fitz would make something happen.

Layla stood in the courtroom next to her highly paid and well-dressed attorney. Fitzgerald Spencer stood with prominence in front of the white-haired Caucasian judge swathed in his flowing black robe and hard eyes on the defendant and her legal representative. Judge Harford had seen it all and handed down over ten thousand years of prison sentences in his thirty-eight years on the bench.

The hearing commenced and immediately Fitzgerald went into battle mode and argued to omit the previous bail ruling. His grounds were that Layla was an outstanding citizen with no violent criminal record. She was a mother who had recently buried three children and was in the process of filing for divorce from her estranged husband. Fitzgerald pointed out that his client and Scott West were living apart when they were arrested and that it was her husband, her codefendant, who had the lengthy criminal past. Fitz did his best to highlight his client's positive qualities and show that she had strong, long term ties to the community and wouldn't skip town if granted bail. He even went as far to surrender her passport. Judge Harford was listening.

The prosecution, U.S. Attorney Gloria Sheindlin, argued against him, highlighting Layla's ties to two violent and murderous drug cartels. She brought up Scott's criminal charges and dug up theft and loitering charges on Layla from when she was a teenager. Sheindlin said that the streets would not be safe with Layla West out on bail.

In Layla's eyes, they wanted the judge to see her as a female El Chapo. She wanted to cut that bitch's head off, but she remained cool, hoping the judge would see things their way. She wished she could throw a bribe at the man—a half a million dollars for her freedom. But he was a stickler for law and order.

It was a pinball game of words between Fitz and the prosecutor. Fitz was convincing with his words and his reasoning, but the prosecutor was fiercer with her fear tactics.

In the end, it was the judge's decision. His cold, blue eyes looked down at Layla and her attorney. His jaw was clenched so tightly that the veins in his temple bulged. "The defendant will remain remanded into federal custody until her trial date."

The judge banged his gavel, finalizing his decision.

It was a harsh blow to Layla. She wanted to cry, but she held back her tears. This wasn't happening to her, but it was. Her attorney was straight-faced. He'd failed her. "This is only a setback, Layla. The odds were stacked against us, but we can—"

"I want my million's worth from you," she interrupted him. "Fix this shit, Fitz!"

"I will. I promise you," he said. "I'll be over to meet with you in a few hours. There are some things we need to discuss."

Layla's eyes were burning with rage. The court officers ushered her from the courtroom and back into the bullpen. She would not be going home anytime soon. She had to accept her new normal.

***

Fitzgerald arrived shortly before lunch. He brought Layla an expensive meal from Nobu. She didn't thank him, as she knew it was purchased with her million-dollar retainer. As she began to devour the delicious shrimp fried rice and three-hundred-dollar oysters, he began speaking.

"We need to have this conversation. It's still early on, but I wouldn't be any good if I didn't broach the subject." He cleared his throat. "We haven't gone through discovery, but I sat with the prosecutor on your case and not only is she good, but she's confident."

Layla stopped eating. "I don't want to hear it! Get me the fuck outta here or so help me . . ."

Her voice trailed off for a reason. She wanted Fitz to imagine what could be done to him.

"Layla, please, no threats. We need to carve out our options. What I can definitively say is that they have a government witness. Someone is cooperating, and that leaves you in a precarious situation."

"Who the fuck is it?"

"I don't know."

"Is it Maxine Henderson? Everything went downhill the moment that snitching bitch came home."

Fitzgerald was well aware who Maxine was. She was a lot of things, but informant wasn't one of them.

"From what I can glean from my talk with Gloria, it's a John Doe."

Layla resumed eating. She stuffed a large shrimp in her mouth and asked, "Do they have anything on my kids? Are they safe?"

"If they had a case on your children, they would have arrested everyone. But that doesn't mean that they aren't trying to build a case. For now, I think their man hours will be devoted to you and your husband."

Layla nodded. "So what's my strategy? Can we blame all this shit on Scott? Let that nigga take the fall."

"Because you're married to him and he's your codefendant, it will be tough for any jury to believe you didn't know about any of his illegal activity. So to point the finger squarely at him would be to your detriment."

"Why would it be hard? Juries do it all the time for white women. Look at Bernie Madoff's wife. That nigga was running a billion-dollar Ponzi scheme. Is she behind bars? But my black ass is being cooked."

"Layla, that's different."

"Because she's white!" Why had he gotten her started? "Name one wife of these white collar criminals that's sitting in jail. Just one! I got plenty of time to wait."

Fitz had to refocus his client. "Let's stay on topic. Whoever the informant is, he will be pointing the finger at you. Do you have any female underlings in your organization that we could use to cast doubt on your guilt? Maybe have this person fall on your sword? I'm just talking out loud. As I said, we are still in the early stages, but if you could give me something to help refute an eyewitness, cast doubt, and confuse a jury that would help. I need a warm body to pin this on."

Layla thought quickly. She was the only female in the West organization. Scott hadn't even let Maxine in. And then she blurted out, "Lucky. She's the only other female."

"Lucky?" Fitz sat back in his chair and placed his hands in a prayer position and began thinking. "How old is she?"

"Twenty."

"Is she currently in the game?"

"Not since the feds shut me down. I gave strict orders for her to stand down until I get through this."

"It could work, but only if she's on board. If I put her up on the stand I would crucify her. Her answers would leave her open for an indictment if the prosecutor found corroborating evidence. She would have to steer clear of the family business."

Layla was desperate. She easily understood his strategy, which was usually used in murder trials. There were trials where, for instance, if the husband was accused of murdering his mistress, the wife would take the stand and allude that she could have done it. Or, sometimes, the defense attorney will name drop a person at trial who wasn't a part of the defense team or strategy. In the O.J. Simpson trial there was a theory floating around that alleged his son was the killer. You just throw out phantom names and hope something sticks.

"She'll do it. Her and Meyer will do whatever I say. I know my baby. She doesn't want to see me behind bars for the rest of my life. She needs me. I'll speak with her."

"Her testimony is only a small step toward getting you acquitted. Have her set up a meet with me in a few weeks as we get closer to trial so I can prep her. Enjoy your food. We'll talk."

Fitzgerald had to quickly leave. His driver was out front waiting to whisk him away to the Hamptons for a cocktail party at a judge's home. There he would hand out his business card to those same white collar criminals Layla had just spoken of.

Maxine dressed down for the task in front of her. Wearing tight jeans, a hoodie, goose coat, and sneakers, she loaded her BMW's backseat and trunk with four large trash bags and two garment bags stuffed with several mink and chinchilla coats. Even with all this merchandise, she still had a closet filled with more where that came from.

Her Michelin tires hugged the road as she headed uptown to pick up Skip. She had her meet her on 125th and Amsterdam Avenue, which was not far from the iconic Apollo Theater and had a lot of foot traffic due to the retail stores in the neighborhood. In her waistband she had a pink handled .22 that Bugsy had given her to help her feel safe. A light snow began to blanket the streets, and Maxine hoped that the weather conditions wouldn't get worse. Right now, it was relatively a warm winter evening, which usually meant that shit was about to be a blizzard.

She sat parked with the car idling for warmth and waited. Skip was supposed to arrive at five o'clock, and it was half past. Maxine called her cell phone repeatedly, but it kept going straight to voicemail. She didn't want to think the worst, but where the fuck was she? Maxine hopped out to get two franks and a Pepsi. The aroma of the grilled hot dogs was making her stomach growl.

The Middle Eastern man with the dirty fingernails was less than polite. "Come on, hurry. What you want?"

"Two dogs with everything and a Pepsi."

She watched as he barely loaded her hot dog with toppings and condiments. "I said everything. Add onions, more relish, more sauerkraut, mustard, and ketchup!" she snapped.

"This is what you get! You want more you pay extra!"

"Then I'll pay extra! Damn!" Maxine turned around to see that a line had quickly formed behind her. People were getting off the train and wanted to grab a quick meal or hot peanuts before heading home. That's what she loved about New York. It was truly the city that never sleeps. Rain, sun, or snow—the weather stopped no one.

"You know what? Give me another order." Maxine heard a female suck her teeth. She turned around and glared at the younger female and then said, "You don't want it." And she didn't.

Max sat in her luxury vehicle, wolfing down her food with Hot 97 blasting. As the clock clicked closer to six, a rage began to grow inside her. She was highly annoyed to be kept waiting this long and without a courtesy call. This is why she hated needing people. They always showed out. Just as she was wiping her hands so she could put her car in drive and peel out, Skip banged on her window, startling her. The anger written on Maxine's face spoke volumes. Skip looked a little frightened but managed a weak smile. Slowly, Maxine unlocked the door and Skip slid in.

"Evidently my five is your six?"

"So sorry to be so late, but the train—"

"I'm not going to waste a second more of my time listening to an excuse. If I can drive from Midtown and make it on time then you shoulda fucking been here too! Especially when you live in fuckin' Harlem!"

"You right, Max. My bad."

Maxine rolled her eyes. She hated that. Here she was way uptown like a sitting duck with hundreds of thousands of dollars worth of merchandise in her car and Skip just didn't give a fuck.

"Why didn't you answer my calls?"

"Oh, because I didn't get them. I was on the train."

Maxine wasn't letting this go. "So let me get this straight. You left your house at five when you were supposed to be here at five? So fuck me, huh? My time don't mean shit?"

Skip didn't allow anyone to talk greasy to her. She was a grown-ass woman, and Maxine was grilling her like she was a child. However, one-on-one, Skip knew she couldn't win. Plus, she wanted to make some money tonight because she was dead broke.

"My bad, you right. Time is money, so how 'bout I lessen my cut from twenty to fifteen percent? This all on me. You good wit' that?"

"I'm good with it." Maxine felt respected again.

Skip smiled broadly. "Now give me a hug, bitch. I ain't seen you in a minute."

The two met in the middle of the console and Skip leaned in and gave Maxine a tight hug. Her arm brushed against Max's pistol, and Skip was even more relieved that she hadn't challenged her in any way.

"I bought you some food."

"Thanks, bitch. This right here gonna hit the spot. I'm starving!"

"Don't spill shit in my car."

Skip paused and looked at the beautiful vehicle as if seeing it for the first time. "This you?"

"All day."

"I need to meet that type of niggas you fuckin' wit'. Like, damn, bitch. You doing it real big."

Maxine nodded and then got down to business as Skip dug into her hot dog. "Where we going first?"

"I got a lot of clients lined up. They expecting me, and they all wear a size four or six just like you, so we should be good on the sizes. This one Puerto Rican bitch is loaded. Her family own a string of beauty parlors, but her man into selling weight. We gonna go there first and then keep it moving. Make a left . . ."

The moment Maxine pulled up to the tenement building in Harlem, shit didn't feel right. Why was someone who was loaded living here in such a basic building?

"You sure about this? I mean, I'm not selling Adidas suits and Steve Madden shoes."

Skip laughed. "We good. Trust me. That's her mom's beauty parlor. They stay packed with the wash and sets. Upstairs are apartments. They own the whole building but keep an apartment for convenience."

"So she doesn't live here?"

"Nah, I don't know where she lives. It's some secret shit. One minute she acts like she lives in Jersey, then Westchester. Not like I give two fucks."

Both ladies got out and unloaded all the bags. Skip rang the doorbell and announced herself, and they were rang in.

A mean-faced old woman answered the door and she was less hospitable than Maxine was used to. She stared at them and walked away. Skip and Maxine dragged the bags into the living room and just stood there. Maxine looked at all the white, red, and pink figurines, several shrines, crosses, lace doilies, and gaudy statues. There were two pictures of young Latino men in caskets taped above several lit candles. The house smelled of oils and incense. It was clear they were into Santería as their religion.

Finally a beautiful woman came into the room. She smiled wide and gave Skip a hug.

"Hola, Skip."

"What's up, Marisol? This is my friend Max. This her shit."

Marisol extended her hand and both women exchanged pleasantries. Marisol looked at all the bags and was completely taken aback.

"All this is for sale?"

Maxine simply nodded.

Marisol opened the first bag and began pulling out garments. Her mouth dropped open when she recognized outfits that Kim Kardashian owned and snapped on Instagram, things that Beyoncé and Rihanna wore to award shows. Quickly, the Latin beauty stripped down to her panties and bra and began trying on the merchandise. She paraded in front of a full length mirror, twisting and turning so she could see her ass, thighs, and profile.

The room was pin-drop quiet. Marisol would take off an item and toss it on the sofa. Soon the pile was damn near to the ceiling. When she got to the fur coats she began speaking in Spanish. She called her mother in the room to watch her model them. The once stern face was replaced with smiles, Spanish talk, and then more smiles. Skip and Maxine didn't understand a word. Nor did they know which items she wanted to buy.

The mom looked toward the women and asked in perfect English, "Would you like something to drink? Juice? Malta? Water?"

Maxine replied, "No, ma'am."

Skip smiled and shook her head. "No, thank you."

Finally the last bag was opened and the Hermes bags came out. Marisol just stared for a long moment. "Are these real?"

Maxine was a little insulted but didn't show it. "They are."

"Where did you get all this? I mean, you could boost all of this?" Marisol questioned.

"Nah, this her shit," Skip answered. "Her ex-man bought it all."

Marisol looked at Maxine skeptically.

They had been there for quite some time watching the fashion show, and Marisol had yet to make a purchase.

"Marisol, do you see anything you like? Cuz we gotta bounce. I have other customers."

Marisol panicked. "No, don't go to anyone else. I want it all. I just have to call my man."

"Everything?"

"Si, si. I want everything for the right price. How much would you sell it for?"

Maxine could not believe that she would sell all her items to one buyer, but she would play along. Between seven furs that cost anywhere between fifteen and seventy thousand, five Hermes bags, and all that other good shit, Scott paid nearly seven hundred thousand, retail. Maxine would be more than satisfied with half that. But she decided to come in a little high and let Marisol negotiate her down.

"Half price is four hundred and fifty-thousand. You can add up the tags and also look on the internet."

"Would you take four hundred?"

Maxine paused, "I guess, but I'm not too happy because Skip gotta eat too."

Skip knew the game. "But she's one of my best customers so if you could look out on the strength of me then I owe you a solid."

Marisol smiled at Skip for taking her side.

"Okay. You can buy it all for four hundred K."

Marisol pulled out her cell phone and called her man, Juan-Pablo. There was a lengthy exchange before she said he was on his way.

The women sat down and waited for nearly three uncomfortable hours. Marisol repeatedly apologized, continued to call Juan-Pablo, and made assurances that he was coming. To pass the time they sat down and had a home cooked meal with the family. Finally, at half past nine, Juan-Pablo showed up with three goons flanking him.

Juan-Pablo was a thug in every sense of the word. He and his goon surrounded Skip and Maxine and instantly they felt threatened. Juan Pablo began looking at all the pricy items while his men just stared at the women. Maxine's heart was beating irregularly. She placed her hands on her hips, one clutched to her pistol. She also noticed that Marisol and her mother had fled the room.

"Where did you get all this shit from?" Juan-Pablo asked.

This time Maxine spoke. "My man got knocked and the feds froze our assets. I'm trying to raise this money on the low to pay a private detective to find out who the snitch is on the case."

This was news to Skip and also piqued Juan-Pablo's interest.

"Who's ya man?"

"You might know of him. Scott West. The West organization."

Hell yeah, he knew of him. Scott West was affiliated with the Garcia cartel. Heavy hitters. Everyone had heard about this case. It had made the national news.

He stepped and took a closer look at Maxine.

"That's your BMW outside?"

"Yeah, that's me. I'm usually driven with my protection, but I told Scott that Skip was taking me to see her favorite client, Marisol on 108th, and that I was in good hands. He gave me permission to come alone. I barely have any mileage on that car."

Juan-Pablo nodded and said something to his men in Spanish. And then, "How much you want again?"

"We negotiated four hundred K."

Juan-Pablo whistled. "Could you do three?"

Maxine quickly noticed that the body language had changed. It felt less aggressive, but still assertive. She wasn't out of the woods yet, but she had to stand her ground and show no fear.

She shook her head. "Can't take less than four."

Juan-Pablo tapped his right-hand man and excused them from the room. When they left, Skip was about to bolt. Her whole body was trembling. Maxine knew that if Skip ran she wouldn't make it far. They were all convened in a bedroom just steps away from the front door, and the front door was locked. Skip was about to say something and Maxine put her finger to her mouth and then whispered, "Stay strong."

Skip nodded.

Inside the bedroom, Juan-Pablo and Marisol were in a heated debate in Spanish. Marisol thought she had the perfect vics for a robbery. When she saw all that high-end merchandise she told her man to come and murder these fools. Marisol was spoiled by family and her man and she wanted what she wanted, when she wanted it. However, there were too many loose ends and Juan-Pablo liked living. If Maxine told Scott West that she was going to meet Marisol and ended up dead they would never be safe. He copped ki's from Scott's twin sons. In fact, the West organization supplied most of the five boroughs. This was so complicated on so many levels. One, he could only get his hands on $250,000, and two, Marisol kept saying in Spanish, "Kill them! Kill them!"—until he had to silence her with a slap. She began to cry. Her mother began to cry.

Juan-Pablo needed her family to understand that they were in grave danger. If the twins on behalf of their father even thought this wasn't an above board deal, there could be repercussions.

The debate continued. His men would do whatever he said, but just saying "Scott West" and "Garcia cartel" in the same sentence brought forth fear.

Juan-Pablo pulled up several articles online and there she was, the night of Scott's arrest, in a nightgown. It looked like her. Maxine was the real deal. He had to pay. When Juan-Pablo told his baby momma that she had to put some items back, she wasn't having it. Spoiled Marisol wanted it all. Marisol's mother agreed to fund the additional $150,000, but both were adamant that Marisol wouldn't see another dime from either one of them for a very long time. Her mother opened a false wall and pulled out the cash and placed it in a shopping bag. Juan would bring her his share in the morning. Everyone agreed that the women had waited long enough.

Marisol never came back into the room to see the women she wanted dead. Juan-Pablo and his goons came back and handed Maxine the heavy bag of money.

Maxine looked down and said, "Do I need to count it?"

"It's all there, mami. But do you."

Skip wanted to scratch Max's eyes out when she bent down and began to count out each stack. Satisfied, they turned to leave when Juan-Pablo said, "What's your man's son's name again?"

"Who? Bugsy or Meyer—or Gotti or Clyde?"

It was his test because it was hard to see so much money walk out that front door. "Yeah, Meyer and Bugsy. Tell them Juan-Pablo said what's up. And that you and I are good peoples."

Maxine nodded.

Once they got safely away from the tenement building, Skip burst out into tears. She was sick with fright. "Skip, that sneaky bitch gotta die! I don't care how long it takes, but she gotta go."

"Max, they was gonna kill us over some fuckin' clothes! Ohmygod, I can't. I got fuckin' kids!"

Maxine was scared too, but she lived to harbor hate. She wanted payback. As she drove back to 125th Street she kept looking in her mirrors to make sure they weren't being followed.

"And you saved us!" Skip continued through heavy sobs. "You thought quickly on your feet."

"We should rob that fucking house and kill everyone in it." Maxine was still amped. If she still had a shooter on payroll it could be done. If Wacka wasn't such a dickhead then this was something she would have hired him to do.

95

Maxine didn't bother to drive Skip home. Let her get home how she got there. Besides, Skip could try to set her up too. Maxine trusted no one. Skip was now whimpering as Max thrust sixty thousand in her hands.

"Get lost, Skip. I gotta go."

"Damn, bitch. I almost died tonight. You ain't gonna take me home? I got all this fuckin' money on me."

"Take an Uber," Maxine replied. "And it's your fucking fault we almost got murdered. That's your friend!"

"You know, Max—no disrespect—but I think I'm gonna take this money and get out of town. You never mentioned your man was a drug lord or what type of heat you got coming around your corner. So after tonight, don't call me anymore because I won't pick up."

"Bye, bitch. I'll call you tomorrow."

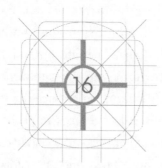

16

Maxine lingered in the backseat of the Escalade for a moment. She needed some time before she entered the federal building. Her two guards sat quietly. They were on her time. This was going to be her first visit outside of the hospital. Scott had been medically cleared and released from Presbyterian, but was immediately thrust into federal lockup to await his trial. Like Layla, he had been denied bail and remanded.

It was late February, and the weather was identical to the wintry January they'd had. It was a bone-chilling 28 degrees in the early morning. Snuggled warmly in her coat and leather boots, Maxine climbed out of the vehicle and walked toward the federal building, her heartbeat pounding like a rock concert was going on inside her body. She needed money, lots of it, and she needed it fast. She didn't have her diamond engagement ring on—a ring that was valued at one million. Would Scott notice it missing from her finger? Of course he would. She still hadn't come up with an explanation for him if he asked about it. On top of all that, walking back into a jail after she'd spent over twenty years of her life in one was a terrifying feeling.

The guards didn't care who she was or who she was there to see. They treated Maxine like any other visitor. She was scrutinized and thoroughly searched from top to bottom—no contraband, weapons, no coats, and no purses—nothing. She was made to empty her pockets, and the female guards felt her up, made her unhook her bra, and examined her tits.

Maxine started to have flashbacks. She was thrust back into her days of serving hard time at the women's prison from New York to Louisiana. She wanted to forget that part of her life, but today she was trying to hold herself together. She struggled with the confinement and the bars of the building and the guards barking orders and escorting her from one area to another. She never wanted to go back to prison. The government had taken away twenty years of her life, and it had been difficult starting over. She took a deep breath and exhaled, and then proceeded forward. She was determined to visit Scott despite the anxiety.

She sat in the visiting room with the other visitors feeling ambivalent. She had vowed to never see the inside of a prison again, but at the same time she knew she had to see Scott. He was the man with the money.

Scott entered the room dressed in a gray jumpsuit. He still looked authoritative and imposing. He coolly walked her way. She stood up and embraced him with a warm hug and rapid kisses, and they exchanged smiles. Lingering displays of public affection weren't allowed. The guards were watching everything and everyone closely.

They sat down across from each other.

"How you been, baby?" she asked him.

"I'm a'ight. One day at a time," he replied.

He had healed considerably from his gunshot wounds. He was a strong man, and he was lucky to be alive. His reputation of cheating death had spread like his reputation of being larger than life. Many inmates were excited to see him, and many were completely intimidated by him. The guards tried to do their jobs objectively and be impartial with West.

Maxine wanted to broach the subject of money, but she didn't know how. She practiced for days, but it always felt weak when she rehearsed it.

Finally, she said, "Money is becoming tight, Scott. I'm a grown-ass woman taking handouts from your son. I don't like the way it makes me feel and I'm a little perturbed that you can't see it from my position."

"Shit is crazy right now, Maxine. My lawyer told me that the feds froze all of my accounts. Which we expected," he said.

Scott knew that the government wanted to cripple him before the trial and take away any line of revenue he had.

Maxine was so tired of this same song. Scott knew she wasn't really talking about his legal dealings anymore. Shit done changed. She wanted to get money from the same place Bugsy was getting it.

"I don't know what to do, Scott. I'm lost. The board is pushing me out. Where am I gonna go?"

"I'm working on something. Give it time."

"I don't have time."

"You think I'm going down for this." It was a realization Scott didn't want to face. Maxine was losing faith in him. That was the only conclusion he could deduce from her constantly bringing up his money.

"I do not," she defended. "Why would you say such a terrible thing?"

Scott stared into her eyes trying to find the truth. "You seem preoccupied, distracted . . . almost in a rush like my end is coming fast and you want to cash out."

"Cash out? I'm not leaving, Scott. It's just that I'm struggling out here and I have bills too."

"Bills? I take care of you, don't I?"

"Baby, I'm here to help," she quickly said. "I know the business just like you, and I can play my part. I can work with Bugsy out there on the streets. I can be a benefit to your organization. I'm not that same girl you met over twenty years ago, baby. I learned a lot inside prison."

Scott was shaking his head before she finished her last sentence. "You? Nah, it's too dangerous. And that's not your world or your business, and I don't want it to become your business. I don't want anyone near my retirement funds other than Bugsy. And he doesn't need your help. He's doing fine by himself."

"And what if something were to happen to Bugsy, God forbid? Then what?"

Scott clenched his fist and replied, "Nothing is going to happen to Bugsy. But if so, I have two other children to rely on."

"Meyer is in no condition to help, and Lucky has sided with Layla. Besides, you and I go too far back for you not to trust me."

"This isn't about trust, Maxine. Things are on a need-to-know basis with you, and as long as your bills are paid and your needs are met, then why do you need access to anything?"

Maxine didn't want to be taken care of. She needed fast money, and therefore, their soft exchange of words started to turn ugly.

"I'm your woman, and you treat me like a jump off!" she griped.

"Maxine, now is not the time for this foolishness!"

"I only want to help you. But how can I, when I don't know shit about anything?"

Through their bickering, Scott looked at her. "You've changed, Maxine. It feels like I'm talking to Layla. What is going on with you?"

His remark bothered her. "I'm not Layla. How fucking dare you insult me like that?"

"And that was always the good thing about you. You weren't her. You were always smarter."

"I just need help, that's all."

She averted her eyes from his, upset that she had to beg for her seat at the table. She wasn't giving up so easily. She desperately needed the cash to pay Wacka.

"Look at me," he demanded. "I said look at me!"

She shifted her eyes back to Scott. His looked showed intensity—anger more than concern.

"Where is it?" he asked angrily.

"Where's what?"

"Maxine, don't play stupid with me. Where's the ring I gave you? It's not on your finger."

Her heart fell to the bottom of her stomach. She knew this was going to happen. She had to answer him. And with his intense gaze fixed on her, she coyly replied, "I lost it."

"What the fuck you mean you lost it? You lost a million-dollar, nine-carat pink diamond ring?" He was incensed at her stupidity and carelessness.

"I wanted to tell you. I'm looking for it. I think it got stolen during the raid at the penthouse—the FBI probably took it."

"Maxine, it was on your finger at the hospital, so that's impossible. That ring cost me a lot of money, and there's no way you suddenly lose a million-dollar ring and act casual about it. Where the fuck is it?"

"I'll find it," she said.

"You better find that fuckin' ring and tell me what the fuck is going on wit' you, Maxine," he said.

She had no answers for him. Maxine could feel the extreme heat from him like he was the blazing sun. She'd never seen him look at her in that way—skepticism mixed with outrage. It was scaring her.

Scott was on an emotional rollercoaster. He was jailed. Layla was jailed too. His son was in the ICU and hanging on by a thread, and Maxine was irritating him about things that shouldn't be important at a time like this. He wondered if she cared that he was incarcerated, his funds were frozen, the feds were trying to crucify him, and that his empire and his family were falling apart.

Lucky peered out the window of the descending American Airlines flight and took in the sweeping view of Miami's pristine, sprawling white sandy beaches and clear blue waters. She was buckled-up in first class, the only way she wanted to travel, and she felt apprehensive about being back in the Sunshine State. Her trip to Miami was purely business, nowhere near pleasure.

Finally, the landing gear roughly connected with the runway and the plane began taxiing toward the terminal. The pilot announced over the loudspeaker, "We'd like to thank you folks for flying with American Airlines today, and we hope you have a wonderful time in Miami."

A surge of passengers started their exodus off the plane. Lucky removed her carry-on from above and was one of the first to stroll through the passenger gateway and arrive into the terminal.

Lucky had reached out to Angel to set up another meeting two days before the shipment. Obviously they couldn't talk over the phone, so she had to fly down to Miami. Lucky had lied to her mother. Layla was under the impression that Lucky was going to meet with Angel to tell him that their deal was off. It was a risk to disassociate from the cartel so suddenly, but under their current situation, Layla felt Angel would understand. Lucky had other plans.

Outside the terminal, she linked up with her goons, who had driven to Miami beforehand in a Range Rover and were there to scoop her up from the airport. She climbed into the passenger seat with her dark shades and her serious expression.

"Let's go," she said to the driver.

It was a sun-drenched and balmy day in the city—85 degrees, a stark contrast to the cold and snow in New York City. The driver navigated the Range Rover to the Marriot Stanton on South Beach. Lucky had booked a room there at Angel's request.

The sophisticated hotel was located in the trendy SoFi area of South Beach—AKA south of fifth. It was an oceanfront hotel surrounded by top shopping, fine dining, and active nightlife.

Lucky checked into her stylish room, which included a spa-like bathroom, platform bed, locally inspired art, and a spacious open closet. There was a private balcony with a view of the ocean and a shimmering infinity pool.

The day was still bright with the sun peaking, and Lucky unwound for a moment, taking a shower with the handheld wand and waterfall showerhead. Soon after, the hotel phone rang and she answered.

"Are you enjoying the room?" Angel said.

"Everything's fine," she said.

"Good. I want you to join me down at the beach in a half-hour." He hung up.

A half-hour later, Lucky was on the sunny beach dressed in a skimpy bikini and flanked by her men from New York. Angel stood near the edge of the beach wearing just his swimming trunks with the waves crashing against his feet. He appeared to be alone, but Lucky knew he had soldiers subtly camouflaged somewhere among the dozens of tourists on the beach.

She approached him evenly with her men not far behind her. But she knew if Angel Morales wanted her dead, she would be dead—her men too.

His back was turned to her and his attention was on the ocean. She stood next to him. He didn't acknowledge her immediately. He continued to gaze at the ocean. There was no one around within thirty feet of them. It was like the section of the beach had been quarantined for his benefit.

"Come, join me in the ocean, and we'll talk there," he said without looking at her.

He proceeded into the water and Lucky followed. Lucky wasn't a fool. She knew he was testing her to see if she was wearing a wire. The beach meant a bathing suit, less clothes to inspect, and the water would most likely interfere with any transmission. They waded into the ocean, the water rising chest deep.

"I know you heard what happened to my parents," she said.

Of course he'd heard. It was his business to know. "The news of them has reached me," he said.

"My mother wants to discontinue business with you. I disagree with her. Despite everything that has happened, I want our business relationship to continue to flourish," said Lucky.

Angel looked her way with a questioning glare. He was silent. He understood the reasoning for Layla's decision. The United States FBI had arrested her, and cartel bosses were always on their radar. She was tainted and could easily be flipped. It wouldn't be wise play for Layla or anyone in her organization to become a snitch, though. The cartel specialized in dealing with informants.

Lucky's voice didn't waver when she said, "But I have one problem. I don't have any access to my mother's money. The feds are freezing her accounts. So I'm on zero."

Angel's eyes shot into her. "Then why are you here wasting my time? I'm a busy man and time is money."

"I understand that. But I can be a benefit to you—continue where my mother left off. I have this vision, and with your product continuing to flow up north, we can grow together. The roots have been planted; all I need is the product."

He chuckled at her ignorance. "You want my business on consignment. You are a foolish little girl. That is not an option."

"You don't trust me because of my mother's situation? I can assure you, Mr. Morales, my mother and my family, we are not snitches! And I'm not in my mother's position. I'm willing to push forward and continue to make us both rich."

"I'm already a very rich man . . . powerful too," he boasted smugly.

It was becoming tougher than she thought.

Angel locked eyes with the pretty young girl with her one flaw, her droopy eye. He'd learned of her ruthless beating which resulted in her slight disfigurement. He could only imagine how beautiful she was before the incident.

"You're young and you're still pretty, despite your blemish. You should think of it as a beauty mark."

Lucky didn't like to talk about it. But it was Angel Morales, and if he wanted to discuss her flaw, then she didn't have a choice.

"Have they ever found the men responsible for your attack?" he asked, already knowing the answer.

"No."

"Such a shame," he said.

She sighed. She was there for business, not to open up old wounds. Was he toying with her?

"You know, you come down here behind your mother's back and you want to play with the big boys. Do you know what you're getting into?"

It was a rhetorical question. Lucky knew. She remained silent.

Angel added, "I'm like a god. I see and know everything. I know your mother is keeping her mouth shut. I know your father is a respectable man having an affair with his old whore, Maxine. She did twenty years for your mother. Now that's loyalty. And your brother, Bugsy, he's smart. I like him. He could definitely be of use to me. But daddy's little girl, she's ready to prove herself by aligning with the cartel." He laughed. "Do you like to get fucked, Lucky? Because the cartel, you fuck us, we fuck you . . . and when we fuck you, it means your life ends and your family's lives too. I have men that like to wipe out entire lineages."

Lucky didn't budge. Her eyes remained firm on him, and she stood firm in the water with extreme confidence.

"Come, we're done in the ocean," he said.

He started to make his way toward the sand, wading through the water as Lucky followed behind him. They walked toward a small cabana situated on the sand. Angel took a seat in a beach chair and lit a cigar. Lucky sat next to him. She didn't want to give up. She was determined to move forward with his business.

"Do we have a deal?"

"No business right now. Relax and enjoy the beach," he said. "In fact, I'm having a party tonight. I want you to come. Invite your friends." He gestured toward her goons in the distance.

Lucky was furious. She didn't want to party. She was about her business, but Angel was skirting the topic. It felt like it was a game to him.

"No disrespect, Mr. Morales, but I'm not in the partying mood. I want your business. I want to build with you. Believe me, I know this business like the back of my hand, and I can make you so much money you'll be able to buy our government. And I'm ready to renegotiate the original deal my mother had with you to appease you. I'll be able to take two hundred kilos at thirty-five thousand a ki. Now that's lessening my profit for you, but it's still a profit for me."

They were strong words from such a young girl.

He chuckled and took a pull from his cigar. His eyes were focused on Lucky. He wouldn't admit it to her directly, but he was impressed by her—her tenacity and ambition were captivating. He remembered when he wanted to make a name for himself and how hard that was. He looked at Lucky, a woman—a young black woman—and wondered if she had what it took. Was she her mother—or better? Was she vicious enough to do what was necessary to survive in a dog-eat-dog world?

He would soon find out. He smiled at Lucky, still puffing on his cigar, and said, "Tonight, dress in something very nice and come down to the lobby at eight."

Angel was done conversing—no more business. He meant it this time. He removed himself from the cabana, leaving Lucky behind wondering if she left a good impression on him. She needed this badly.

***

Lucky emerged from her hotel room dressed in a sexy, curve-hugging red dress with a plunging neckline and side-tie skirt. Her hair fell in soft waves past her shoulders, and with her four-inch red bottom sandals, she felt picture perfect and ready for Angel's party. She felt that she'd made some traction with him, but there was more work to be done. She wanted to make an impression on him with her wit and confidence.

She stepped into the elevator alone and descended to the lobby. She found the lobby littered with several of Angel's henchmen. Her own goons were nowhere around. She wondered where they were and what kind of ploy she was stepping into.

"Angel sent us to accompany you to the event tonight," one of them spoke, his voice rolling deep with a Latin accent.

She looked at him and felt an unwelcome chill percolate through her body. He had boorish looking eyes and he was muscular and intimidating with his large, meaty hands. He stood six feet tall with tanned skin and a balding head. He didn't smile. His eyes locked onto Lucky, and she didn't have a choice but to leave with them.

The men shepherded her out of the lobby and toward an idling black Navigator. She was helped into the backseat and sandwiched between two men. She felt like a hostage. The driver pulled off and traveled from South Beach via the MacArthur Causeway.

It was a beautiful view of the city at night, but Lucky didn't care for the scenery. Her mind was racing. Where were they taking her? Was it to a party or to a gloomier location? She noticed that all the men were armed and she wasn't. The only thing she could do was sit calmly and hope for the best—and that meant surviving the night.

They drove for almost an hour to Homestead and arrived at a desolate warehouse on Palm Drive. Surrounding the location was miles and miles of shrub swamps, and there were no residences around. It was a hell of a place to throw a party, but Lucky deduced that there wasn't going to be a party. Angel definitely had something else planned for her.

The driver steered into the warehouse garage and the gate closed behind them. The place was barren besides a few luxury cars, including a Bentley and Ferrari, aging pillars, and scattered crates. It appeared the building had been abandoned for years.

The Navigator doors opened, and Lucky was escorted from the vehicle. Her stomach dropped when she realized what they were leading her toward. Angel was standing over a man who was gagged with duct tape with his arms bound behind his back and his legs tied to a metal chair. Lucky didn't take her eyes off them. They were situated in the center of the building. The captive was Latino, and he was sweating profusely with his wide, panicky eyes hooked onto Lucky as she approached. He had been beaten. She didn't know who he was or what this was about, but it wasn't going to end well for him.

"Welcome," Angel greeted with a smile and politely kissed her on the cheek. He wasn't hostile toward her, so it was good news so far.

"What's this about?" she asked.

"Business," Angel replied.

Angel was dressed in a dark tailored suit and bowtie, looking remarkable in such a grim looking place. If this was the type of party he was talking about, Lucky wanted to be uninvited.

"Who is he?" she asked him.

"He's an innocent man," said Angel. "He's a stranger we kidnapped from his home for our benefit—and yours."

Angel tossed the man's wallet at Lucky to verify his story. Inside was a picture of his beautiful wife and his two sons. She was taken aback by everything happening, but Angel's response was far from the truth. Unbeknownst to Lucky, the man tied to the chair was the nephew to Javier Garcia of the Garcia cartel. But he was a civilian, living an ordinary life with his wife and kids. He wasn't part of his uncle's vicious cartel.

"Have you ever taken a life, Lucky?" Angel asked her.

What kind of question was that? She looked at him strangely. He was waiting for her answer.

"Of course," she uttered. "You know my family."

He chuckled at her comment. "Yes, I do. But do I really know you?" he said. "I need for you to be honest with me. And I don't mean giving orders for another man to murder for you. Have you killed someone with your own hands? I know your brothers have . . . but have you?"

He no longer was laughing. His stare was intimidating.

"No," she answered.

"Thank you for your honesty," he said.

Things became tense. Angel's men surrounded him and the tied-up man. Angel soon had a pistol in his hand and he placed it into Lucky's.

He said, "I have a test for you, and in order to move forward with our business I want you to kill this innocent man—a family man—someone that has never wronged you and someone that has a lot to live for. Think about it—he will never get to see his wife and kids again because of you."

The man squirmed wildly in the chair, desperately trying to free himself from the restraints. His eyes were pleading for his life as tears started to stream down his face. He repeatedly mumbled something underneath the duct tape, but it was incoherent.

"When his life ends, then our business can begin," Angel said in a soothing voice. He was deceitful and sneaky. His words were encouraging.

Lucky gripped the gun and stared at the man while Angel circled her, his voice hypnotizing her with peer-pressure and masked aggression.

"Can you really kill this man for your own gain, just to have access to my yayo? How desperately do you want it, Lucky?"

Lucky said, "I can."

She lifted the firearm to the man's head and squeezed—*Bak!* A single bullet ripped through his forehead and he was dead instantly. His head slumped forward to his chest as his body lay flaccid in the chair.

She dropped the gun and directed her attention toward Angel. He showed no expression. He picked up the gun and said, "Well done. You're a treacherous and cold-hearted bitch. You know, my father gave me the same test and I failed it, miserably."

She didn't believe him.

"You don't believe me, huh? I see it in your eyes. How can a seasoned killer have to be coerced into committing murder?" he said. "But it is the truth. I couldn't pull the trigger."

Hector, one of Angel's OG's and a former lieutenant for Angel's father, confirmed his story.

"Long ago, I was a different man, Lucky, and my father saw me as weak and he beat me and ridiculed me," Angel said. "I wasn't ready for his organization. But that's another story. We still have some work to do."

Lucky thought she was done, but Angel indicated there was more. He walked away and she followed him. Next, they entered a dark room. Angel turned on the lights and Lucky received the shock of her life.

"What the fuck is this?" she exclaimed.

He smirked and handed the gun back to her.

Lucky stood inside the room with her eyes wide-eyed in shock. There they were—her three goons on their knees and tied up with their hands bound behind their backs and duct tape covering their mouths. The moment they saw Lucky, their eyes pleaded for help and they started mumbling something incoherently. They all hoped that Lucky would be their savior. They had no idea why were they being held captive by the cartel.

Angel looked at them and then at Lucky. "Your test isn't over."

"What is this? Why are my men tied up?"

"Business can cost, as you know." He stood between Lucky and her men and added, "Killing a stranger is easy to get what you want. But can you murder your own men? Men who've sworn allegiance to you and your family? Men who put their lives on the line to save yours?"

Lucky stood there and watched her men moving to free themselves, and their eyes were swamped with terror. But they were in a no-win situation. Even if they did manage to free themselves, they would be met with a half-dozen of Angel's murderous triggermen.

Angel nodded to one of his men, and he at once tore the duct tape from each of her men's mouths. To see them tied up was one thing, but to hear them plead and beg for their lives would make it a lot more difficult for Lucky to pull the trigger. Her test had just gotten harder. All three begged Lucky not to kill them.

"Please, we done nuthin'!"

"He'll kill yuh too!"

"Don't trust him! Please, you don't have to do this!"

"No, not like this! I'm beggin' you, he's playin' you."

Despite their pleading, Lucky knew that her hands were tied and there wasn't anything she could do for them. They continued to drown her ears with begs for mercy. She gripped the gun tightly, holding it parallel to her side. It was hard to look at them. They were soldiers—her soldiers—but soldiers were meant to die in war, and she couldn't take hearing their pleas any longer. She quickly stepped closer to the first one and put the barrel to his head and fired—*Bak!* He collided backwards with the concrete in death. She repeated the same action with the other two—*Bak—Bak!* Each man went down with a bullet to the head. Their slain bodies coiled in their restraints as thick crimson spurted and pooled around them from their wounds.

Lucky stood over their bodies with the smoking gun in her hand and felt some contrition. It had to be done. She needed to progress forward by any means necessary. The end result for them, whether she had pulled the trigger or not, was death. Her heart was heavy, but it didn't mean anything to the newly departed.

Angel laughed and clapped his hands. "Well done. You are a vicious bitch, I must admit." He removed the smoking gun from her hand.

She turned to him with a callous look and asked, "So, when do I get my kilos?"

He said, "Soon . . . real soon."

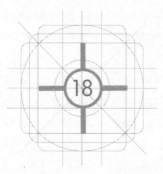

T he thin Jewish man wearing a kippah held the 10x loupe to his eye and meticulously inspected the large Tiffany diamond ring. Wacka and Tarsha stood in front of him waiting for the results of his inspection. This was big for them. They knew the ring was costly, but just how big of a payday it would be for them was up to the jeweler.

They were in the Diamond District in Midtown Manhattan, home to nearly 2,600 independent businesses. Just about all of them dealt in diamonds or jewelry. When Tarsha showed the jeweler the ring she wanted to sell, he grew excited and directed them into a back room.

The crooked jeweler took his time inspecting the diamond and was amazed by the quality—knowing the ring was hot and a high quality brand. He remained expressionless in front of the ignorant couple standing there and waiting for his verdict. It felt like *Wheel of Fortune*, with the wheel spinning and them hoping for the needle to land on big money. Tarsha was eager for a huge payday. She could already see it—Gucci, Prada, Chanel, Fendi—all the expensive brands. The famous 5th Avenue was nearby, and she was ready to indulge herself in a shopping spree.

The man removed the loupe from his eye and looked at the apprehensive couple with a stoic gaze.

"So what's up? How much can we get for it?" Tarsha asked.

"Where did it come from?" the man asked.

"Why do you care? It's yours for the right price," Tarsha said. "You the fourth jeweler we seen today. If you ain't interested in it, then we can take our business elsewhere."

He said, "Seventy thousand."

"Boy, bye. Gimme my fuckin' ring," Tarsha shouted.

He panicked. "Okay, okay, okay, okay." He took another look at the precious stone.

"I'll give you three hundred thousand for it. Final offer."

They had no idea the true value of the ring, and they both felt they had made a killing.

"Three hundred thousand," Tarsha said. "We want that in cash."

"Of course."

The jeweler disappeared from their view for a moment, went into another back room, and shortly emerged with their cash stuffed into a leather briefcase. Tarsha was the first to reach for it. For a moment, it felt like she had an orgasm. Wacka was amazed by how easy it was for this middle-aged Jewish man to come up with $300K. He looked at the jeweler with a predator's stare. If this was back in his glory days, it would have been easy money for him. He would have taken the mark for everything he had—probably his life too.

And that was it; the deal was finalized by a simple handshake and the Yiddish expression—*mazel und brucha*.

The couple exited the jewelry shop situated in the middle of a one-way street lined with jewelry shops, boutiques, and retail stores. Tarsha could feel her pulse thumping in her clenched hand on the handle of the briefcase. From the Diamond District, it was over to 5th Avenue for some shopping. In an hour she spent close to forty thousand dollars on furs, jewels, clothes, jackets, and shoes.

***

Wacka and Tarsha rented a five-bedroom, two-bath home on E. University Parkway in Baltimore. The place was 1,800 square feet with parquet flooring, a fireplace, and a sizable kitchen. The neighborhood wasn't the greatest, but it was a step up from their previous one. Their loot was dwindling from expenses and all the shopping they'd done for the past several weeks. There was a high-end stereo system with large speakers in the living room, and the entire home was tricked out with big flat screen TVs, king size beds, and oversized sofas. They bought two refrigerators and stacked them with food, beer, and liquor. There was a grill on the small deck out back and a pool table and cases and cases of Hennessy and Grey Goose stacked in the basement, Tarsha's two favorite liquors.

It was party time. In fact, almost every night was a party. Their home would be full of folks, the music blaring, the alcohol flowing, the men playing pool in the basement, and the ladies gossiping and laughing. Tarsha played hostess in her stylish designer clothing and jewelry.

This was it, the good life. It was what she wanted—to boast her fashion and wealth in front of her family and friends and prance around her new home in red bottoms like she was the shit. Maxine's extortion money had Tarsha sitting pretty on her pedestal.

She tossed back her fourth Hennessy of the night, and she didn't plan on slowing down anytime soon. Her nieces and nephews were running around the place and playing video games, and there was Wacka, flaunting his large bankroll for everyone to see.

He was generous to the family, giving the kids a hundred dollars each, and the adults soon came begging behind the kids with their hands out with promises to pay him back. Some told Wacka their heartbreaking stories—looming evictions, cars breaking down, doctor bills, child support, and so on. Wacka, with his new direction in life, became their Santa Claus and handed out a thousand there, five hundred here, and maybe five grand over there. Wacka felt like a baller again. The money was a high, and feeling needed felt good—damn good!

Tarsha downed her fifth drink and laughed with her girlfriends. She was the life of the party. She looked good and she felt great. But looking around, seeing everything they'd bought, the new house, their bills, her clothes, and their wild parties, she knew their stash was becoming smaller and smaller. Soon they would have to reach out to their lifeline again for their five million dollars, and Tarsha wasn't taking no for an answer.

19

I f there was a God, Bugsy was thankful. It was a Friday night when he witnessed a miracle happen. Meyer awakened from his coma. Immediately, the doctors and nurses were in the room to analyze his condition and check his vitals. Though his eyes were open, he looked spaced out. He had no idea why he was in the hospital. At first, he couldn't respond to anyone. He didn't speak and he barely moved.

"What's going on with him?" Bugsy asked the doctor.

"It could be many things—the medication he's on or a brain injury. You have to keep in mind, your brother has been through a traumatic experience, and emerging from a coma is not like waking up from regular sleep. We will monitor his condition for a few days and run some tests."

It was good news and bad news. Bugsy worried if his brother would ever be the same again, but he planned on being there for him either way. Although they had their differences, they shared a twin bond.

Day one out of his coma, Meyer had trouble focusing his eyes and responding to Bugsy. However, after several days, he was able to keep his eyes open for longer periods of time, and, fortunately, he didn't experience any paralysis.

His muscle functions were slow, but they were fine. Movement of his toes, legs, and fingers were signs of improvement, as was the visual and auditory trailing. He was starting to follow sights and sounds. Bugsy would get up and walk around the room, and Meyer would turn his head, his eyes transfixed on his brother. Seeing and hearing his brother was the best form of healing.

Bugsy had sat right by his brother's bedside every day of his coma. He would talk to Meyer, and though it was a one-way conversation at times, it was therapeutic for them both. Now, they were starting to have shared conversations.

"You've been out for months now. You remember anything?"

Meyer looked at his twin, and his memory was still in a haze. Parts of him still ached and he was out of it from time to time, but he knew that he was lucky to be alive.

He shook his head. "I-I . . . don't remember anything."

Bugsy didn't push him. Luna was dead, and that's what mattered. Now they had to move on and recover from this. He had never seen Meyer so calm before—so humble and unassuming. It felt like Meyer was a different person. Bugsy would closely watch him, trying to see if that fire and that murderous muthafucka were still in there somewhere. Would this change him? Would he be able to get back to business and run the streets again?

"A lot has been happening out there, Meyer. Pop and Ma are locked up, the FBI raided their places, and shit's been hectic ever since," Bugsy said.

"Wow . . . that's crazy," he simply replied.

"Yeah, it is."

Meyer showed no anger or empathy behind his words. It almost felt like Bugsy was talking to a stranger. But it had only been a week since he'd awakened from his coma, so Bugsy knew he had to give him some more time to recover.

Bugsy spent an hour or two each day with Meyer, and the rest of his time was spent on the streets handling the organization's affairs. Now that Scott was incarcerated, Bugsy had a lot more responsibilities. He had to keep an eye on the product from the Garcia cartel, manage his lieutenants and his triggermen, run the trap houses and stash houses, and deal with his father's attorneys. He did all this while having to be extra careful, making sure he wasn't being followed by the feds. He was always looking over his shoulder. He didn't talk on the phone, and he changed up every day—different cars, different routes, and no routines. He couldn't be caught slipping, not at a time like this. If he went down, then the entire organization was going down.

Heavy was the head that wore the crown.

Since he had taken over, his men started to deeply respect him. Bugsy was a king for sure—able to multi-task the streets, business, and his brother's recovery. He ruled differently than his father. Scott was a cruel and ruthless man—shoot and ask questions maybe, then came the smarts. But Bugsy was sharp and witty from the get-go, and violence came secondary to him. He believed if everyone wanted to kill each other and was always shooting at each other, then how was money going to be made? There was no business in always going to war. He understood that bloodshed always brought trouble—the feds and agitated rivals. But that didn't mean he was passive. When violence and murder were necessary, he did it just as viciously as his father.

Bugsy continued to sit by his brother's bedside and talk. He had one of his lieutenants posted by the door, keeping an eye out. It was that kind of party. Everywhere he went, he needed security.

"We miss you, bro," Bugsy said.

Meyer looked at him. He was extremely grateful to have his brother by his side. He was still very weak and was constantly going in and out of consciousness. He closed his eyes, sleeping again.

The next day he opened his eyes and there was Bugsy, sitting right beside his bed.

Scott sat down on the green cot in his jail cell and stared at the thick gray stone walls. The paint had started to chip over time. The window was a small opening fitted with thick metal bars, and the air was stale and carried the stench of raw sewage. It was a hellish looking place—bleak and ugly, where souls were trampled with inhumanity and despair. Scott knew if things didn't go his way in court that this would be his life for many, many years—maybe for the rest of his life.

He was alone—immersed in absolute confinement. There was nothing to do but stare at the walls and wait. He wanted complete silence, but the ruckus of the inmates locked in their adjacent cells sounded like monkeys in a zoo. He wanted to be left alone to contemplate his options.

The meeting with his attorney didn't go so well. His charges were serious—from RICO to attempted murder. There was no bail, and the U.S. Attorney for the Southern District of New York planned on hammering his ass to the wall and leaving him there to rot. The feds had frozen his legitimate accounts, so there was no legal money to depend on, and his name was being slandered in the media. And with Layla stealing his fifty million, he was less forthcoming about his illegal money.

What was on Scott's mind the most was Maxine. There was something off about her—she had changed. The FBI was watching him and he didn't trust his woman knowing where his cash was and risk her carelessly being followed by the feds. Bugsy was smart and stealthy. He knew the game and he knew how to move. Besides, that was his son. Bugsy was born and bred to fill his shoes, but he hoped it was no time soon.

Another thing that bothered Scott was why Maxine was so concerned about what he earned without her. She wasn't around when he'd built his empire. And where was her engagement ring? No woman loses a million-dollar ring without a logical story behind it. Did she think he was stupid—that he wouldn't notice it missing? The questions echoed on and on in his mind. What was different about her? Did she really love him, or was it all a ploy to get closer to his money—his empire? Did she have an agenda? Had she played him? Maybe. Scott was sure that she had some kind of motive. Was it revenge?

He had to think about it. In 1994, he completely fucked her over and left her to rot in jail for over twenty years—and he didn't visit her one time once she went upstate. To add insult to injury, he fucked and married her best friend and had six kids with her. Was Maxine really that forgiving? Could anyone forgive anyone for that?

Scott couldn't shake the feeling. Worried about Maxine's true intentions was weighing him down, and he needed to make moves and phone calls.

***

The next day, Scott made his phone call to Bugsy. Knowing the phone was monitored, he would have to watch what he said.

"I need you to do me a favor and keep an eye out for Maxine for me."

Bugsy was surprised by the request. "Why? What's going on?"

"I just need you to keep eyes on her twenty-four seven. I think this bitch is seeing another nigga on the side."

"What? I don't believe that, Pop. Not Maxine. That woman loves you, and I don't think she's the type to step out on you."

"What the fuck I said to you? Just get it done and don't question me about it. Understand?" he growled.

"Yeah . . . I understand," Bugsy replied.

Scott ended the call. He didn't want to say too much on an open line. He felt confident that his son would get things done. Maxine needed to be watched vigilantly. He didn't need or want any surprises. He hated them.

"You ready to go, Mr. West?" CO Mahan asked him.

Scott nodded.

Mahan escorted him from the kiosk of pay phones in the dayroom back toward his cell. Scott marched through the corridors of the jail like he was the President of the United States—and the inmates were treating him like he was. The respect was overwhelming, and overnight, Scott had a crew of men behaving like the secret service. They were ready to protect him from any inside threats. He casually moved through the corridor like it was a walk in the park, and passing inmates immediately averted their eyes from him. They didn't want to inadvertently disrespect him.

Before Scott stepped foot into his cell, Mahan slyly slipped a burner phone into his hand. Scott looked at it like it was an alien device from the future.

"For you, Mr. West. Courtesy of some friends," said Mahan. "You have plenty of them inside."

Scott stood there expressionless. The guard seemed infatuated by him. Mahan and CO Karen Jones were becoming his two flunkies. Mahan was a young CO in his early twenties with three years on the job, and Jones was a veteran with a decade on the job. Unbeknownst to her co-workers, she had developed a strong crush on Scott, and she would risk her job to help him get whatever he wanted. Power and money was her turn-on. The two guards brought him unsanctioned meals and contraband without him even asking.

"I'll have my son look out for you," he said to Mahan.

"It isn't about the money, Mr. West," replied Mahan.

Scott smirked. "It's always about the money."

With nothing else to say, he entered his cell and the gate closed behind him. Mahan walked away. Once the guard was out of sight, Scott tossed the phone to the side. He didn't trust it. So the following day, he passed the burner phone to an inmate—a gift from him for a price. Nor did he eat the food. For some reason, Scott didn't trust the two guards.

***

The unassuming brown van sat parked on the Manhattan corner for several days. Traffic pedestrians went by the van without giving it a second glance. It was just another ugly vehicle parked on a crowded city street. NYPD traffic had given the vehicle several parking tickets, yet, it still remained—not yet towed away like routine. There was something odd about the vehicle.

An African-American man in his late twenties walked toward the van carrying a brown paper bag containing bagels in one hand and a big traveler of coffee in the other. He observed his surroundings for a second and then he tapped on the sliding door. It quickly opened and he climbed inside.

"Anything yet?" he asked his team.

"Not a damn thing," one man replied with frustration.

The man sighed. "Fuck!"

"He's smart," said another man.

"He's a fool, and I want to nail this son of a bitch to the wall with everything we have."

The van was fitted with wireless security cameras and state-of-the-art listening equipment. From where they were parked, they were able to hear a fly fart and a gnat sneeze. Headphones stayed glued around one or two agents' ears daily.

The three federal agents occupying the brown van parked near the jail were listening in on conversations made from a certain cell phone.

They had been on the West case for nearly a month, and they sat day in and day out listening to the conversations from the tapped cell phone. They wanted to make a stronger case against Scott West. He was a very dangerous man and a very wealthy man, and although his accounts had been frozen, they understood he had plenty of money elsewhere.

For all the days of listening to the cell phone, the agents heard nothing relevant to their case against Scott. It was a lot of gibberish between various inmates, but not one voice matched Scott's. They deduced that he wasn't using the cell phone at all and had likely given it away. Was he on to them and the corrections officer? They were a bit worried.

They heard phone sex with inmates and their girlfriends or wives, certain confessions that would be labeled as misdemeanors, and a few idiots using the phone to further their criminal enterprise, but it wasn't what they really wanted. The big fish they wanted to pull in was West, and he was smart enough not to go near it.

"What now?" an agent asked.

The black male in charge of the operation looked away. He didn't know what to do next. A bugged cell phone had seemed like a good idea. They were still trying to make a solid case against the West organization, but Scott and Layla weren't slipping up. They ran a tight ship, and their minions rarely snitched. Still, the feds still had one secret weapon under wraps.

Maxine scurried around the penthouse trying to prepare for her meeting with her extortionist. She needed to keep Wacka quiet, but his blackmail was driving her crazy. She couldn't function and she couldn't think straight. Every day it felt like she was living on borrowed time. The pressure was building and building. She thought, if she managed to pay them their five million dollars, what would stop them from coming at her for more? They were always going to want more money from her as their greed continued to grow. She was their meal ticket to a life of luxury.

Maxine stared at the leather satchel that was filled with money—$990,000 to be exact. It was enough cash to run away with and start a brand new life somewhere in another state. She could say fuck this and leave—somehow ditch the men who were watching her and get on a bus and travel far away—maybe the west coast, maybe the Midwest. Who would think to look for her there? She could live a simple life under a new identity, change her look and change her lifestyle.

Maxine turned her eyes away from the satchel of money and started to think realistically. If she ran away with loose ends, she would always be looking over her shoulder no matter what state she was in. Once the truth about what she had done was out there, Scott wouldn't sleep until he had her murdered. Yes, he would most likely be confined to prison for a lifetime, but he still had clout and resources everywhere, and, most of all, there were his children. They would want to hunt her down and avenge their siblings' deaths. Lucky would probably become the most relentless and vicious one to try and track her down. She never liked Maxine in the first place.

Running away was not an option. She would have to deal with Wacka and her secret until she came up with a permanent way of handling it. There was only one way she could think of, and that was somehow killing Wacka and his bitch.

Maxine grabbed her long mink coat for the cold outside but quickly put it back. She wouldn't make the same mistake twice. She wrapped her wool pea coat around her petite frame, picked up the satchel, and left her penthouse suite. She was to meet with the extorting couple in an hour.

The cold air was aggressive, so Maxine hurried into the backseat of the SUV with the tinted windows and closed the door. Her two armed guards were up front. Avery turned toward her and asked, "Where to?"

She needed them to take her to West Side Highway, at Pier 86. Once again, Tarsha wanted to meet in a public place.

Maxine didn't reply right away. The SUV sat idling in front of her building. She wanted to ask them a question. She was desperate to do something. "I need to ask you two a question."

"What is it?" Mason asked dryly.

"If I needed y'all to do something for me, would y'all be able to do it and keep it a secret between us?"

They had no idea where this was going, but Mason responded first. "Whatever you need from us, we gotta clear it with Bugsy first, and Bugsy might gotta clear it wit' Scott. We do what they tell us. You understand?"

Maxine needed to push further. "I'm Scott's woman and I need something done that doesn't need to get back to Bugsy or Scott."

Again, Mason replied. "Miss, we have strict orders from the top, and unless the boss tells us differently, then we react on that. No disrespect to you."

Maxine continued with, "And I don't want anyone to feel disrespected. Bugsy is like a son to me, but I don't want to involve him in this petty issue that I have going on. He already has too much to deal with. And Scott has his own problems. What if I say there's money in it for y'all? Could we keep it among ourselves?"

The driver, Avery, spoke. "How much we talkin' 'bout?"

Mason rapidly uttered, "It don't matter how much money you throw at us, the boss made it crystal clear that we don't answer to you. We're only here to protect you! *Capisce!*"

Maxine cringed inside. She wanted to rip his throat out. He was making things difficult. He was truly loyal to the family, but it was easy to see that she had Avery's interest. But he didn't say another word because of Mason. Mason sat in the front seat with a frown. He was doing his job, but he didn't care for Maxine at all. He was completely loyal to Scott and Layla. He felt that Maxine was trouble from the beginning. The moment she came around was when everything started to fall apart.

"Just take me to the damn west side—Pier 86," she snapped.

Avery drove off. Maxine sat in the backseat and frowned. Avery answered to Mason, Mason answered to Bugsy, and Bugsy answered to his father. That was the chain of command. So where did that leave her?

It was early afternoon when Avery stopped the truck in front of Pier 86 in the Hell's Kitchen neighborhood. The place was open to the public and home to the Intrepid Sea, Air and Space Museum.

"I'll be right back. Stay here," Maxine told the two men.

"We need to come wit' you," said Mason.

"I said I'll be okay. Stay here!" she commanded harshly.

Mason looked reluctant, but he relented. Maxine climbed out of the truck and looked around. It was cold and the area was sparsely occupied with folks. She walked toward the pier carrying the satchel. She could feel Mason and Avery's eyes tracking her from behind. She knew they were watching her closely. She felt nervous and reluctant to pay these fools again, but she didn't have a choice. Until she could find someone to handle her problem, this was going to be it.

She paid the admission and walked into the museum. There were a few folks inside the massive structure, mostly tourists exploring the place—wholesome families with children. Maxine looked at the white folks for a few, thought about her own future, felt some sadness, and then she proceeded with her business. She was to meet Tarsha at the food court.

There the bitch was, seated at a table alone. Maxine locked eyes with her and felt reluctant to hand her nearly one million dollars in cash. She had to take a deep breath. Maxine walked toward her, her eyes transfixed on Tarsha. She noticed since their first meeting at One Police Plaza, Tarsha's upkeep had significantly improved. She observed the Jimmy Choo heels, the Prada purse, the diamond earrings, and the diamond rings and bracelet, and the fifteen-hundred-dollar leather coat. Maxine knew it all came from her money. That bitch was living well off of her, buying nice shit. It bothered her.

Maxine sat opposite Tarsha, and their hatred for each other was palpable. Maxine placed the satchel on the floor near her feet and nudged it closer to Tarsha's reach. She secured it in her hand. The smirk on Tarsha's face started to make her angry.

"This is it. Nothing else will come after this," she said.

"Bitch, you don't give out demands. We say it ends when we want it to end. And this don't look like five million," Tarsha replied.

"It's almost a million. Be grateful!"

"You think this is a fuckin' game?"

"No, but until Scott is either acquitted or convicted, I have nothing else to give you."

"We will fuck up your life, bitch! You keep comin' up short wit' our money, and we will destroy you," Tarsha griped.

"Look, I'm done! So you can go ahead and tell Scott. But let me remind you of something. If you do, then your gravy train with me ends. Because he will kill me and he will kill you and Wacka, and your son. At least with me alive, there will be more cash coming in if he gets acquitted. Besides, if you've been watching the news, then you would understand that his money is tied up right now. The feds froze his accounts, and I don't have access to any of his illegal funds," Maxine explained.

"Bitch, I don't want to hear all that. That's your fuckin' problem, not ours! Now you better start coming correct, or we—"

Tarsha didn't get to finish her threat. Something inside Maxine snapped. She leapt from her seat and charged at Tarsha like a beast from the jungle. Her clenched fist collided with Tarsha's face and it felt like she broke her nose. Tarsha toppled over in the chair. She couldn't get her footing quick enough. Maxine was on top of her with repeated punches. It was weeks of frustration and pent-up anger finally being released, and Tarsha was on the end of an ass-whooping. Blood flew everywhere.

"Fuck you, bitch! I'm tired of your shit!" Maxine yelled.

Her punches were solid, like Iron Mike Tyson. Tarsha had never felt anything like it. She'd underestimated the bitch. She felt her face smashing into the floor, her eyes swelling, and her beautiful wardrobe being torn up by Maxine's abrupt attack. She was being pulverized.

"Get off her!" Maxine heard him yell.

It was Wacka coming out of nowhere to aid his woman. He tried to attack Maxine, but he couldn't get a grip around her with missing fingers.

Tarsha was still underneath her attacker, screaming her head off. "Get this bitch off me! Get her off me!" she yelled.

A slight crowd started to gather around the altercation. They stood aghast at the scuffle happening in such a family oriented place. Who were these two women? And why were they fighting each other? It was chaos and they weren't going to stand for it.

"Someone, hurry and call the police," a voice shouted from the crowd.

"You bitch! Don't fuck with me!" Maxine screamed. Her fist smashed into Tarsha's face one last time before two men rushed in to break up the scuffle and pull them apart.

During the chaos, the satchel filled with the money remained unattended; it had been kicked around and tossed to the side. No one but the two girls was any wiser to what was inside. Now that they had been pulled apart, Maxine was able to compose herself, while Tarsha looked a bloody mess. Max breathed heavily and knew it was time to go. She noticed the satchel nearby. She picked it up and could have easily left with it, but she decided to throw it at Wacka, shouting, "Take your fuckin' money and leave me the fuck alone!"

Clumsily, he tried to catch it, but his hands failed him and he let it fumble to the floor. Maxine was keen and watched him try to pick up the bag with his gloved hands. It was awkward. He seemed all thumbs. Why? She shrugged it off and made her escape before the cops came.

Tarsha and Wacka fled the area too—almost a million dollars richer. But Tarsha was fuming. Maxine had put her hands on her, and now she really wanted to make that bitch pay.

22

Lucky sat in the backseat of the Navigator in a slight daze. The city went by her in a blur as the vehicle did 70mph on the highway. Her men were dead by her hands and she felt alone and dismayed, but she also felt that she'd left a good impression on Angel. Her connection with him started shaky, but she felt confident that he was a man of his word.

Angel's men felt that it was foolish and unwise to get into business with Lucky. They thought for sure that he was going to murder her along with her men. And yet, he hadn't. They had to admit to themselves that the girl really had heart. Killing four people in one night was nothing to sneeze at.

Angel wanted to test Lucky for two reasons. One, he only dealt with men. He felt their world was a man's world and women shouldn't be allowed in it. The only reason he did business with Layla was because he knew she helped build her husband's empire. Layla had been making moves for decades and she had a strong reputation for being ruthless. Angel needed to know if Lucky was just as ruthless and tough as her mother—maybe even crazier.

The second reason he made her kill four men was to test if she was working for the feds. If so, it would have been asinine for her to commit a quadruple homicide. Angel had secretly recorded her murderous deeds, and the video was a smoking gun if she ever tried to get cute with him.

Angel was known to have an arsenal of evidence against all kinds of people, from criminals to cops. If he ever got jammed up, he was going to use his evidence to get out of jail free or take some serious drug lords down with him. Now Lucky was one of many he had tangled in his web.

It was early morning with dawn approaching in two hours. The driver smoked a cigarette and soon neared Lucky's South Beach hotel. It had been a short ride, but it felt like it'd been hours. Lucky released a deep sigh and slouched in the seat. It had been a long day for her, and her outfit was wasted on murder and deceit—no party at all. Despite the hour, South Beach was still alive with bustling nightclubs. Lucky wanted nothing to do with partying and the nightlife. She'd had enough of Florida and she wanted to fly back to New York ASAP.

The truck stopped in front of her hotel and Lucky made her exit and strutted into the lobby fatigued.

She went up to her plush room and peeled away the red dress from her petite brown frame and went into the bathroom to draw a hot bath. The hot water poured from the pipes into the sunken tub and it was filling quickly. Though she literally didn't have blood on her hands, in her mind, she did. Her first murders by her own hands were somewhat overwhelming for her, but she would get through it. She justified her actions as the cost of doing business and nothing else.

The tub was soon full and her bath was waiting. Before she could enjoy it, she heard a faint knock at her hotel room door. Trepidation swelled in her as she donned the white cotton hotel robe and went toward the direction of the knock. She wasn't expecting any company, especially at this hour, and she didn't have a weapon, since she'd had her bodyguards in town. She felt extremely vulnerable.

Carefully peeking through the peephole, she saw that it was Angel standing outside her room door. *What else does he want from me?* she asked herself. She couldn't ignore him. He knew she was inside. She inhaled and sucked in a deep, calming breath to galvanize her nerves before slowly opening the door.

Angel smiled. She stepped aside, and he walked inside.

"Is everything okay?" she said, closing the door.

"I should be asking you that," he replied. "I know it's been a rough day for you. I'm just here checking to see if you're good."

"I'm fine."

"You did good tonight . . . impressive," he said.

"I want this to work between us."

He smiled. "It will."

Lucky stood before him in her white robe, while he stood there in his white linen shorts and top and white Gucci loafers, with his dark shades off and in his hand. He admired her sexiness.

It felt like he was about to put her through another test—a more intimate one. "You have no reason to be afraid. I adore your company."

Angel stepped closer. Lucky didn't move. The look in his eyes showed what he wanted from her—sex. She took another deep breath to steady her nerves.

"I find you quite intriguing for a black woman," he said.

Wow!

Angel wasn't attracted to races outside his own. He didn't consider himself a racist, but when it came to mating, he believed you stick to your own kind. But there was something about the pretty black girl with the droopy eye and a cold heart. He couldn't allow her to leave the state without sampling her goods.

He wanted to kiss her and she didn't deny him. Their lips pressed together and he kissed her passionately. She didn't resist. In fact, his lips against hers felt kind of good. But why did he want to have sex with her? Lucky's mind was spinning with reasoning, but his hand against her breast distracted her. It had been a while since she'd had sex.

Slowly, he untied her robe, removed it from her shoulders, and let it fall to the floor. Her nakedness was beautiful. He kissed her again, and they soon found themselves in the bedroom.

Lucky felt the great pleasure of her nipples being licked and kissed softly. He sent electric signals down to her clit, making the entire area wet. She felt overwhelmed with sensation. She moaned and wondered how she could fuck him after he made her kill three of her men. Her emotions to be appeased sexually were too strong, though.

Angel undressed, and Lucky was impressed by his hefty eight-inch cock. She became fearless and spread her legs for him. He placed himself between her inviting thighs and thrust inside of her. Lucky gasped and clenched her body against his. She felt every inch of him. Feeling him move inside of her, she had no second thoughts or doubts.

He was pressed against her in the missionary position like a hot iron to clothes, and for an average sized man at five-eight, he became a gigantic lover. His dick felt hard and smooth inside her, and his kisses were like magnets to her skin. The friction against her hardened clit twisted her body against the bed.

Her eyes were shut and her body wriggled against him. "Oh shit!" Lucky cried out.

She moved from beneath him, saddled up, and rode him cowgirl style, gyrating on his fully erect dick as it stimulated her G-spot and clitoris to a brewing orgasm. She felt in control, but in actuality, he was the one in control of her. He thrust up into her and she leaned forward as he massaged her breasts and toyed with her nipples. Her breathing started quickening. Her legs quivered and there was no holding it back.

"I'm gonna come!" she announced breathlessly.

They both came multiple times that night, and they knew that this would only be a one-night stand. Three hours after his entrance, Angel left the room, leaving Lucky asleep on the bed.

Later that day, Lucky boarded an American Airlines flight back to JFK. She sat in first class and laid her head back against the chair. She heaved a sigh, thinking *What's next?* She still felt some lingering remorse for killing her men, but the good news was, she achieved getting her independence from her mother.

Two weeks later, a shipment of two hundred kilos on consignment arrived from the Juarez Cartel via two 18-wheelers. Lucky knew that there was no turning back now.

The charges were official for Layla—attempted murder and the RICO act. Layla felt she was fucked. But she was baffled by the attempted murder charge. Who did she try to kill, and whoever it was, how were they still alive? If she wanted someone dead, then they would be dead. So who was still alive? She bothered her attorney with tons and tons of questions, but Fitzgerald had nothing for her yet. "I can't go to prison! Get me the fuck outta here!" she cursed.

"They have a witness, but the identity hasn't been made clear yet," said Fitzgerald. "I have someone who can go underground and dig out whatever I need."

"I don't care what you gotta do, make it happen. Make it all go away."

"He's expensive."

Layla sighed. "How much?"

"Fifty thousand," he said.

"Nigga, I gave you a fuckin' million on retainer, take it out of that," she growled at him.

Reluctantly, Fitzgerald nodded, and their meeting concluded.

Layla felt that she was rotting away in a jail cell while Maxine was mocking her. She couldn't shake the feelings of hate and disgust for the bitch. She didn't trust Maxine. Everything started falling apart the moment she came home from prison. There were questions like, how did Maxine get an early release? Parole?

Layla felt in her bones that Maxine was the snitch. She had to be working with the feds. But what did she know that could possibly get her and Scott locked up? Was Scott running off his mouth to that bitch and jeopardizing everything they'd worked so hard for? Layla surmised that Maxine made a deal with the feds and infiltrated their organization to disclose information. It all made sense to Layla—befriending her and getting back into her good graces before stabbing her in the back would be the ultimate revenge. All the years she helped Maxine because she felt sorry for her, and it came back to bite her on the ass.

But no one was listening to her. No one believed that Maxine needed to go immediately. Layla needed someone to do what her own family wouldn't do. Scott was a fool to fall back in love with Maxine, and Bugsy was an idiot to think she cared for him like she was his mother. Meyer was in the hospital, and Lucky was becoming detached.

***

It was visiting day, and Layla walked into the visitor's room to see Lucky smiling like she'd won the lottery or something. Lucky looked fabulous and bossy, and it pissed Layla off. It felt like Lucky didn't care that her parents were locked up, or that her mother was in a legal battle for her life.

"Bitch, why the fuck you grinning so hard for? Like you visiting me at the Ritz or something?" Layla berated after taking a seat across from her.

"It's nice to see you too, Ma," Lucky replied sarcastically.

Layla took in her daughter's fashionable outfit, hair and nails done, eyebrows threaded and shaded in. "I see you're living well."

"I'm doin' me."

"Well, I need for you to take care of something really important. I want for you to put two of your best goons on Maxine and take care of her," she ordered in a low tone. "She's the one snitching on us. I know it.

It all started to fall apart the moment she was released from prison. That bitch is out to destroy us."

Lucky rolled her eyes and sighed.

"Bitch, you got a problem?" Layla said angrily.

"I'll think it over."

"You don't need to think shit over. I gave you an order, you execute it. I'm the boss bitch here!" Layla growled through her tightened jaw.

"You *were* the boss bitch," Lucky replied matter-of-factly. "Your men, they now answer to me."

Layla clenched her fist and narrowed her eyes at Lucky. Was Lucky saying she was now wearing her shoes—stealing her queen pin position? But how? There was no fucking way, especially without a connect.

"You listen to me, you fuckin' dead-eye bitch," Layla exclaimed. "Don't fuck wit' me!"

Lucky had never heard that nasty remark from her mother. It stung like alcohol in a gunshot wound.

Layla continued to berate her. "I made you, I made all of y'all. And if you fuck wit' me, if you go against me, I'll bury you, you fuckin' dead-eye cunt. This is my empire—I built it, and I will burn it down before I let an ungrateful bitch like you take control over it."

For a black woman, Layla was turning red and it looked like smoke was about to bellow from her ears. However, Lucky kept her cool. Her mother wasn't a threat to her, but she did have one thing she needed—the fifty million she hid somewhere.

"Where is it—the money?" Lucky asked. "You tell me where you hid it and I'll take care of Maxine for you."

Layla chuckled at the proposal. "Bitch, you think I'm a fuckin' fool? You wanna play games wit' me, little girl? I'll take away your livelihood."

"How? You don't have any clout in here and no access to any funds. I met with Angel in Miami, and we negotiated a new deal. He's mine now.

Checkmate, bitch."

"Angel would never get in bed with you!"

Lucky chuckled. "You don't know how naive you sound right now."

"Fuck you, you fuckin' cunt! Don't underestimate me, bitch!" Layla retorted.

"Then don't underestimate me! You better recognize who has the upper hand." The torch had been stolen, and now she was the one carrying the flame.

Layla paused and reexamined her position. She needed her daughter's help, so she called for a truce. "Okay, look. I didn't mean to get so upset with you. I apologize for getting heated. It's just that I'm scared, Lucky. Despite what you've heard on the streets, this isn't Club Fed. I'm surrounded by a bunch of phony, stink bitches. It's cold in here and the food is lousy. I just want out."

"And I want you out too."

"I'm glad you said that. Because my attorney said that you might be able to help me do just that."

Lucky was perplexed but replied, "Sure. Anything I can do, I will."

"It's not complicated. First you need to immediately stop doing business with Angel just like I ordered. Second, we need to put you up on the stand and convince a jury that you're the female West who's into racketeering and helping to run a corrupt drug organization. We need to give them reasonable doubt."

"Say what now?"

"We need to make you a part of my defense. You shouldn't have a problem with credibility because you *are* a part of our organization. You're just not me—the head bitch in charge, but after listening to you today you obviously wanna be. So get your ass up on that stand and help your mother get found not—"

"Are you crazy?"

"Not yet, but I will be soon if I stay in here!"

Lucky immediately felt nauseous. A rush of emotions overwhelmed her and she had to blink repeatedly to stop the tears from flowing. She refused to cry in front of anyone. She clasped her clammy hands together to stop them from shaking and momentarily averted eye contact with her mother. How could Layla ask her such a thing?

"You just asked me to get up on the stand and implicate myself in a fed case for you? You know how those people play, Ma. Sealed indictments, snitches, and phone taps would be in my future if I placed myself on their radar. Whether you got acquitted or not, that act alone would ensure that my life as I know it would be over. The feds would make it so that the air I breathed was shallow until they got a conviction on me."

"You're jumping too far ahead in the story, Lucky."

"One question. Are you willing to gamble my today for your tomorrow?"

Layla gritted her teeth out of frustration. She wasn't used to begging or being in a position where she had to explain herself. But she did. "There's no one else that I can trust to get up on the stand and say the right things convincingly. And it's too risky involving strangers in our world, exposing them to family secrets. This has to be done in-house. I wouldn't come to you if I had a choice."

"You have a choice. And you chose you!"

"I'm your mother!"

"Not anymore!"

"Oh, stop being a gotdamn drama queen. You know I'd always protect you."

"Just like you protected Bonnie, Clyde, and Gotti?"

"Bitch don't ever bring my kids into this bullshit."

Lucky stood up, an indication to the guards that she was ready to go. "I'm going to make you regret this day for the rest of your miserable life!"

"Don't you ever fuckin' threaten me, Lucky West! I brought you into this world and I'll take you out! You hear me! You fuckin' hear me, bitch!"

Layla yelled and ranted, creating a scene for everyone to see. She gave her daughter an earful of threatening words while she could only watch Lucky walk out of the room and, perhaps, out of her life for good.

Lucky walked into the hospital room and smiled at her brother. She was thrilled to see Meyer awake and recovering from his wounds. She kissed him on the cheek and said, "I brought you some soup."

He managed to smile back. It was good seeing her. He took in her appearance and sensed that there was something different about her. She stood in front of him dressed in her black mink coat, diamonds, and pricey heels. She had this aura and maturity about her that said—*Boss!*

"You look good, sis," he said.

"Thanks. I'm feeling good," she replied.

She helped Meyer raise his bed up to eat the soup. Lucky looked at him and could see he'd lost weight. His face was thin and his body looked frail. It was her brother, but then again, it wasn't. His mannerisms were a lot feebler. She needed that monster back. He was critical in the streets, and Lucky knew that without him, things were going to be harder for her.

"I need you, Meyer. I need you to get well and get back on this grind wit' me. A lot of things done changed."

He nodded. "I'm here, sis."

"I know you are."

She helped him eat his soup. They had the hospital room to themselves, but Lucky knew she had to be careful with what she said and when she said it. But she needed to pull her brother's coat to what was going on. She stood up from the chair next to his bed and closed the room door. She had one of her men posted outside the room for security. She put her iPhone's music on shuffle, sat back down next to his bed, and looked at him.

"I'm working with Angel now," she started. "I flew down to Miami a few weeks ago, and we had a lengthy meeting that went very well."

Meyer was listening. She had his undivided attention.

She continued with, "I had to do something, Meyer. Layla wanted to discontinue her business with him, and that would have left us with nothing. She doesn't care about us. Her main concern is getting herself out of jail. The feds froze her accounts, and we had no product to put out on the streets."

Meyer wasn't shocked by the news. "It's always been about her."

"That's not even the craziest part. She basically asked me to take the heat off of her by getting on the stand and suggesting that I was the real queen pin—not her—to establish reasonable doubt."

Meyer whistled. It was unbelievable, even for his mother. "You serious?"

"Like a shot to the dome. You can't make this shit up!"

"She's always been a selfish bitch, though. And you know I love her more than my strippers and limited edition kicks, but this right here? I dunno. It's foul."

"Yup. And you know I can be a crybaby sometimes, but when I left MCC all I felt was rage and revenge. Like fuck Layla for real. She wanna do this to me? Her kid? After I rode hard for her over what Daddy did to her—even had her back after what she made you do to Bugsy! You and I have always held her down, and when the heat came around her corner she offered me up as a sacrificial lamb."

"I'ma curse her ass out when I speak to her."

"Nah, don't even. I can handle her. I *need* to handle her on my own. Besides, don't talk over those phones. I don't want my name circulating through any phone taps."

Meyer nodded. "I gotchu, sis."

"Yeah, that visit with her is why I made the Angel deal," she lied. "To protect us from her bullshit. We need our own money."

"I understand your position with Angel. You had to do what you had to do . . . but I don't feel comfortable with you having to deal wit' him, and alone. I'm not there to protect you right now. And I don't trust him."

"I can take care of myself, Meyer."

"I don't doubt that, but the cartel ain't nuthin' to fuck with," he said.

Lucky knew firsthand how dangerous they could be. She flashed back to that night they made her kill her three men in cold blood—and an innocent family man.

"I need to tell you something else," she said.

Meyer was staring at her intently, ready to hear what was about to spew from her mouth. "What is it?"

"I fucked him," she blurted out.

"Fucked who?" He was clueless for a split-second, and then it dawned on him. "No . . . get the fuck outta here! What the fuck were you thinking?"

"It just happened," she said.

"He didn't rape you, right?" Meyer asked with a hint of anger in his voice.

"No, he didn't. He came by my hotel room and it just happened."

Meyer couldn't see the attraction. Why would she fuck him? He felt that Angel was too effeminate for his sister with his soft hair and pale skin. He wasn't Lucky's type. Did he take advantage of her, or did his sister think throwing her pussy at Angel would put her in his good graces?

"Wow, a nigga's in a coma and wakes up to all kinds of surprises," he said. "You actually fucked that Mexican? Hey, don't think that your pussy is gonna spare you if shit goes wrong with him. Don't trust him, Lucky. I don't."

Lucky nodded.

25

Bugsy stepped into the jail visitation room with a strong stride and was assigned to a table near the back. The place was mostly jumbled with elderly women visiting daughters or granddaughters and children tagging along to see mothers, sisters, or cousins. He tuned out the chatter and glanced at the signs posted throughout the room. Some warned that it was a drug-free institution and lawbreakers would be prosecuted to the fullest extent of the law. Another sign warned of littering—anyone who litters shall be denied visitation privileges. Smoking, eating, and drinking were prohibited in the visitation lobby. So many restrictions, so many rules. He laughed lightly at them.

Before long, Layla and another female inmate were escorted in by a clean-cut male guard. The look on Layla's face indicated that she wasn't too happy to see him.

She sat across from him and spat, "That bitch is still alive, right?"

He didn't kill Maxine, and he didn't want to hear her fuss about it. "We're not gonna start with that today. I didn't come here to hear you gripe about her."

Layla didn't argue with him. She didn't want him to leave. She didn't want him to abandon her too. So many things were going wrong in her life. At night, all alone in her cell, she would cry and cry. But in public, she personified her bad girl, gangster bitch image.

The conversation shifted to Lucky. "Your sister is a bitch. She's treating me unfairly and fuckin' with my finances."

"What's going on?" he said.

Bugsy was listening, although he had places to be and there were other things to talk about. He sat there and allowed Layla to grumble about her issues with Lucky.

"She's out to destroy me," said Layla. "She cancelled the two-year lease on my Manhattan suite and collected the prorated funds without my permission. And I have no idea where the money went," she said.

"How did she do that?" he asked.

"A foolish mistake on my end. I gave that little bitch power of attorney on my behalf when I branched off from your father and started my Boss Bitch corporation. I thought she could be trusted."

Bugsy chuckled at the lunacy of his mother's decision. It was petty shit between two women, but he continued to listen.

"She's getting rid of all my personal belongings—jewelry, clothing, and shoes, everything—without my permission. She's leaving me with nothing! She's acting like I've already been tried and convicted and sentenced to life."

Bugsy shook his head. "I'll talk to her."

Lucky was doing some foul shit, but why? Something was going on, and he was in the dark.

"I want you to break her fuckin' neck for me," Layla said angrily.

"Now you know I can't do that. She's my sister."

"And she's my daughter, and look how she's treating me. I'm telling you, Lucky can't be trusted."

"Whatever issues you two got going on, y'all need to work it out. But like I said, I'll talk to her," he replied.

He had issues of his own, and the last thing he needed was to get caught up in their situation—*girl shit*, he felt.

"Well, before you get all dismissive and preachy with that 'sister' shit, let me pull your coat to this. And this is some serious shit, Bugsy, so that's why I'm coming to you. I need your help convincing my hardheaded child. I swear she's just like your father."

Bugsy exhaled. "What's up?"

"My attorney said that with an informant things are complicated. He's working on a defense, but with your father tied to my case, his shady drug past could spill over into my pristine record."

Bugsy gave his mother his full attention. "What you need me to do?"

"We need to create reasonable doubt. So, at the advice of my attorney, I asked your sister to testify on my behalf."

"Oh, like a character witness? And she has a problem with that? Don't worry, I'll speak—"

"Not like that, damn. And, I thought you were the smart one. He needs Lucky—and this was his strategy, not mine—to get up on the stand and give the jury an impression that she was really the person making all the illegal moves while I was at home raising my kids."

If Bugsy were a crying man, he would have cried for his sister. How could a parent even entertain such an asinine idea? He could only imagine how hurt Lucky was hearing this selfish proposition. He knew she looked up to Layla just as he looked up to Scott.

"Are you fucking insane? She's your daughter, not some underling!"

"Ain't shit gonna happen to her ass! It's just a ruse!"

"She's a fucking kid!"

Layla smirked. "Lucky? She came out my pussy wearing heels and lipstick. She can handle a few questions on the stand. I mean, if she can't, she's in the wrong business."

"I could say the same for you." Bugsy shook his head in disgust. "This is Maxine all over again. Anyone can do the jail time just as long as it's not you."

Bugsy got up. He couldn't leave fast enough. He exited the jail and was greeted by his men lingering around the Escalade. Bugsy climbed into the backseat and said, "Get me the fuck out of here. I hate this place."

His lieutenant, Choppa, looked at him with something important to tell him. "What the fuck you gotta say to me, Choppa?"

"I got word from Miami. They found the body of Javier Garcia's nephew. He was shot in the head," Choppa said.

Bugsy was stunned by the news. "What the fuck! They know who did it?"

"Nah, but shit is about to get heavy. His nephew was a civilian—a family man with kids."

"Garcia reached out to us yet?"

"Nah, no word."

Bugsy sighed and threw his head back against the headrest. Who would be bold or stupid enough to assassinate one of Javier Garcia's family members? Was it an act of war, or just a random killing by a walking dead fool?

"This fucking day keeps getting better and better," Bugsy said. "Just take me the fuck home. I'm tired."

26

Spring was almost in the air in New York City. Many were praying for an early spring, ready to climb back from life from the ice, cold, and snow. But it was early March, and there were going to be few more cold days and snow in the forecast.

Although it had been a bleak winter for many, it had proven a profitable winter for Lucky. She reigned over her mother's empire, and business with Angel was thriving. She was moving so much weight into the city, that some were calling her Snow White. She had reinvested her profit and taken fewer kilos on consignment. It would take a couple more flips before she wouldn't need consignment at all, but Lucky felt like she was moving in a good direction.

But there were always distractions.

It was a sunny Monday morning, and Lucky couldn't get any sleep. She constantly felt a rumbling and steady vibration in her stomach. It felt like her tummy was on a rollercoaster ride. She hurriedly removed herself from the bed and ran barefoot into the bathroom. She dropped to her knees and floated her face over the toilet and immediately hurled chunks. She was sick. Was it the flu? Or was it something worse? She feared the worst.

After cleaning herself up and downing a bottle of water, Lucky got dressed and headed to the nearest pharmacy and purchased several pregnancy tests. She went home and took all of tests in the privacy of her bathroom. Time seemed to crawl by as she sat on the toilet waiting for the results.

"Oh shit, I'm pregnant." They were all positive, and it was Angel's baby. She had brought more than a drug deal back with her from Miami.

She calculated the time since her one night stand with Angel, and it'd been seven weeks. She was carrying Angel Morales's baby inside of her. Angel Morales, head of the Juarez cartel. Being pregnant by him probably brought advantages. The brilliant idea grew inside her head of how powerful she could be if she became his wife. She, Lucky West, married to one of the most powerful men of the underworld. That's what it was about—power and money! Lucky wanted to climb to the top and be more successful than her mother ever was. She wanted to become that queen bitch everywhere—an international shot caller.

She stood up and went to look at herself in the mirror. Still young and vibrant, now pregnant. She lifted her shirt and examined her stomach. She had a baby growing inside of her. She thought of Whistler and how she'd once thought she would someday have his baby.

Lucky placed her hand on her stomach and took a deep breath. Her estranged parents were going to become grandparents—their first grandchild. She wondered what their reaction would be once they heard the news from her brothers, because she wasn't fucking with either one of them. Especially that heartless bitch Layla.

The following day she went to see her private physician, and it was confirmed. She was seven weeks pregnant. Now all she had to do was tell the daddy.

27

The knock at her apartment door made Maxine grab her robe that was hanging off the back of the bedroom chair and throw it around her naked body. She was getting ready for bed when someone decided to show up late night. She had an idea who it was. She tied her robe together and walked barefoot to answer the door. Opening it, there was Bugsy smiling at her.

"Hey Bugsy," she said with a smile.

"Hey, Maxine. I just came by to check up on you. Can I come in?" he said.

She nodded. "Sure."

Bugsy stepped inside the penthouse suite, and Maxine closed the door behind him. He stood there looking handsome in his black overcoat, his facial hair neatly trimmed. She could see the butt of his holstered 9mm slightly showing from the inside of his coat.

"Everything good with you tonight? You doing okay?"

"I'm doing fine."

But she wasn't stupid. Maxine realized that Bugsy was only coming to visit her late at night or early in the morning to keep tabs on her for his father. He wanted to see if she had another nigga in his father's bed. But there was no one.

Though Bugsy was against spying on Maxine, Scott made it clear that he wanted it done. For the past two weeks, Bugsy had been coming by unannounced. But he was always extremely nice to her and he was a gentleman. Maxine didn't mind it; she loved his company. She was lonely. She didn't have any friends, and her parents were dead.

Bugsy removed his overcoat and took a seat on the sofa. He made himself at home.

"Do you want something? Coffee? Hot chocolate?" she asked.

"I'll take a hot chocolate," he said.

"Coming up."

Maxine disappeared into the kitchen, and Bugsy's eyes lingered on her longer than needed. He looked around the place and it was always the same—tastefully decorated, relaxing, and no indication of another man's presence. Maxine had done a wonderful job of picking up the pieces and cleaning up after the FBI left his father's place in disarray.

She soon came back into the living room holding two cups of hot chocolate. She handed Bugsy his and took a seat near him.

"Thanks," he said, taking a few sips.

"So, how's it going out there?" she asked him.

"Hectic. But I'm managing things," he said.

"I commend you. You took on a lot. I know Scott is proud of you," she said.

"I do what I need to do."

"Don't we all?" she said.

"I guess so," he replied.

"Scott is a good man with a lot on his plate right now, and I'm gonna always be there for him because I love him. I don't want him to ever second guess that," she said with sincerity, giving Bugsy direct eye contact. Meanwhile, she couldn't give two fucks about Scott's fate.

"I know. I see it in your eyes—more with you than my own mother," he said.

She was thankful to hear that.

He sighed heavily. He had something on his mind too, and Maxine picked up on it.

"So what's going on with you? I can see it in your eyes that something is bothering you. There's a deep sadness behind them."

He chuckled. "What, you a psychiatrist or something?"

She chuckled with him. "No, I just know the signs all too well."

"Everything's cool," he lied.

"Have you seen or spoken to Alicia lately?" she asked him out of the blue.

He was taken aback by the question. "How did you know I was thinking about her?"

"A girl can tell. The way your mood shifted right after I said the things about your father, how I loved him. I know you loved that girl deeply."

"I did. I still do," he admitted.

"She's a good woman. If it's meant to be, Bugsy, she'll come back to you."

"I don't know. Her world and my world, it will never mix. She's a good girl. And if anything was to happen to her because of me, I would never forgive myself for it."

"Love can be a complicated machine."

"I don't need it to be complicated. I wanted it to work with her," he said.

"Have you seen or spoken to her lately?" she asked again.

"I parked outside her home a while back and watched her from the truck. It was difficult for me. She's moving. I don't blame her."

"You're a good man, Bugsy. I'm sorry it didn't work out with her."

"I chose this life, and she has hers. That's life, right?"

Maxine tried to encourage him. "You'll find that special girl one day, and she's going to love you unconditionally."

"If I don't die out here first," he uttered.

"Don't talk like that," she said. "You're gonna live forever!"

He laughed. "You believe that, don't you?"

"I believe we make our own way, no matter what, and those who are determined to survive will, no matter what," Maxine said.

"I respect you because you're a survivor. Twenty years inside, not a word to give up my mother. If it wasn't for you, I probably wouldn't even be born," he said.

"Fate is a funny thing, you know? You never know where it might take you, good or bad."

"Speaking of bad," Bugsy wanted to shift the conversation from Alicia. It hurt too much. "Layla is at it again. I don't want to bring up bad memories for you, but she wants Lucky to take the fall on her case."

"Take the fall?"

"Yeah, I don't know why I'm mentioning this, but I guess it's because you can relate. She wants Lucky to take the stand and undergo a line of questioning that could place her on the FBI's radar. Can you believe that?"

"With Layla? Yes. She will always put herself first."

"Over her kids, though?"

"She's frightened, and when she's scared no one around her is safe."

The two finished off their hot chocolate and talked for a while longer. Maxine always provided Bugsy with good conversation. He felt that he could talk to her about anything. He felt that she was honest with him and she offered good advice.

Bugsy looked at the time and it was getting late. He'd spent nearly an hour at her place. He stood up, and she stood up too. They looked at each other and smiled.

"It's been real with you, Maxine. Thanks for the hot chocolate," he said, throwing on his overcoat. "I feel like I'm twelve years old again."

She chuckled. "You're far from twelve years old, Bugsy. You're a very handsome young man."

There was lingering eye contact between them, but no words. She continued to smile. He started to walk toward the door. There was nothing for his father to worry about. Maxine was a wholesome woman, he believed. Scott was being paranoid, and Bugsy would report back to him with the good news like he always did. But Scott would continue to look for something that wasn't there at all, and Bugsy would warn him to fall back. Scott was determined to find something on Maxine—something that he felt wasn't right with her all of a sudden.

Maxine followed him to the door and opened it. Before Bugsy left, there was more lingering eye contact between them—smiling eyes and a shared connection. Before Bugsy made his exit, they hugged, and it was a lasting hug. Maxine pulled away from him, feeling her heart flutter suddenly. His hold around her started to become a little bit too enticing for her. Then he accidently brushed up against her backside. They both felt it, their emotional exchange. He looked at her and she looked at him. There was desire between them, but it felt awkward.

Bugsy left and Maxine closed the door behind him. She sighed and remained by the door. *What the fuck am I thinking?* she asked herself. The fuse had been lit. She felt something with Bugsy. There was this cumbersome spark that somehow ignited inside of her. He left moments ago, but she still felt him.

She retreated into her bedroom, removed her robe, and lay naked on her king size bed. Her body felt built up with a need to release. She spread her legs and moved her hand between her open thighs and rubbed her clit and fingered herself, all while thinking about Bugsy. He was the younger, smarter, more loyal version of Scott. His charisma, kindness, and swag had left a mark on her.

***

Bugsy briskly walked out of the building and climbed into the backseat of the lavish GMC Yukon. His men had been patiently waiting outside. They didn't question his extensive time inside Maxine's apartment. It wasn't their business.

Bugsy sat back in the seat, knowing what he suddenly felt for Maxine was surreal. Something unspeakable had started between them. She was a real woman and his father was lucky to have her. He respected that—the love they had. It made him envy it and made him upset that he didn't have that with Alicia. He needed to forget about Maxine somehow. It was immoral.

"Take me to this nigga right now," he said to Pluto.

The man nodded and drove away from the building. Bugsy stared off in the distance in a daze. He remained silent as Pluto navigated the SUV to Brooklyn in the middle of the night. The traffic was sparse, and it was familiar territory to Bugsy. Brooklyn was his parents' stomping grounds, their home, and it was the place where everything started for his family. It was where his parents made a serious name for themselves the hard way, literally through blood, sweat, and tears. The West name was known in every ghetto and project building. The streets were unforgiving at times, but his folks built a legacy.

Still, the wolves were at their ankles, snarling and hungry to devour what his family had built. With Scott and Layla locked up, there were more wolves emerging and trying to test their strength and looking for cracks in their foundation. They wanted to see the family and the organization torn apart and crumbling so a new team could rise from the rubble.

One particular wolf was named Gambino. He was becoming a heavyweight on the streets and a problem, like Spank. However, Gambino was a lot more organized and connected, and he was older and more influential in the streets. Scott's arrest made it appear that Gambino would become the next major drug lord in Brooklyn and beyond, and Bugsy couldn't allow that to happen. The West organization couldn't look weak. Bugsy and his father had just eliminated Deuce and his crew from the face of the earth, and now Gambino was their next threatening rival.

The Yukon came to a stop in front of a corner bodega on Myrtle Avenue in the Bed-Stuy section of Brooklyn. Bugsy stepped out of the truck and went into the store with his two goons following. There were no customers in the store, and Bugsy was met by the store clerk. The man nodded and watched Bugsy walk by toward the back area. He trekked through a short, narrow hallway and descended narrow concrete stairs to the basement. He was met by Choppa, who looked like he had been putting in work.

"Is he talking?" Bugsy asked Choppa.

"Nah," Choppa said.

Bugsy frowned and entered the concrete room and saw the victim lying on the floor. His name was Mackie and he was a higher-up in Gambino's crew. Mackie had been severely beaten by Choppa and the other hoodlums in the room, and there was more to come. Bugsy approached Mackie with his hard gaze and felt no remorse for his condition. His face was bloody, eyes swollen, and skin bruised. Choppa had put a serious hurting on him. His right-hand thug loved his job a bit too much.

"I swear y'all muthafuckas are like weeds. Cut a few down, more pop up somewhere else in the backyard and fuck up my grass," said Bugsy.

He removed his overcoat and suit jacket, unbuttoned the cuffs on his shirt, and rolled up the sleeves.

Mackie looked up at Bugsy and scowled. Bugsy nodded to Choppa, and right away an aluminum baseball bat was put into his hand. He towered over Mackie like a hungry cat to a cornered mouse.

"I'm tired of y'all muthafuckas thinking y'all can just come and take food out of our mouths. Nigga, do you think we're gonna allow that to happen?" Bugsy exclaimed.

It was a rhetorical question.

"What—you see this nice suit, the expensive shoes, and the pretty face and you think I'm a pussy?" Bugsy threw out another rhetorical question. Next came the not-rhetorical question. "Where's your boy at? Gambino? He and I really need to have a face-to-face. He's overstepping his boundaries because my peoples are down—like he can just come into Brooklyn and do whatever the fuck he wants!"

"Fuck you!" Mackie growled at Bugsy with contempt.

"Seriously? Fuck me? That's your comeback line? You disrespect my business and you insult me?" Bugsy retorted.

Yeah, he meant it. Mackie wanted to be tightlipped and hardcore to the end.

Bugsy wanted to teach him some manners, and the baseball bat was his lesson plan.

"My boys beat you down pretty badly, but that's nothing compared to what I got in store for you if you don't speak up and tell me what I want to know," said Bugsy coolly.

Once again, Mackie glared up at Bugsy and retorted, "Fuck you, nigga!"

Bugsy shook his head in disbelief. "Y'all niggas are never gonna learn. This shit isn't a fuckin' game!"

He took an angry swing, and the baseball bat slammed into Mackie's lower back. A deep howl emanated from Mackie as he cringed from the blow. But Bugsy wasn't done yet. He swung that bat again and struck Mackie in his knee cap, then on his shin, and he worked his way up the body.

"You have nothing to say, muthafucka?" Bugsy screamed.

Still, Mackie showed noncompliance, and that further fed Bugsy's rage. He swung the bat again and hit Mackie full-force on his forehead. The blow was so heavy that it nearly sunk his skull in. Blood started to trickle down his face. Bugsy hit him again, the bat colliding with the man's face, spewing more blood and knocking out teeth. Then there was another hit and another. Each forceful bash was disfiguring the man's appearance as Bugsy's men watched. Mackie's face started to look like chopped meat, and he wasn't moving. Mackie was dead. Bugsy had hit him like he was a hanging piñata—ready to have his guts spill out instead of candy.

When he was done, Bugsy was breathing heavily, and the bat was dripping with blood.

"Get rid of this muthafucka," he said.

Choppa nodded.

"I want you to dump the body on the street—send a message to that muthafucka Gambino," Bugsy added.

"I got you," Choppa replied.

Bugsy's actions were in complete contrast to who he was earlier with Maxine—Mr. Nice Guy and a gentleman. Bugsy had a lot of pent-up hurt and anger that he needed to release, and Mackie made a fine punching bag. Plus, he wanted to get his hands dirty to remind his men not to be confused by the suit and tie. He was still a very dangerous man—a killer—and he needed to show it from time to time.

He dropped the bat and cleaned his hands. He then fixed his shirt and tie and donned his overcoat. He turned and left the basement, leaving his men to exchange silent glances.

28

Angel invited Lucky to join him in sunny California. He loved his warm weather states. Lucky flew first class to Los Angeles, alone this time. She wanted to see Angel face-to-face and tell him about the pregnancy. How was he going to take it? It'd been nearly twelve weeks since they'd seen other in Miami.

The plane landed at LAX in the early afternoon. It was her first time in the Golden State. The nearly six-hour flight went smoothly, and Lucky walked through the terminal with anticipation of seeing Angel. There was a three-hour difference between New York and L.A., and Lucky experienced minor jet lag. Her pregnancy wasn't helping either. So far, she'd kept it a secret from everyone. She wanted Angel to be the first to know about his baby growing inside of her.

The only baggage Lucky traveled with was her small carry-on bag. She walked toward the terminal exit behind the dozens of other arriving passengers looking ravishing in her dark blue pantsuit and heels. She looked like a professional woman in L.A. on business, but her cleavage was spilling out of her blouse. She didn't look twelve weeks pregnant. She was carrying small, her waist only slightly thickened.

Outside the terminal, there was an idling black Range Rover with tinted windows parked near the curb and a tall, intimidating Latino male wearing a dark suit and dark shades posted by the vehicle with his arms crossed in front of him. Lucky knew he'd been sent by Angel to greet her at the airport. She looked at him and he looked at her, unsmiling. She took a deep breath and walked his way. He immediately opened the back door for her to climb inside. There was no welcome—no formal greeting from the henchman. He was standoffish and didn't even help her with her small carry-on bag. He was simply there to escort Lucky to her location—nothing more and nothing less.

Lucky sat back and eyed the scenery. It was busy, busy, and busy. Cars and people swamped the area, and L.A. traffic was already in full effect right outside the airport. There were two men with her inside the Range Rover. Both of them were quiet. The driver navigated the vehicle toward the airport exit. It was a slow crawl, but eventually, they made it onto the 405 Expressway and headed north toward Santa Monica. Lucky was floored by L.A.'s palm trees and beaches, and the weather was flawless.

The driver came to a stop in front of an attractive hotel on Ocean Avenue. The passenger got out and opened the back door for Lucky. She stepped out of the vehicle and looked around. The street was lined with towering palm trees, and the people were sexily dressed for the sunny and warm weather. It was like Miami all over again. The luxury hotel featured oceanfront tranquility, European-style spas, and fine dining.

Inside, Lucky was guided toward the elevator and she rode it to the top floor and stepped out onto the rooftop pavilion with exotic floral arrangements, a rooftop garden, and deck chairs. The place seemed a world away from everything else. The only occupant was Angel. He was seated by the bar sipping on a clear drink. He was dressed for the warm weather in white shorts and white loafers, but he was shirtless with a thin gold chain decorating his neck. He spotted Lucky and smiled.

"You look beautiful," he said to her.

She smiled. "Thank you."

"You must be hungry after your trip. I already had the chef prepare you a nice meal," he said.

Lucky was famished. She was eating for two and she was soon going to tell him the news. Angel snapped his fingers, and a white male chef came into her view with eagerness to appease. He set before her a plate of chicken parmagiana and a plate of salmon. He went to pour a glass of white wine, but Lucky waved her hand and said, "No, thank you. I'll take a glass of water."

"You don't drink with me?" said Angel.

"Not right now," she said.

He wanted to toast with her because business had been really good. Lucky was a shrewd bitch when it came to business and the streets. Together, they were moving more cocaine than there was snow in the Himalayas. Angel was sorry that he'd doubted her. She was better than her mother, a lot more resourceful, and the sex was good. In fact, he was looking forward to a second encounter with her tonight. But for now, they had a late lunch and talked.

After lunch, Angel took Lucky on a tour of the hotel, which he owned. It was a beautiful place. Her room was a luxurious suite, and Angel wanted to put the soft bed to good use. He made it unequivocally known to Lucky that he wanted to have sex with her tonight. She remained nonchalant toward him.

Lucky stood out on the balcony gazing at the sea. The sun was gradually setting and creating a golden glow over the ocean and the landscape. Angel approached her from behind and wrapped his arms around her. It felt good, and she groaned faintly. He started to fondle her breast and kissed the side of her neck, and she could feel his erection growing behind her. His hands reached under her shirt and he felt how swollen her tits had become. They felt plump and juicy in his hands.

"I'm pregnant," she announced to him abruptly.

The movement of his hands against her breasts suddenly paused. He removed his arms from around her and took a few steps back. Lucky turned around to face him. She lifted her shirt and he didn't see much. If she were pregnant the telltale sign was her breasts. Angel's mood quickly shifted from lover to interrogator.

"By whom?" he asked her.

"By you . . . it's your baby."

"You lie to me, Lucky?"

"No, I'm not lying. You're the only man I've been with—no one else," she told him.

"So sad for you."

"Sad? I don't understand."

"You need to get an abortion immediately."

An abortion? She was shocked to hear those words come from him. She was already twelve weeks and soon to enter her second trimester. She could feel her body changing, and the nausea had subsided.

"I'm not killing my baby," Lucky said to him.

"Either you'll get an abortion or I'll give you one myself," he said harshly.

Lucky was taken aback by his reaction—his words. Protectively she placed both hands over her stomach. She glared at him and was ready to fight back if he came to attack her. She was willing to protect her unborn child by any means necessary, even if it meant going toe-to-toe with a powerful kingpin like Angel.

Angel saw her tense up. "That baby is going to get you killed."

"I will die before I let you do anything to it." Lucky's chest heaved up and down from the stress.

Angel took a deep breath. Things were growing hostile. He realized that he was being too harsh with Lucky. He wasn't in love with her, but that one night together had formed a connection. And although they were business associates, he would contact her from time to time to check on her.

"You can't go full term with that baby," he warned her. "They won't let you."

No one was going to tell Lucky what she could and what she couldn't do. It was her baby and her body.

"If you have that baby, its life will be in serious danger. There's a long standing tradition in the Juarez cartel that you don't muddy the bloodline. Children in my family must be a hundred percent Mexican. We don't mix races. If anyone finds out about your pregnancy, they will come for you."

"But you're Angel Morales. You *are* the Juarez cartel," Lucky replied.

"I'm a major part of it, but there are others out there that I have no control over," he said.

"I won't tell anyone that it's your baby," she said.

"Why would you take that chance? If my wife ever finds out about you—"

"Wife?" It was the first time she heard that he was married.

"Yes, my wife. If she finds out about the pregnancy, she will surely come for you and terminate you and the baby."

"I'm not afraid of your fuckin' wife," Lucky replied brazenly.

"You should be. She scares me sometimes," he said.

Lucky wasn't in a joking mood. "If that bitch comes near me or my child, I swear, I'll kill her."

Angel frowned. "Don't be foolish, Lucky. This will be too much for you to take on. You can avoid all of this with a simple abortion. Why risk members of the cartel coming for you and your baby? Or risk my wife coming after you? It's not worth it. I don't want to see you harmed."

Lucky placed her hands against her stomach and looked brooding. Angel didn't take his eyes off of her; he was waiting for her to make the right decision. Right away, she was put into a difficult predicament—her baby or her continued business with Angel. She was making money hand over fist with him. She sighed heavily and said, "I'll have the abortion."

He smiled. "Wise choice. I want our business relationship to continue. You can have a baby some other day. But not with me."

Angel realized that he'd dodged a bullet himself. His position in the Juarez cartel could have been jeopardized if it came to light that he had a half-nigger child. The Juarez cartel, like most illicit empires, also had legal businesses, and an heir could have legal rights. Angel made a mistake with Lucky three months ago, and it would be a mistake he wouldn't make twice. Even kings can be dethroned, and in his case, they'd sooner chop his head off than have a half-black baby connected to the Juarez cartel.

Their evening together was ending. Angel was no longer in the mood to be intimate with her. He told her that it was best to keep their relationship strictly business and not to call him for social reasons.

Lucky agreed.

Bugsy told himself that he wasn't going to go back there—to her home—but he did. He needed to see her again. *One last time*, he told himself. It was borderline stalking, but he couldn't help himself. She was the only perfect thing in his life. She was once his sunshine and his muse, but now there was nothing. Bugsy stared at the dark and empty house. She had finally moved out. He had no idea where she had gone. He didn't want to know. Alicia was now completely out of his life, but she was still in his heart. There would be no more visuals of her, only memories and nostalgia.

Sitting parked across from her home on the quiet suburban street, it was a world he thought about a few times—having a family of his own and regular living. Would he have given it all up for her? Was that even possible with his background and his family? A deep sigh escaped from him and he kept his feelings contained. There would be no tears or anger, just what-if's.

While seated in the backseat of the Yukon, his cell phone rang. It was his sister calling. He wasn't in the mood to speak to her. He had been trying to see her since he had spoken to his mother, but Lucky was always too busy for him. She was going her way and he was going his. He was hearing about Lucky a lot. Her name was ringing out on the streets faster than the wind could blow. His sister was a cold and calculating bitch.

She had a great source somewhere, and Bugsy knew it was most likely an opposing cartel. So far, they hadn't bumped heads.

She called again and this time he answered. It had to be important.

"What?" he asked roughly.

"I need to talk to you," she said.

"I'm busy."

"This is important."

"Life or death?" he said.

"Just come by to see me right away," she said in almost a demanding tone. "I really need to see you. I need your help."

Bugsy could hear the desperation in her voice. Something was going on, and it had to be critical for her to call him during the night and ask for his help. She rarely needed his help. She was capable of handling her own and surviving in this game. Layla had taken her daughter for granted. Bugsy was smart enough to know that his sister was never to be underestimated. She was a beast, like him. But he was smarter than her.

"I'll be there in about an hour," he said. "Come to think of it, I need to speak with you too."

"Life or death?"

He chuckled and hung up. Bugsy looked over at the vacant house one last time and then instructed Pluto to leave. For him, there would be no more harping on the past. Alicia was gone.

Two hours later, he arrived at Lucky's new penthouse apartment on the west side of the city. Bugsy walked into his sister's lavish place. It looked like something out of the *Scarface* film—gaudy, ornate furnishings, floor-to-ceiling windows with a scenic view of New Jersey, the Hudson River, the bridge, and beyond. Bugsy was impressed, but he hoped his sister was smart enough to know that everything had to be accounted for. It wasn't the feds that they had to worry about most times, but the IRS. Everything needed to be legit—every penny, nickel, and dime—and she needed to have a reasonable income to explain her wealthy living. Despite that she'd come from a wealthy family, Bugsy knew that legitimacy was the key to maintaining. Without it, they would be living in a house of cards and the IRS and the feds could easily come in and knock it down. The West money was far and wide, and it was cleaned and legal. The company filed tax returns yearly, but Bugsy was the one behind the scenes putting all the pieces together. He knew business and he knew how to make money, from the streets to the boardrooms.

"Nice place," he said to Lucky.

"Thank you," she said.

She walked around in a silk robe and house slippers, diamonds dripping around her neck and wrist. The image of her reminded him of Layla. It was ironic.

"You got correct paperwork for everything?" he asked her.

"I'm not stupid, Bugsy. I know how to conduct business and explain my income," she said.

"You and I are connected, so they come for you, they'll damn sure come for me," he said.

"I didn't call you over here to criticize me."

They stood in the center of her extravagant living room. Bugsy didn't take a seat because he didn't plan on staying long.

"What's so important that you called me over here?" he said.

Lucky took a deep breath and locked eyes with him. She could tell him the news because she trusted him and knew he would be there for her. Meyer was recovering, but it was a slow show and Lucky's life was moving on fast-forward.

"I'm pregnant," she said.

Bugsy's eyebrows shot up. "Pregnant?"

She nodded.

"How far along?" he asked.

"I'm in my second trimester."

He looked at her and didn't see anything that indicated her pregnancy. She slowly opened her robe to reveal her small baby bump. Though she was carrying small, it was there.

"Whose baby is it?" was Bugsy's next question.

Lucky sighed and answered. "Angel Morales from the Juarez cartel."

He couldn't believe it. How did she get pregnant by that fool? The Juarez cartel was at war with the Garcia cartel. Javier Garcia was shrewd and lethal, and his little sister was pregnant by his adversary. It was a serious situation that could get very ugly.

"What the fuck, Lucky! Are you kidding me?" he exclaimed. "How could you be stupid enough to get in bed with our rival? You know we've got ties to the Garcia cartel!"

"It just happened."

"What the fuck you mean it just happened? How do you accidentally get pregnant by Javier Garcia's archenemy?"

"What more do you want me to say?"

"How about you start with how y'all met?"

Lucky decided not to tell the whole truth. Luckily for her, it was always hard for Bugsy to tell when she was lying.

"Our mother needed a connect, and the Juarez pipeline would have been a lucrative deal. But those racist, chauvinistic fucks don't do business with women—said women are only good for pussy and carrying babies!"

"So you fuck him?" Bugsy felt something wasn't adding up.

"It was one night, Bugsy. Damn, you act like I'm trying to be wifey."

"The Juarez cartel is your connect and you're fucking Angel to make sure it stays that way."

"What are you talking about connect? I have no business dealings with that man. I shut it down."

"You think I'm stupid?" Bugsy was incensed that she would lie to him. "You out on the streets making money moves, Lucky. Don't play with me!"

"I'm not! And why are you yelling?"

Lucky started to get emotional. She averted her look from him; her eyes were ready to leak tears.

Bugsy knew by the heavy emotions and the poignant look on his sister's face, that there was more. She wasn't telling him everything.

"What the fuck else, Lucky? I know there's more," he said.

"Angel wants me to get an abortion. He warned me that if anyone finds out about my pregnancy with his baby, that they'll come for me and kill me and the baby."

"We can't afford to go to war with the Juarez cartel, Lucky. There's too much going on already. So, what are you going to do?"

She remained silent. She was thinking, but her hesitation already gave Bugsy his answer.

"You plan on keeping the baby, huh?"

"It's my baby, Bugsy."

"And does Angel know this?"

"I lied and told him that I would get an abortion."

He sighed. "And he believed you?"

She nodded. "Nobody's going to know anything. You and Angel are the only two that know about this. I'm goin' to hide my pregnancy for as long as I can. And I'll live my life in private. You didn't even know I was pregnant until I told you."

"So you got it all figured out, huh? It's gonna be that easy?"

"Yes! My baby is gonna have the best of everything, from nannies and bodyguards. It'll be my secret and no one else will know about my child."

"And you believe that's any way for a child to live—sheltered and in private, not knowing his family—me?"

"At least my baby will live! And it's gonna have me around. And I will kill anyone before they harm me or my child," Lucky said with a fierce look at her brother.

He sighed again. The room was growing thick with concern for his little sister, but he didn't want to argue with her. He was going to be an uncle. Lucky really wanted to have this baby, and it wasn't his right to tell a woman what to do with her body. But the concerns were major. She was running a drug empire, and being pregnant would be seen as weakness—and she could become an easy target. Bugsy understood this, even if she didn't comprehend the grave danger she had placed herself and those who loved her in. However, he would protect her life with his own. No harm would come her way as long as he could help it. But Lucky's love life was an added aggravation that the West empire did not need.

Now that they were in the same room talking, Bugsy felt it was the right time to ask Lucky about Layla and what she did.

"I went to see our mother and she told me a story that you took everything from her. Where is everything, Lucky? Her personal things—pictures, clothes, furniture, and money? You surrendered the penthouse back to the management company?"

"Fuck her! She's not my mother anymore. I'm done wit' her. I put everything in storage because it was money wasted having that place sit while she's locked away. I made a business decision to vacate it," she said. "And if I told you what she wanted me to do you wouldn't be on her side!"

"I know she wanted you to take the stand, and I told her she was fucked-up for that. Dead fucking wrong on so many levels. But you did this shit to her belongings before she had even crossed the line. Why?"

"I just told you why. To save money, that's all."

Bugsy suspected that she was lying; he needed to push. "We're not standing on line at a soup kitchen. Don't insult me."

"You wouldn't understand! She hurt me, Bugsy."

"How?"

"She called me a dead-eye ugly bitch." Lucky stared at her brother looking pitiful. Her low eye was something that she couldn't come to terms with, and when someone you love and trust tells you you're ugly, you believe it.

"You're just as beautiful, Lucky, as you ever were. And believe me, I'm a man. I know. You have the most beautiful face I've ever seen. Don't let Layla get under your skin. You're stronger than that."

Lucky nodded and then gave her brother a tight hug. She needed to hear someone say the word "beautiful" in the same sentence as her name.

They had more pressing things to talk about, and the issue of her pregnancy took precedence. Bugsy spent the majority of the night with his sister, talking and being there for her. They only had each other, because everyone else was locked down, dead, or in the hospital.

Each day alive and above ground was a promising day for Meyer. He took a deep breath and started to walk slowly, taking his road to recovery one step at a time. On his first attempt to walk again, his legs felt like jelly. His strength wore out so quickly, he wanted to collapse and give up. His legs ached with every movement, and he didn't think he would ever get back to his old self again. His physical therapist pushed him to his limit and encouraged him. He was the best, supposedly, and he was very expensive. It was helping significantly, but it was still one long road ahead. The bullets had done major damage to his system and shattered not only his flesh, but his quality of life. If he couldn't be 100% healthy and strong, what good would he be to the streets—to his sister and their organization? Meyer accepted that though he carried the West name, what made him useful and respected was that he was feared. His reputation preceded him.

Meyer made a vow to himself, that if—no, when—he got completely healthy that there would be no more fucking remorse. He made one mistake, and that mistake came back and nearly killed him. He trusted Luna. They were like brothers, but they weren't blood. Luna made a mistake by attacking Bugsy, and Layla wanted him dead. She wanted to send that message that no one messes with her sons. But Meyer felt Luna deserved a second chance, so he lied to his mother and allowed Luna to live. Now, if he was supposed to kill someone, then he was going to pull that fucking trigger. Luna had betrayed him—gunned him down when Meyer spared his life. Meyer knew he would never be that weak or ignorant again.

So, he took his first steps in physical therapy, and they were his hardest and longest. But each day he progressed forward. He needed to make himself useful again. So long in a coma, drowned by medication, and his body severely damaged, Meyer was angry with himself. Everything seemed to be crumbling.

Meyer was desperate to get back to normal before the summer. The weather was becoming warmer, the clothing outside was changing, and the greenery on the trees started to develop little by little. Each day he would gaze out the window and observe the transformation happening around him.

Another thing that was bothering Meyer was Zoe. Not once did she visit him in the hospital. Where was she? Why wasn't she around when he needed her? He really liked her, but he felt that her absence from his side was a sign of betrayal. He made another vow to find her and see what she was hiding. They spoke often once he was well enough, and he explained that he didn't show up for their trip because he had gotten shot. Zoe told him she knew all about his shooting; it was all over the news.

"My parents don't think it's safe to visit you," she said. "My dad doesn't want me connected to that life."

"And what type of life is that?"

"You know . . ." her voice trailed off.

"The same life your family is into?"

"I told you that I didn't want to date someone in the pharmaceutical business. I told you that."

Meyer repeated his same cover story. "And I told you that's not me. I'm a businessman, Zoe. Why can't you believe that? I get shot and I'm the villain? I thought you loved me."

"I do."

"Then come see me."

She exhaled. "I will—I'll try. . . soon."

In the meantime, he would play therapist to his sister and sometimes his twin brother. Lucky visited him frequently and told him about Layla and her foul proposition. But today she came by to tell him that she was pregnant and it was Angel Morales's baby. Meyer didn't like it one bit. How was his little sister knocked up by the head of the Juarez cartel? He felt that she was stupid to get pregnant by him. But the part that infuriated him was Angel threatening Lucky.

"He wants you to get what? An abortion?" he spat.

"I'm keeping the baby," she said.

"Yeah, that's your choice, sis—not his. Fuck that nigga! I swear, when I get better, I'm gonna see that muthafucka," Meyer exclaimed.

"You gonna go up against an entire cartel, Meyer? That's foolish!"

"He threatens you and my unborn niece or nephew, then fuck yeah, I will," Meyer replied.

It's what Lucky loved about him, his tenacity and boldness. He didn't fear anyone or anything, and that was the reason Lucky needed him completely healthy and killing again. She smiled at him. Meyer gave her assurance. It felt good to know he had her back all the way in this. Meyer understood her drive and determination. She was a hothead, just like he was. But in his feeble state, he was worried. Until he was out of the hospital and able to protect his family, he was vulnerable to anything.

"How's the therapy coming along?" she asked.

"It's good. This dude is on point. I be wanting to kill him sometimes, because he aggravates me wit' these fuckin' exercises, but he got me mobile again. I can't get mad at that," he said.

Lucky smiled. "You do what you need to do so we can be strong together. I need you out here, Meyer."

"I'm here."

"I'm gonna let you get some rest. I love you." She kissed him on the cheek.

"I love you too, sis. You just be careful out there. I'll be out soon."

***

Lucky stepped out of the hospital into the spring air with her two armed guards. She took a deep breath and felt her baby moving around inside her stomach. It felt surreal. She was going to be a mother. It was becoming difficult for her to hide her pregnancy. She was in her second trimester and her stomach protruded more. She didn't want her underlings to know about her pregnancy, so she made herself scarce and trusted her lieutenants to overlook production and supervise incoming product shipments and the streets. The last thing Lucky wanted was for word to get back to Angel that she was still pregnant. What she needed was a buffer between herself and the streets and organization, and it had to be someone she could trust completely. Meyer would have been perfect for the job. She needed him healthy and she needed him by her side ASAP—like yesterday.

Bugsy took a deep breath and exhaled. He had been drinking, but he wasn't sloppy drunk. He was a bit tipsy, and he had some things to think about and get off his chest. What he suddenly felt for Maxine, it was surreal. The feelings for her came out of nowhere and he couldn't shake them off.

He lingered by her door and made sure his appearance was up to par before he knocked. The cold air faded as spring blessed the city. And it wasn't just the weather changing; it was his relationship with Maxine. He continued to visit her on certain nights to "check in" on her, as his father wanted him to do. But what was developing between them was happening fast, and it was unexpected. They didn't have sex—not yet—but the sexual tension continued to build between them. Maxine took great pleasure in teasing him with her sexual innuendos. It was nothing overt; just subtle exchanges between the two of them, and it was becoming hard to overlook.

The other night when he was over there, her robe opened suddenly, as if it was inadvertent, and her naked body peeked out at him. Bugsy kept his cool and remained expressionless at the sight of her nakedness, but he took in an eyeful and it was a glorious sight. Maxine was a forty-something with the body of a twenty-something. She kept herself in great shape. She was a cougar at its finest.

She would answer the door in a towel or in a cotton bathrobe before running into the room to get dressed and later coming out fully clothed with her hair soaking wet. She cooked for him and talked to him like an equal. She listened intently to him and became like a therapist or sounding board for Bugsy. She showed him patience, empathy, and support.

At first, Bugsy wondered what her ploy was. What did she have to gain by seducing him? She belonged to his father. Scott loved her—but damn-it, Bugsy couldn't ignore the attraction. The enticement continuously taunted Bugsy; even the way she ate her king crab legs one day when they had lunch, stuffing the meat into her mouth with the hot butter sauce running down her chin. It was all driving him crazy.

So tonight, he stood in front of her door, waiting for it to open and yearning to see Maxine again. Tonight, he didn't want to talk. He didn't want her to listen or cook for him. He came there for one thing only, and that was to have sex. The sexual urges he felt for her couldn't be contained any longer.

The door opened and there she was, dressed in her short cotton robe with a smile aimed his way. "Hey," she greeted.

Bugsy immediately took charge. He marched into the apartment, closed the door, and wrapped his arms around her and kissed her passionately. She didn't resist, and their kiss deepened. She wanted his body on top of her and to feel him inside her. He continued to press her fondly into his arms and undid her robe.

"Bugsy, I . . ."

He lifted her into his arms and she straddled his waist. Their minds drowned in waves of lust for each other. He carried her to the couch and dropped her against it. Maxine stared up at him, and he was the finest thing around. He started to undress himself, removing his jacket and unbuckling his pants, and she opened her legs for him.

He sank between her legs and his dick throbbed as she teased the head with her pussy's wet lips, which seemed to pulse around it. It was commanding him. He wanted to feel her completely. It was sexual torment just lingering near the pussy. He aggressively pushed forward. He didn't want to be teased anymore. She could feel the head of his dick slowly pushing against the opening of her pussy. He was finally inside of her and there was no turning back. This was it! Maxine shuddered and moaned from the feel of him pushing inside. He continued to press the mushroom tip past her taut lips and soon was completely inside of her. The movement of him against her and his large erection sent bolts of pleasure through her abdomen and down to her wet, pulsating pussy.

She moaned into his ear, her legs straddling him and tightening around him. He quickly found his rhythm with her and they fucked hard and long on the couch.

"Oh shit . . . fuck me, Bugsy. Damn, you feel so fuckin' good," she whispered to him, her warm breath flowing across his ear as her sweet nectar coated his erection.

Her hands slid up and down his back, her manicured nails decorating his skin with scratches. Her body writhed beneath him. Her suction pulled him deeper and deeper into her, and his strokes grew faster and faster.

From the couch, to against the wall, to the bed, and to the carpeted floor, their tryst continued. Bugsy continued to show off his stamina—his strong back and sturdy legs twisted Maxine into different sexual positions. His dick was repetitively buried into the tightest, but softest, pussy he had ever been inside. He groaned as her body kept his dick firm within her soft walls. She purred in his ear like a cougar as he bestowed her with multiple orgasms, and she granted him a mind-blowing orgasm of his own. He released deep inside of her, and she moaned into his mouth and gripped him tighter. In the end, she didn't feel an ounce of guilt.

***

The next morning, Bugsy was already dressed and sitting in the chair near the bed watching Maxine sleep. He was consumed with guilt. What had he done? He was supposed to check in on her and make sure there wasn't another man in her bed. Ironically, the man in her bed was him.

Maxine awoke to find Bugsy staring at her. She sat up and said, "Is everything okay? Why are you dressed? Are you leaving?"

"Soon," he said.

"You want me to make you some breakfast?"

"No, I'm fine. I apologize for last night. I'm sorry for my behavior. I shouldn't have come on to you like that. I took advantage of you, and I don't want my father to find out. He would never forgive me for this."

"What? No, I'm fine. You didn't take advantage of me; we both wanted it, Bugsy. And I'm not going to tell him anything. What happened between you and I will stay between us. I can promise you that."

He was relieved to hear her say that. Maxine knew how tense it was between them. If Scott found out about her and his son, he would certainly have her killed. No question about it. As if she wasn't in hot water already, she had journeyed on to risky grounds by having sex with Bugsy.

Bugsy stood up from the chair. His presence in her bedroom was stimulating. There was something about him that Maxine really liked. She wanted to do it again, but he was dressed to leave.

"I'll see you later," he said.

He left the room and she remained in bed naked and thankful for the satisfying night he gave her. Maxine's mind started to spin with ideas, and she wondered how she could use this situation to her advantage. She still had a major problem out there, and that was Wacka. She needed him dead, and Maxine figured out that Bugsy was just the man to do it. It was going to take some finesse and pussy, but it could be done—and finally, no more Wacka and his whore to deal with. The extortion and blackmailing was taking its toll on her.

Maxine smiled widely at the idea. It had to work. She didn't have any other options.

Money, money, money. Wacka and Tarsha couldn't get enough of it. Three brand new Range Rovers sat parked outside their rented home in a rundown neighborhood of B-more. The third Rover was a mini Range Rover, a toy car for Junior. He had the best toys and video games money could buy. They also bought themselves matching Rolex watches, jewelry, and they splurged in the nightclubs, popping champagne bottles, partying, and laughing it up while dripping in designer duds. Tarsha repped herself like a diva. She wore nothing but the best and wasn't shy to show off her newfound wealth in even the most dangerous places in B-more. She felt that Wacka's fierce and murderous reputation still ran deep in the streets, although he hadn't been active in a while. He still got the respect when they were out and about. Not too many folks knew about his accident. They tried their hardest to keep it hidden.

The party music would blare, and Tarsha would step out onto the dance floor and live it up, dancing like she was in a 1970's disco—twirling and spinning, twerking and grinding. She drank liquor like it was water, and people were watching—even some of the wrong people.

Tonight was no different. Tarsha finished off a bottle of peach Cîroc and giggled against Wacka in the VIP area of Club Maroon in West Baltimore. She was dressed in a short Fendi skirt that showed off her long legs, the most expensive shoes in the club, and her tits were spilling out of her low-cut shirt. Her diamonds sparkled inside the dark nightclub. Yes, she definitely stood out and she was having a good time. She didn't want the night to end.

It was two hours before daylight when Tarsha and Wacka finally left the nightclub. They both had a good time and wanted to continue their fun, but the club was closing and the last call for alcohol at the bar was an hour ago. Tarsha was tipsy and bubbly. She staggered against Wacka and giggled continuously as they walked toward the Range Rover parked a block away on the dim Baltimore street.

The liquor in Tarsha's system was making her horny. She wanted some dick tonight, and her baby's father was the only viable option. His hands may have been fucked up, but at least his dick still got hard and it worked.

"You wanna fuck me tonight, baby?" she slurred.

Wacka chuckled. "Yeah, baby, I want you tonight."

Her body squeezed against his and they walked closely together toward the Range.

"I'm driving," said Wacka.

Tarsha didn't argue with him. She stumbled into the passenger seat and leaned her head against the headrest. Wacka started the ignition and pulled away from the curb. Their black Range Rover was one of the nicest vehicles in the area. He sat high up while driving and was proud of it. Their home wasn't too far away. He was getting used to dealing with his handicap, but he still had some ways to go.

They weren't a mile away from the club when he noticed that Tarsha was fast asleep. She was slumped in the seat, snoring with the side of her face propped against the window. He frowned at her condition. She'd made his dick hard tonight with her wild dancing and promises of pussy, and now the bitch had fallen asleep on him.

Wacka made it home and helped his woman from the truck and into the house. She tripped and stumbled, but managed to make her way inside. Tarsha just wanted to flop on her bed and sleep straight through the next day. The babysitter was sleeping on the couch and their son was asleep in his bedroom. Wacka woke up the young girl and told her she could leave. He gave her a hundred dollars for her services and she was happy with it. She collected her things and made her way out of the house.

Tarsha wasn't in the house one minute before she made a beeline to the bathroom, dropped to her knees, and threw up into the toilet. It sounded like she was puking her guts out. It echoed throughout the house, and it was disgusting. Wacka stared at her and shook his head. *Drunk bitch.*

After fifteen minutes of spilling out everything she previously ate and drank, she finally stood up from her knees and sloppily wiped her mouth. Tarsha looked at her man with a drunken smile and said, "You still wanna fuck me, baby?"

She was all over the place, her outfit and long hair in disarray. Wacka stared at her with disgust. He wasn't in the mood anymore.

"Just take your fuckin' ass to bed," he barked at her.

Tarsha sucked her teeth and stumbled to her bedroom. "Fine, nigga. I was gonna give you some, but your loss."

The door closed. If Wacka had all his fingers, he could jerk off, but it was frustrating to not be able to please himself correctly. He was still a man with needs, and lately he felt he wasn't getting what he needed from his bitch. He was providing Tarsha with everything she needed and more. They were seeing more money now than when he was a notorious stick-up kid and cold-blooded killer. They were overdosing on the money coming from Maxine. More than nine hundred thousand dollars in one day was more money than he could dream of.

Wacka sat on the couch and smoked a cigarette. He chose to sit in the dark and think about some things. He wanted complete silence.

Parked and idling outside his home was a black Dodge Charger with tinted windows. Three men intently watched the place.

"We gon' hit that nigga tomorrow night, a'ight?" said the passenger up front.

"Yeah-yeah, I'm ready to get this money," said the driver.

The wolves were right outside Wacka's door, and he had no idea what was coming his way. He was slipping, not paying attention to his surroundings, and the stick-up kids were coming for him. The old Wacka would have seen them coming from a mile away—always alert, trigger finger on speed dial. But Wacka wasn't as on point as he used to be.

***

The following night, as Tarsha and Wacka slept in their bed and their son was sound asleep in his bedroom, three black men wearing ski-masks kicked in the back door and charged into the house carrying automatics and assault rifles. They came prepared for a battle, knowing Wacka's reputation, and they weren't about to take any chances with him.

The three men rushed upstairs to give Wacka and his bitch a rude awakening. The master bedroom was dark, and they could see the silhouettes of two people lying in bed together undisturbed from the break in. The third man went into their son's bedroom to take him hostage. Immediately, Wacka and Tarsha were awakened by violence. The masked gunman struck Wacka over the head with the butt of his pistol and he hollered from the blow.

"Wake the fuck up, nigga!" one of the men shouted.

Tarsha stared wide-eyed at the two men in her bedroom and screamed out for her son. As if on cue, the third man dragged Junior into the room with them and pushed him to the floor.

Tarsha cursed, "Get your fuckin' hands off my son!"

She was ready to charge at them like a bull seeing red, but the assault rifle aimed at her face stopped her dead in her tracks. The men got an eyeful of Tarsha dressed in her panties and bra.

"Chill, bitch, or we fuck him up right in front of you! And then we fuck you up!"

"You know who the fuck I am?!" Wacka shouted.

"A dead man if you don't chill out and shut da fuck up, nigga!" the alpha male replied. "You think we fuckin' playin' wit' you?"

"Fuck you!" Wacka shouted.

The man started to pistol whip Wacka, and he fell to his knees with his face covered with blood. Wacka was dazed and helpless with a small gash across his forehead. He scowled and growled at the masked men in spite of the beating he took. He refused to be intimated by them, but with his son in harm's way, his hands were tied at the moment.

"Chill, muthafucka, or I swear I'll kill you and that bitch right now and rape ya fuckin' son," he said.

His words were chilling to Tarsha—rape her son. She trembled with rage and fear and glared at the men with so much hatred that it felt like her head was going to implode with anger and wrath.

"Please, don't hurt him . . . don't touch him!" she pleaded, having to humble herself and surrender her rage.

She could feel them smiling wickedly from behind their masks— enjoying their suffering. She had no idea who they were. She didn't recognize their weird, muffled voices. They made her get down on her knees next to Wacka. They restrained the couple and the child with duct tape around their wrists, feet, and mouths to keep them from screaming. Now the attackers were in absolute control.

"Where it at?" they asked Wacka. They removed the duct tape from his mouth so he could speak.

Wacka scowled at them. "Fuck you!"

"You wanna go there, nigga? I'll cut off your other fingers too, you crippled muthafucka! Where the money at, and the jewelry? We want it all, nigga! You think we playin?"

They continued to be met with resistance from Wacka, but the men weren't leaving empty-handed. They knew there was a fortune somewhere in the home. But Wacka and Tarsha didn't have any intention of giving up the money. They still had nearly six hundred thousand left.

It was then that the third gunman holding the young boy hostage came up with the ultimate idea. "Fuck it. You don't wanna talk, nigga, then we cut off your son's fingers too. Like father, like son, muthafucka."

He pulled out a large knife and said, "Grab that little nigga's hand. I'm 'bout to put some work on him right now."

Junior hollered and cried from beneath the duct tape. Tarsha frantically wriggled in her restraints, desperately trying to free herself, but to no avail. She screamed underneath the duct tape, but she was incoherent. Her tears started to trickle down her face as she stared in horror at the men attacking her son. She couldn't do anything about it.

"Talk, nigga! Before we starting cutting," the man shouted

Tarsha was ready to burst open with information before they could cut off her son's fingers. It was too much for her to take. They pulled away her duct tape, and she submitted to their demands at the protest of Wacka. "It's in the kitchen. Everything's underneath a cutout under the kitchen sink. The money's all there."

The alpha male nodded to one of his men and left the room to see if she was telling the truth. They continued to hold everyone at gunpoint. Tarsha was seething with rage. Her chest heaved up and down, and she refused to take her eyes off her baby. He was against the floor in his underwear and at the mercy of the gunmen. She wanted to shield him, but became sick with worry and regret.

"It's gonna be okay, baby. You gonna be all right. Mommy's right here . . . I'm over here, baby," Tarsha cried out to him.

Wacka stood there on his knees, still bleeding, and his eyes cut furiously into the two men. The rage on his face was murderous. He doubted that they were going to leave them alive. How many victims had he put in the same predicament he was now in? He rarely left anyone alive during his stick-up days, and now it felt like karma was coming back on him.

The third man came back into the bedroom with the bag of money and the jewelry. When the other two saw it, their eyes lit up.

"That's what the fuck I'm talkin' about," said one of the masked men.

Wacka felt his heart sink into his stomach. This was it—the moment his world would come to an end. They had what they'd come for, and he and his family were no longer needed.

"I swear I'm gonna fuck y'all niggas up!" he shouted with pure rage dripping from his voice.

But it felt like an idle threat. Wacka knew they had the advantage. They could kill him right now and that would be it—game over.

"Nigga, fuck you! What you gonna do, muthafucka, huh?" The man thrust the barrel of the gun in his face and taunted him with death. "You ready to hear that bang, nigga? Huh, muthafucka?"

Wacka glared up at the man. They locked eyes. Wacka wasn't going to beg for his life. If he was going to die, then it'd be with dignity.

"Let's go! We got what we came for," said the other man, moving toward the door and eager to depart the scene.

"You lucky tonight, nigga—you and your bitch and that bastard child," the man said.

With the blink of an eye, all three men disappeared from the bedroom, leaving them all alive. It was a miracle that they hadn't killed them, but it was still a tragedy. Tarsha immediately tried to free herself from the duct tape around her wrists. She needed to get to her son right away.

Wacka simply remained there on his knees, bound with duct tape and looking cold and upset. He was going to remember their eyes—what they looked like and sounded like. They should have killed him, because he was personally going to hunt them down and destroy them.

B ugsy thrust his length and thickness inside Maxine, painting her pulsating pussy with pure gratification. Her eyes closed, and every inch of her body started to quiver. He drove deeper and harder into her in the missionary position as her walls constricted around him. She pulled him closer and wrapped her legs around him tighter and breathed into his ear. She was on the threshold of a mighty orgasm.

"Oh shit, I'm gonna come!" he yelled, huffing and puffing against her.

"Come in me, baby! I'm gonna come too!" she cried out.

Bugsy wanted his orgasm to sync with hers. Their mouths met passionately and their breath became one. It didn't take long before they magically came together. It was satisfaction at its best. Bugsy removed himself from the sexual position and rolled on his back. He exhaled. Sex with Maxine was more mind-blowing and intense every time.

Maxine had to catch her breath. Her entire body felt spent as she nestled against his chiseled frame, placing her head against his heaving chest and feeling secure in his arms. It was another great night of lovemaking, and one of many, many nights of wicked sex. They'd been sexing for nearly two weeks now, and Scott was none the wiser.

Maxine lay quietly against him for a moment. Things felt great with Bugsy, but that black cloud was still lingering over her head. She sighed with unease and removed herself from his snug embrace and the bed and donned a robe.

Bugsy stared at her. "You good?"

"I need a cigarette," she said.

Maxine lit a Newport and started to pace around her bedroom. Bugsy propped himself up against the headboard and watched her. He knew something was bothering her.

"My father doesn't know anything about us. I saw him the other day."

"It's not him I'm worried about," she replied.

"What is it then?"

She stopped pacing and looked at him. She had to tell him. She couldn't go on another day without finding a solution to her problem.

"I have a serious problem, Bugsy, and I don't know who to turn to for help," she said to him, perfectly portraying the damsel in distress.

She had Bugsy's undivided attention. He got out of bed to come closer to her. He cared not to cover up, his flaccid dick swinging away.

"Talk to me. What's going on? Who or what do you need help with?" he asked her with concern.

She looked at him and puffed out. "His name is Wacka, and he's been threatening to kill me."

"That same fool that kidnapped you a while back?"

She nodded. "He's back in town. And I don't feel safe with him around, even with the security you provide me. He's still dangerous."

"I wanna know everything about this fool. How did you get involved with him in the first place?"

Maxine understood that if she wanted his help, then she would have to tell him the entire story but leave out critical details. He could never know about Max.

"When I got convicted for murder it didn't take the inmates long to see that I was no murderer. I was bullied, beaten, and I constantly feared for my life."

"I'm sorry to hear that."

"Don't be," Maxine said and touched his hand softly. "I've moved on and Layla was there for me. For years your mother was paying the family of an inmate named Shiniquia for my protection."

"Layla?"

"Yes. Your mother does have a heart."

Bugsy was surprised that his mother would do such a humane thing, but then again, nothing surprised him anymore. She'd paid people to protect Maxine while incarcerated. It was the least she could do for Maxine not snitching on her.

She continued on with her story.

"For years this arrangement worked out until Shiniquia got greedy and wanted Layla to send additional money. This is around the time someone was targeting your little brothers and sister. Your mom was grieving and here I was asking her to save my life when she had just lost three children."

Maxine took a deep breath and momentarily closed her eyes as if this was too much to take. "Layla came to visit me and on the visit she explained that as I sat there with her, Shiniquia was being murdered. And just in case that news wasn't ground shattering enough, your mother also arranged to have Shiniquia's family killed. Just like that."

Bugsy whistled. "Everybody?"

"That was the plan, but Shiniquia's brother Wacka survived."

Bugsy shook his head. That was more like his mother, cold-hearted and ruthless. He chuckled at the thought.

Maxine feigned disgust. "She killed his entire family," she said in a meek tone. "Were you a part of that?"

Maxine showed hurt and sadness over the death of an entire family but it was all a ruse to lure Bugsy into feeling sorry for her and making it all go away once and for all.

"Nah, I had nothing to do with that. Most likely, that has Meyer's fingerprints all over it. He did all of our mother's dirty work," he said.

"Well, Wacka blames me for it. He wants to avenge his family's death and I'm the scapegoat. And with Scott locked up, I feel alone out here. A few weeks ago he pointed a gun in my face and nearly broke my finger ripping off my engagement ring. Your father noticed immediately that I wasn't wearing it, but I can't worry him about this man. Scott has enough on his plate to deal with. And this is Layla's mess, not Scott's."

"That clown got that close to you! Where was your security? I don't want you to be alone ever again. You hear me?"

"I do. I realize now that my life's in constant danger. Another time when I wasn't with my security detail he took a shot at me. I have no idea where he is. He's coming for me and he wants me dead."

She was pouring it on thick. She gave Bugsy some good pussy followed by a heartbreaking story that ended with her life being in danger. He seemed to be falling for it. As smart as he was, it seemed like he was no match for the damsel in distress routine. Maxine put on an award winning performance.

Bugsy stared at Maxine with his eyebrows furrowed in anger. There was a glimmer of fury in his eyes, and his hands were clenched into tight fists. He was ready to kill someone.

"Do you know where he stays?" he asked her.

"No."

"I'll find out and I'm going to take care of him. I promise you that," he assured her.

"He's dangerous, Bugsy, and I don't want to see anything happen to you."

"Believe me, you have nothing to worry about. I'm gonna handle this," he said.

Maxine was smiling inwardly. She had him exactly where she wanted him, doing her dirty work and solving a serious problem for her. Bugsy was somewhat whipped—or had very strong feelings for her. It was easy for him to fall for Maxine because he was still broken up over Alicia. He didn't realize that he had redirected his feelings to Maxine. She reminded him of Alicia.

Maxine didn't want to say anything else. She didn't want to complicate things. Bugsy believed Wacka was trying to kill Maxine, and Maxine wanted him dead quickly, no questions asked. It had to go down swiftly. The last thing she needed was for Wacka to start talking and exposing everything to Bugsy.

Maxine gave Bugsy Wacka's number and told him that's all she had. Bugsy knew that there was a lot he could do with a number. He started to get dressed. Their intimate time together had ended. Bugsy had business to take care of and people to kill. When he was done dressing, he looked at Maxine and said, "You're not going to have to worry about this nigga for too much longer. I'm going to handle this."

He kissed her lips and Maxine felt in high spirits. She smiled at him and said, "Thank you, baby. I really do appreciate this."

"I got your back, so go to bed and sleep well tonight." He planted another kiss on her lips.

He left the apartment, and Maxine closed the door behind him and sighed with relief. It had actually worked. She'd actually persuaded Bugsy to kill Wacka for her. She threw a smile and some pussy his way, along with some charm and innocence, and she had Scott's son eating out of the palm of her hand. Now, she needed the results.

***

The next morning Maxine was back up and scheming. Bugsy had planted a seed when he confided to her that Layla wanted Lucky to take the stand. It was a clever play, and it was bugging Maxine that it might just work. Maxine lived for the day that her nemesis was either dead or doing life behind bars. Retribution was just a trial away, and she'd do whatever she could to sway the scales of justice in her favor. She thought about the dead-eye diva with the slick mouth and knew that the jury would automatically dislike her. If Layla's defense attorney could get the jury to hate someone more than the defendant, then it could create the reasonable doubt that Layla needed. Maxine didn't think Lucky would agree to take the stand, but she needed reassurance.

It was time to help pit mother against daughter.

She called Skip. Before she could speak, Skip said, "Bitch, you gonna live a long time! I was just thinking about you."

Maxine snorted. "Me? Last time we spoke you said to never call you again. Were you thinking 'bout how foul that was?"

"You don't ever let shit go, do you?"

"Nope."

"Well I don't wanna be on your bad side because you've helped me more than you know. I really want to apologize for acting ungrateful. I took that money and bought myself a house in South Carolina for me and my kids. They got big houses there with land for forty or fifty stacks. And I'ma get myself a good job too."

Maxine didn't care to hear about her happy ending. "I called for a reason. We need to meet."

"Meet?"

"Yes, meet."

"I can't, Max. We in the middle of packing—"

"Now, Skip! Same spot in an hour and this time don't keep me waiting!"

This time when Maxine arrived Skip was already there waiting in a pink Adidas jacket with a foul look on her face. Any other bitch and Skip would have gone HAM. She knew she had to bite her tongue until she was safely out of town, in her new house raising her children. They deserved the new start. She was going to give them what she had neglected to give going in and out of prison. They deserved love and stability.

Skip slid into the passenger's seat ready to get this day over with.

"What's good, Max?"

"I need help with this bitch ASAP."

"Help?"

"I'm going to get to the point. There's this bitch that I need you to scare with this pistol." Maxine pulled out an untraceable .45 and placed it on her lap. "If you threaten her, I got two large for you. If you kill her, then ten stacks."

Skip was conflicted. She wasn't a killer, but that ten large would help her in South Carolina. She could decorate her new home and buy herself a hooptie car. But she couldn't do it; kill someone. And the two grand just wasn't enough for her to get involved with whatever mess Max had going on. She declined.

"I can't, Max. We already have the U-Haul almost packed. I'm hitting 95 South at four in the morning. I need to get back home, finish packing, and get some sleep."

"Skip, this isn't a negotiation. I need your help and you owe me. I could have died on a deal you put together. Now if you turn your back on me then I'ma start thinking that you were a part of the shit."

"You know I don't get down like that!"

"Are you in or out?"

"In what? What is it that I need to do?" Skip lips were poked out. Her whole demeanor expressed her anger. Her heaving chest and her scowl were clear indicators that she was pissed.

"All you need to do is point this pistol at this young bitch and say this, 'Your mom wants you to take the stand or else you die.' I need you to scare the shit outta her!"

"Who is this bitch?"

"Don't matter."

"Why can't you do it?"

"You actin' pussy right now. The less you know, the better. Do this and then bounce."

"Max, I got a bad feeling about this."

Maxine lied, "Listen. Real talk. Soon I'm going to come into a large sum of money. Leave me your address and I promise I'll bless you with six figures. You my girl and I'ma look out."

Suddenly, Skip's frown turned around. Thoughts of easy money gave her comfort.

"Show me this bitch. I'ma do her dirty." Skip leaned in and gave Max a hug. "Thanks for always looking out for me. You good peoples, for real."

It didn't take long for Maxine to spot Lucky across from her building. It was just after two in the afternoon and it was cool for late spring. Lucky ran out of her building wearing six-inch heels, yoga pants, and an NYU hoodie, and her long mink coat swept the ground. She was going on a food run. Maxine parked far enough back to not be spotted but close enough to see the action. She handed Skip the gun and told her to meet her several blocks over for her escape.

"She's crazy about Asian food. There's a Thai restaurant a couple blocks over on Seventh Avenue. Scare the shit outta this bitch, but be careful. She may be carrying too."

"I got this."

Skip caught the unsuspecting Lucky coming out the restaurant. She quickly snatched her up by her hoodie and pulled her off to the side. She parked the .45 in Lucky's ribs and whispered, "Your mother said you better take the fuckin' stand, bitch! If I have to come back then you're a dead ho!"

Skip was so close spit flew in Lucky's eyes, temporarily blinding her.

"Understand, bitch?"

Lucky nodded feebly, which empowered Skip.

"In fact, run ya shit! Give me this fuckin' coat!"

The coat meant nothing to Lucky. She took it off without incident and handed it to the dead bitch on borrowed time. Skip draped it over one arm. Lucky's burner was tucked in her waistband. She was about to reach for it when Skip stopped her.

"Oh, you's a bold bitch, huh?"

Skip was doing too much and had gone off script. She grabbed the girl's pistol and placed it in her free hand like it was a western, pointing both guns at Lucky.

"Stay here for five minutes! If you move my partner gonna blow your fuckin' brains out!"

Skip backpedaled away as Lucky stood there glaring. With the mink coat safely hiding the burners she turned around and did a jog away from the scene of the crime. What she didn't expect was, "Stop her! She robbed me! That's my coat!"

Skip began running as a superhero civilian stepped in to tackle her. Skip pulled out her gun just to back him down when two beat cops turned the corner and took in a frightful scene. Both cops pulled their guns and yelled, "Police, drop the gun!"—before unloading both their clips into her.

It all happened as Maxine watched in horror. Lucky slid away, not wanting to be attached to the bizarre crime scene.

Layla had crossed yet another line, and the goon she had sent to threaten Lucky was dead. It had been a while since Lucky had stepped foot into the Metropolitan Correctional Center to visit her mother, and, undoubtedly, this would be her last. It was a visit Lucky wasn't really looking forward to, but she couldn't wait to tell Layla the good news— well, good news for her and bad news for her mother. Since her last visit, Lucky had accomplished a lot. Whoever doubted her could kiss her ass.

She went through the security procedures a confident woman looking fabulous in her $900 Manolo Blahnik heels. Her expensive jacket covered her growing stomach, and her long, sensuous hair was flowing. She was glowing as a pregnant woman, but also as a very rich woman. Her mother's imprisonment was the best thing that had ever happened to her.

Lucky sat down at the square metal table and waited for her mother to show up. The room wasn't too crowded, and things weren't hectic. The corrections officers were situated throughout the visitation room like statues watching everyone. Ten minutes later, Layla was escorted into the visitation room by a male guard, and the look on her face wasn't friendly.

Layla sat across from her as routine, and their greeting wasn't pleasant.

"Bitch, you got some fuckin' nerve showing your face after what you said to me," Layla growled at her.

"What I said? You send a thug to threaten me and you're the victim?"

Layla was perplexed. "Thug? You tryin' to be fuckin' funny? Lucky, don't try this bullshit or I'll beat your fuckin' ass myself! You know I ain't do shit but sit and wait for you to start actin' like my daughter!"

"I knew you'd deny it."

Layla frowned. She knew Lucky was calculating and was cooking up something to justify turning her back on her when she needed her most.

"There ain't shit to deny 'cause I didn't do shit!"

Lucky locked eyes with her mother. She wasn't there to talk about her run-in with the ghetto bitch or what she did or didn't do. She was there to gloat. She smirked at Layla, leaned closer to her and said, "I found it!"

"You found what, bitch?"

"The money—your money. Or shall I say, *my* money," Lucky said.

The reaction on Layla's face was priceless. The news almost made her faint. Layla didn't want to believe it. There was no way.

Lucky continued to grin and said, "You don't believe me, huh?"

Layla didn't respond. She could feel her heart beating and her mind spinning with the possibility of it being true. Lucky had to be lying.

"It was tedious work, but I'm smart—something you feel only describes Bugsy. I went through all your paperwork and properties and I had to think, where would you be able to hide millions of dollars and think it would be safe from everyone, including your own children? Then it dawned on me. You bought part of a cemetery, the same place where my sister and brothers are buried. You purchased part of that business without anyone knowing, and you had the money stored in a refurbished, climate controlled mausoleum. Guess what? I got the cash, every last dollar of it. I've gotta give it to you. It was a genius plan. Who would think, millions and millions of dollars stored among the dead?" Lucky said with a smirk.

The look on Layla's face was anger and shock at the same time. Her eyes burned into Lucky, and with her teeth gritted, she angrily grumbled, "You better not fuck wit' me, Lucky. You touch my money, I'll kill you."

"You ain't killing shit. You're broke, with not a dime to your name. I got it all! Me! I did it! I outsmarted you and took control of everything," Lucky retorted. "See, you let this dead-eye bitch beat you."

Lucky couldn't let that insult go. Her mother's words hurt her deeply and Layla didn't understand how sensitive Lucky was about her eye. Calling Lucky a dead-eye bitch put Lucky on a new path of vengeance, but asking her to take the stand put Lucky on a mission to break her mother, and she finally did by finding that money.

"You better spend that money fast because when I get out, I'm gonna fuck you up. And guess what? Not just me, but the Juarez cartel is gonna fuck you up too. You jump into bed wit' them with your inexperience, it's gonna be your death sentence," Layla said. "You gonna need me, bitch!"

Lucky shook her head at the remark and giggled calmly. Surprisingly, her mother was still trying to put up a fight with words. It was all she had—unkind and harsh words. But her visit was over. She came, she saw, and she conquered. Her only reply was, "You always been a self-centered, selfish, and evil bitch, and Meyer would have never gotten shot up had you not forced him to rob Bugsy. It's your fault everything went to shit. You're the one who put Bugsy in the hospital, not Luna, and you're the one who almost had Meyer killed. But you're not gonna fuck up my life. I'm done with you, bitch. No more visits and I hope you rot in jail."

She stood up, indicating she was done visiting.

Layla cursed, "Bitch, you wanna go to war wit' me! I'll give you a fuckin' war! I will destroy you! If it wasn't for me, you wouldn't have shit! Lucky, don't walk away from me! This ain't over! It ain't fuckin' over!"

Their quarrel caught the attention of the COs and other visitors and inmates. There was trouble in the West house.

Lucky was done. She didn't need to reply to her mother's angry outburst. She walked away and several corrections officers rushed over to contain Layla from charging at her daughter.

Lucky stepped out of the correctional facility feeling empowered.

want that bitch dead!" Tarsha shouted. "She has some thugs come into my home and attack us and our son! She's fuckin' dead!"

She furiously paced around her bedroom cursing and carrying on. Wacka understood her rage. She wanted Maxine dead, and he wanted to find the three thugs that broke into his home, attacked his family, and took everything they had from them. Tarsha was convinced Maxine was behind the robbery, but Wacka didn't subscribe to that theory. It didn't make any sense to him. Why would she leave them alive? No, he was sure it was stick-up kids that'd caught them slipping.

"I want you to find them niggas, baby. I want you to fuck them up! I want you to gut them like pigs and bring their guts to me. They fucked wit' our son and our home! They put their hands on our baby and threatened to rape him! I swear you better find these niggas!" she yelled.

"I'm gonna find them, baby. I swear to you, they already dead men."

"And that bitch, she gotta fuckin' go! I want her DEAD!" Tarsha was highly emotional. Her tears of upset and rage wouldn't stop. The thought of three men violating her family and taking everything they had replayed over and over again in her head.

Wacka suited up for war, despite his handicap. He wasn't about to let anyone get away with this. Tarsha called over reinforcements, her two cousins Speedy and Trick. The moment they heard what had happened, they rushed to the house.

"What these niggas look like, cuz?" Speedy asked.

"I don't know. They wore masks," she said.

"You got a clue who these niggas might be? I swear, we gon' find these niggas and handle these muthafuckas," said Trick.

"There were three of them—tall and I don't know, but I know who sent them, this bitch named Maxine. She sent them," Tarsha said.

Speedy and Trick were down for whatever. They had much respect for Wacka, knowing his pedigree and they loved their cousins. Whenever their cousin Tarsha needed something done, whether a beat down, help in the streets, or a murder, she could depend on her cousins when Wacka wasn't around.

"Y'all niggas ready?" Wacka asked the two men.

"Nigga, yeah . . . let's do this," Speedy said, lifting his shirt to reveal the 9mm tucked in his waistband.

The men left with Wacka to search B-more and beyond for the fools that robbed him. They took nearly six hundred thousand dollars from them and some expensive jewelry, and Wacka was determined to find them and get his money back. That type of score would have niggas talking.

Alone in the house, Tarsha continued to fume. Her son was with a friend. She didn't want him in the house. She vented by smashing things and yelling. She was biased because Maxine had beaten her ass. Revenge was inside her heart, and she wanted Maxine to suffer like she had. There was no turning back. She felt that bitch pushed her over the edge and Tarsha wasn't thinking logically. She believed that the home invasion had Maxine's fingerprints all over it and didn't once consider what Wacka said—why would Maxine leave them alive? Tarsha wasn't thinking with reason; she was thinking with emotions and vengeance.

"That bitch wanna fuck wit' my family and play games? A'ight, bitch, I can play games too and fuck your entire world up. See me, bitch!" she said to an imaginary Maxine.

Tarsha sat down at the kitchen table and started writing. Pen to the paper, she spilled it all in a letter to Scott, outlining all the evidence and explaining Maxine's role in his children's deaths. It was emotional and it was detailed. Wacka had told her everything, and it was all coming out in the letter.

Fuck that bitch, she told herself as she wrote and wrote.

"You wanna play games, bitch? I can play games too and tell all your dirty secrets, bitch."

She couldn't shake the image of men threatening to cut off her son's fingers and rape him while she watched. It infected her with rage and insanity. No way she was letting that go. Maxine needed to be put down.

When she finished writing, the letter was four and a half pages long. It was ready to be signed, sealed, and delivered to one of the most notorious men living. Tarsha couldn't wait to see the outcome of her tell-all. She mailed the letter off and it somewhat helped her anger and rage. Still, she wouldn't be completely pleased until she saw the three men who invaded her home killed in a very gruesome way.

***

Bugsy sat in the backseat of the Yukon and looked at the New York City skyline from over the East River via the Brooklyn Bridge. One World Trade Center, standing erect over everything else in the city, caught his attention. What was once the World Trade Center was now a towering, gleaming structure. What terrorists knocked down on 9/11, the city rebuilt as the tallest building in the Western Hemisphere and the sixth tallest in the world. It was a statement to the world—no matter what you throw at us, this city will continue to stand and continue to show power. One World Trade Center represented power and strength, and it was precisely what Bugsy wanted to show to his enemies and everyone else. They were trying to knock him down, he and his family, but the Wests weren't going anywhere. Bugsy was that bright, shimmering tower—standing erect in the air, towering over the city's skyline and standing out above everything.

But there were planes ready to knock him back down and wipe him out completely. They were circling him like vultures and ready to slam into him on a takeover mission.

One headache in particular was Gambino. He had gotten the message from Bugsy with Mackie's bloody and beaten body found in Brownsville. Gambino lashed out by shooting up one of Bugsy's trap houses and killing three people. Then there was a West soldier Gambino's men threw off the rooftop of a ten-story project building—and it got gruesomely ugly below. The bloody war was spiraling out of control, and the last thing Bugsy needed was the negative spotlight. With his parents under federal indictment, he knew that he needed to calm things down or he was going to find himself in the same predicament his father was in.

Bugsy sighed as they arrived into the city. It had been a stressful day and the saying was fitting for how he was feeling—heavy is the head that wears the crown. His head felt heavy and leaning. He was sleeping less and worrying more. If it wasn't one thing, it was another. His only relief was being with Maxine. She made him feel good and forget about his troubles. But that was stress itself, knowing Maxine was forbidden grounds, knowing every night he spent with her was a profound betrayal to his father.

And her problems became his problems. Wacka needed to be dealt with immediately and he was on top of that crisis. It was one of many crises he had to deal with.

First, he put the word out that he wanted a face-to-face meeting with Gambino to talk civilly. Maybe they could work something out. Bugsy wasn't waving the white flag, but he needed shit to settle down.

Second was Wacka. He wanted Maxine to have peace of mind. The West family had connections everywhere, and Bugsy was determined to use his clout to find Wacka by any means necessary. He had someone inside all the cell phone companies—Verizon, Sprint, T-Mobile, and AT&T. He handed out significant amounts of cash for anyone who could track down the location of that cell phone number. He gave his contacts the number, and a day later, he had an address in Baltimore. The place was registered to a girl named Tarsha Smith. Right away, he sent two expert killers to the address and gave clear instructions to kill everything inside that house—nobody lives.

***

It was two in the morning when the black Tahoe slowly turned the corner of the urban Baltimore street and came to a stop in the middle of the road. The home they stopped in front of matched the address provided to them, and parked outside were two black Range Rovers that stood out among the ordinary vehicles parked on the street. It was quiet outside, and the late-late hour made the area sparse of residents. Two black men sat in the front seat of the SUV and scoped out the front entrance of the home. The house was dark, indicating to them that everyone was asleep inside. The driver puffed on a cigarette, exhaled the smoke, and flicked it out the window. The passenger nodded and put on a pair of black latex gloves and gripped a Glock 19 in his hand and twisted the six-inch silencer onto the end of the barrel.

The driver repeated the same action, putting on gloves and he gripped a 9mm with a matching silencer. They were dressed in all black, and being stealthy and lethal was a common thing for them. They were being paid a lot of money for this particular task. It hinted to them that this was personal. Bugsy wanted it handled with proficiency, and they were the epitome of adept killers. The area was clear, and they coolly climbed out of the vehicle and approached the house. They ascended the front steps but quickly disappeared into the backyard. They briefly scoped the area and spotted the motion lights, bars on the windows, and a steel door. The situation wasn't going to be a problem for them. With the right tools, they disarmed the door and slid inside the home undetected.

They were like shadows as they moved from the kitchen and ascended the stairs to the bedroom where Tarsha was sleeping, but they didn't see Wacka in the bed with her. There was supposed to be two targets.

The room was dark and still, and the first gunman took aim at the body under the bed sheets and fired—*Phwet-phwet*, killing Tarsha immediately in her sleep. Then, chaos erupted—*Bak! Bak!* The gunfire came from the closet and struck the first gunman in the chest, pushing him back into the hallway. Wacka had been too late to save Tarsha, but he wasn't going down without a fight. He held the automatic awkwardly with two hands and was able to get off a couple of shots. The second gunman unloaded a barrage of shots into the closet, riddling it with bullets. He glanced back to see his partner on the ground. He rushed forward to make sure Wacka was dead. But he wasn't. Wacka burst from the closet firing his gun wildly, but his accuracy was off without a proper grip. He'd gotten lucky with the first rounds, but the second shootout proved difficult. The gunman took cover behind the door frame and Wacka snapped.

"You come for me, muthafuckas! Here I am! Come get some! Come get some!" he madly screamed.

Bak! Bak! Bak! Bak! Bak!

He continued to shoot at his attacker, splintering the door with bullets. Just a foot away was the body of his baby's mother, shot in the head. He had the second gunman pinned down behind the door. He was ready to blow his head off.

"Fuck you! Fuck you!" Wacka shouted. "I'm right here, muthafucka!"

And then it happened. Three bullets rapidly slammed into his chest and lifted him off his feet and dropped him on his back to the bedroom floor. He was gasping for air, and his deafening heartbeat thumped in his ears like thunder. His chest was coated with blood. He knew this was his end; there was no escaping it this time. Wacka didn't know the first shooter was wearing a bulletproof vest and, after regaining his composure, had a clear shot of Wacka's insanity.

The killers coolly approached their victim. Wacka was still alive, barely, and his fading eyes locked in on the two hitmen hovering over him. He showed nothing but contempt for them in his grizzly stare. He could feel his body fighting not to die, but the blood loss was massive and he could feel his vital organs shutting down.

Gurgling off his blood, he managed to get out a harsh, "Fu-fuck you!"

They had no words for him. The second gunman aimed his weapon at Wacka's face and shot him twice at close range. It would be a ghastly mess for homicide to clean up.

When the men turned around to leave, they were immediately taken aback by a small child gazing upon them in shock. The boy stood in the threshold of the bedroom dressed in his pajamas and clutching his teddy bear. He didn't scream, but his young, innocent eyes were glued to his parents' murder scene. He had seen their faces. He was a witness to his parents' murder. The killers glanced at each other and spoke with a professional gaze—like grasping for the shortest straw. Then one did the unthinkable. He lifted his gun and fired, shooting the boy in the face. His young body crumbled at the threshold of the bedroom. It was a savage act, but Bugsy had said he wanted everyone dead.

The killers left the scene and headed back to New York. They called Bugsy and told him that everything had been taken care of—Maxine no longer had a problem. But there was one snag. They killed a young boy—their son.

"Fuck!" Bugsy uttered.

"You said everyone inside the house."

"I know," said Bugsy. He sighed heavily. "But not a fucking kid!"

"The boy was a witness."

"Fuck it—collateral damage." Bugsy convinced himself.

He was blinded by the experienced pussy of a seasoned cougar. Although he was somewhat broken up about the kid, he had to charge it to the game. He justified that it was the boy's parents that put him in danger—just as his parents put Gotti, Bonnie, and Clyde in harm's way.

***

Maxine was sitting and reading in her apartment when she got the phone call that she had long been waiting for.

"You don't have to worry about that problem anymore. It's been taken care of," said Bugsy.

She was ecstatic. It was the best news she'd heard in a while. But she kept cool and nonchalant. She simply replied, "Thank you."

"I told you, I got your back."

"Are you coming by to see me tonight?" she said.

"Not tonight, maybe tomorrow. I got some things to take care of."

"Okay."

Their call ended. Maxine stood up and walked toward the window and stared out at the city. She sighed with titanic liberation. A huge weight had been lifted off her shoulders. She couldn't help but to smile like the Cheshire Cat. She wanted to celebrate, but she drew a hot bubble bath and submerged herself into the large tub with a glass of white wine and peace of mind. Her problem was officially dead—literally—and she could finally put her past behind her.

Enjoying the soothing, warm water and her opulent bathroom, she hollered, "Free at last, free at last, thank God Almighty, I'm free at last! Don't fuck with me, bitch."

She lingered in the tub and drank the wine and let her body soak. *No more secrets,* she told herself. Well, except the secret affair that she was having with Bugsy. The boy was a fantastic lover. He made her toes curl every single time they had sex. But she knew she had to put that to bed and soon. If Scott ever found out about them, her life would once again be in jeopardy.

***

Baltimore city police cars flooded the urban street with their blaring sirens and lights. Homicide detectives and crime scene techs meticulously investigated every square inch of the crime scene. The medical examiner concluded that the family had been killed a few hours ago—they were in the early stages of rigor mortis. The looky-loo's crowded behind the yellow crime scene tape that encircled the area. Word had traveled through the community that, along with the parents, a child was killed. It was heartbreaking news.

The media came to report on the murders, especially because of the young child. It was headline news, even for a murderous city like Baltimore—a child dead in a bloody home invasion. Reporters swamped the area with their cameras and microphones, filming the scene and interviewing witnesses. They wanted to know how old the child was and about the parents' backgrounds.

Pulling up to the hectic scene in their Dodge Charger were Tarsha's two cousins, Speedy and Trick. They stepped out of the car and were shocked to see the heavy police activity in front of their cousin's home.

"Yo, what da fuck happened?" Speedy asked someone.

"Home invasion—they killed the parents and their son too," said a neighbor. "Shit is all fucked up."

"Muthafucka!" Trick yelled in disbelief.

Speedy and Trick looked at each other and they both felt some guilt. Though they didn't kill Wacka and Tarsha, they were two of the attackers who robbed them and took everything they had. Neither felt any remorse for torturing and beating Wacka and Tarsha, nor the psychological damage threatening their son would cause. They were stick-up men; that's what they do.

The couple was flashing too much money and showing off too many nice things in a city that was hungry to take it. Speedy and Trick felt that they were owed something more than the peanuts being thrown at them. So they decided to take action and take what they felt was rightfully due—everything.

But this? The entire family killed, even their son? They both figured it was over that same paper.

Both men climbed back into the Charger and drove toward the interstate. Later, they would load up the trunk of the car with a bag full of money, jewelry, and guns. Speedy and Trick were ready to leave Baltimore and set up shop in another state. It was time to move on. Their cousin was dead and they wanted to get far away from the city—maybe Atlanta or Charlotte. The south seemed like a good place to start over with their newfound wealth.

36

Maxine sat in the visitation room feeling nervous but looking sexy in her classy wrap dress, the top showing just enough cleavage to excite her man. But in reality, she didn't want to be there. She didn't want to see Scott, but she tried her best each week to sit through the visits with him. Whenever he would hug her or squeeze her hands, she would cringe inside. She would sit there talking to Scott and she would be thinking about Bugsy. Had she fallen in love with his son?

"I missed you, baby. Has Bugsy been taking care of you like I asked—looking out for you?" Scott said.

Oh, he was taking care of her, all right. He took care of her the other night, had her legs around him, his dick swelled inside of her, and he came inside her so hard that she felt her pussy was going to drown in his semen.

"Yes, he's been taking care of me," she said.

"That's good," he said.

Again, visions of Bugsy's thick dick and his long tongue plunging inside of her induced daydreams. She managed to smile for Scott and put on a show for him. But this was the same muthafucka partially responsible for half her life being taken away from her. All types of ill feelings swirled around inside her head. A nigga locked up brought back all types of animosity. How could she forgive him? How did she forgive him?

"You okay, Maxine?" Scott asked her.

"I'm fine," she replied dryly.

"You seem different—like you here, but you ain't here," Scott said with suspicion in his voice.

"Baby, I'm here. I'm always gonna be here," she said with a thin smile.

Scott stared at her closely. She looked beautiful. Her eyes were sparkling and she had this radiance—but for what? And her irritability toward him didn't go unnoticed. He studied her actions and lingered on her every word. When he saw her, she was glowing about something, and he felt it wasn't about him. When he gave her a deep embrace at the beginning of their visit, Maxine felt a little healthier in his arms than she should have. She was eating well, it appeared.

Also, she wasn't talkative. She seemed aloof and distracted by something else. Scott was a seasoned vet. He knew Maxine's feelings were someplace else. His conclusion was that she was fucking another man. But he had no proof yet. The fact that she had stopped wearing her engagement ring was another red flag. She kept saying it was lost, then misplaced, and that it was probably somewhere in the penthouse. It had him vexed. He continuously jumped down Bugsy's throat each week. "Find out who she's fucking!" he would growl. "I wanna fuckin' know who's in my home!"

Calmly, Bugsy would reassure his father that Maxine was clean. He informed Scott that she spent majority of her time indoors, and no one went to see her. He advised his father that he was becoming paranoid. Scott somewhat believed his son. Maybe he was overreacting. Bugsy was their only line of defense. He had to instill into his father's head that Maxine was a good woman and he had nothing to worry about.

"I love you, baby," Maxine said sincerely. "And I miss you so much."

Maxine had to keep up the show for him. She found herself slipping and thinking about Bugsy too often, and she could feel that Scott was noticing something was wrong.

"I don't know what to do without you, baby. I'm lost," she added. Her eyes started to water and Scott looked at her with empathy.

They held hands across the table. He squeezed her fingers into his and said, "We gonna get through this, baby. I promise you. I'll be home soon."

She smiled. "I just want to be with you again."

"I know. I want you too."

Scott took a deep breath and stared into Maxine's eyes. He knew why he fell in love with Maxine. Since the beginning she was die hard for him and she was smart. He felt that maybe it was the money that had Maxine worried and feeling distant. She didn't have access to anything he owned. *Am I being petty?* he thought. Why didn't he trust her? He knew that she was a good woman and he didn't always treat her as such—especially over twenty years ago. He'd put money before their relationship and had children with her best friend. He made a vow to himself that he was going to make it up to her once he got out. It would start with having Bugsy give her fifty thousand dollars to buy herself something nice to cheer her up.

"Baby, I need to use the bathroom," she said.

"Again? You just used the bathroom less than a half-hour ago."

"I think I might be coming down with something."

"You getting sick?"

"I don't know."

She hurried to the nearest bathroom. The COs were watching carefully. Scott sat there and pondered. Once again, he strongly felt that something was off. He tightened his fists on the table and his eyes narrowed into an angry gaze. He hated to be made a fool of. He knew when someone was lying to him, and it wasn't what Maxine was saying as much as her body language. Yes, she knew all the right things to say to throw him off her trail, but using the bathroom twice in a half-hour and her inattentiveness spoke volumes. Even the outfit she wore today, was it to distract him?—to show her cleavage to take attention away from her lying eyes?

Maxine returned looking a bit under the weather.

"You okay?" he asked her coolly.

212

"I'm fine."

"You sure?"

She nodded.

During a moment of silence between them, Scott came up with an idea. The visitation room had two vending machines and he instructed Maxine to get him some Planters Honey Roasted Peanuts. She did. Scott opened the package and ate a few peanuts, but the aroma of the nuts suddenly made Maxine nauseous and Scott fixed his eyes on her. Her rapid nausea told him everything he needed to know—she was pregnant!

"You fuckin' whore! I'm gonna fuckin' kill you!" He lunged at Maxine with the insanity of a demon.

Maxine flew back and jumped out of her chair just in time, away from his murderous grasp. She was shocked by his sudden outburst of rage. He had seemingly lost all control. His eyes danced with madness.

"I'll fuckin' kill you! You're pregnant, bitch! You think I wouldn't find out!" he screamed.

Scott's wild actions sent the room into panic. Other visitors and inmates stared at the ensuing squabble with wide eyes, and the corrections officers hurried to restrain Scott and regain order inside the room. They grabbed Scott forcefully and dragged him away from a frightened Maxine and back into detention.

Maxine was astounded. Things went from good to ugly in a heartbeat. But she was more surprised by what he shouted to her—pregnant! She couldn't be pregnant, and at her age. How would he know before her? She stood there in the room bewildered and placed her hand against her stomach.

Pregnant?

***

Bugsy sat in the visitation room and waited for his father to show up. When Scott came through the doors, the look on Scott's face told

Bugsy that something had happened. Although Scott had caused a scene the day before, his clout and reputation served him well. The warden had overlooked the incident, as long as it wouldn't happen again. Scott promised the warden that it wouldn't and requested a visit with Bugsy.

The heat of rage and betrayal was pouring from Scott's body. As soon as he sat down opposite his son, he leaned in closer to rattle off his demands.

He angrily whispered to Bugsy, "I want that bitch Maxine dead."

Bugsy leaned back. "What? Why?"

"Nigga, don't fuckin' question me. I gave you a fuckin' order and I want you to carry it out. That bitch is pregnant and I ain't the daddy!"

"Pregnant?" Bugsy was stunned. "Did she tell you this herself?"

"Nigga, what I tell you? I want her dead. I could see it all over her, the bathroom trips and the nausea, the plump breasts and flushed face. I put six kids into your mother. I know the symptoms."

Bugsy did everything in his power not to show his shock or fear. Maxine was pregnant, supposedly, and he knew it was his baby. But he couldn't show nervousness in front of Scott. The man was masterful at picking up on body language and facial expressions.

Scott glared at his son like he was the anti-Christ. "You ignorant muthafucka, you're not doing your job watching her or you're lying to me. Either way, you fucked up! And I won't tolerate disobedience."

Bugsy quickly found himself in a difficult position. Scott continued to rant, saying, "I want that bitch tortured until she gives up the baby's father, and I want him dead too."

"Pop, let me talk to her and see what's up. Maybe you're wrong."

"I told you, find out the father and you get rid of her now—her and the baby, or I'll hammer you down, muthafucka! That's a direct order, so don't fuckin' defy me!" he said with unquestionable authority.

Scott stood up and nodded to the guard. He was done talking. Either Bugsy killed Maxine or he'd suffer for disobeying the chief's command.

37

Maxine opened her legs and placed her heels in the metal stirrups for the OB/GYN. Dressed in a pink gown, she was nervous. She'd made an appointment to see the doctor the next day. She prayed Scott was wrong, but he rarely was. What made him so dangerous was his ability to know if you were lying to him or not, and how he picked up on body language and signals. He was subtle with it. He watched Maxine's every move like a hawk and was able to pick up on the slightest change. It's how he advanced in the underworld and became a multi-millionaire—studying, watching for anything out of the ordinary, and knowing who was and was not nervous around him. Maxine had screwed up.

When the examination was over, her physician drew blood and had her pee in a cup. It was confirmed by the doctor that she was five weeks pregnant. Maxine was stunned. She was definitely carrying Bugsy's baby. She was over forty years old, and it was her first pregnancy.

"It doesn't happen commonly with women of your age," said the physician. "Congratulations!"

Congratulations? Maxine wanted to smack the taste out of her mouth. Her mood was far from celebratory.

The physician explained the risks of being pregnant in her forties, such as high blood pressure and gestational diabetes and how the odds of genetic problems jumped higher after forty. But Maxine didn't care for any of that right now. Her biggest risk was Scott and losing her life.

What a tangled web we weave, she thought.

What was she going to do? She couldn't very well tell Scott that the baby was his. It wouldn't add up, and Scott wasn't going to fall for any okey-doke. Shit, he'd figured out that she was pregnant before she had. She needed to tell Bugsy, but she didn't know how to approach him. How was he was going to take the news?

That evening, Maxine arrived home with butterflies swimming in her stomach. It all felt surreal. She had the option of an abortion, but she'd always wanted kids, and in the beginning, she wanted to have them with Scott. But times had changed. She was in love with Bugsy. But every step she took felt like it was going to be her last. She was nervous and scared. She didn't feel protected any longer.

Maxine stepped off the elevator onto the carpeted hallway and slowly walked toward her suite. It felt quiet and still in her building. She knew if Scott wanted her dead, she wouldn't see it coming. *Leave town*, she thought. But with what money? Wacka took nearly everything from her.

She entered her apartment and turned on the lights, only to be startled by Bugsy's presence in her living room. He sat composedly in a chair with his eyes fixed on her. Maxine could feel her heart in her throat.

"Ohmygod, Bugsy, you scared the shit out of me. Why are you here?"

"You're pregnant?" he asked nonchalantly.

She didn't answer him right away, but locked eyes with him and knew that the shit had hit the fan.

"You went to see your father?" she said.

"Today, and he gave me the order to have you killed," he said. "He warned me sternly not to disobey him, or he's gonna fuck me up."

Maxine stood in the center of her living room like a tree, her feet rooted to the floor. "Are you here to kill me?"

Bugsy stood up from the chair. Suddenly his presence inside her home was frightening. The look in his eyes seemed unpleasant and deadly. Gone were his warm, pleasant mannerisms toward her. She'd heard the horror stories about him and she didn't want to experience them personally. He stepped closer. Maxine reacted fearfully by stepping away from him.

He said, "No, I'm not here to kill you."

Could she believe him? She didn't know, but she didn't feel reassured by his words.

"Your father knows already, so how we gonna play this out?" she asked him. "He wants me dead."

He looked prudent in front of her. He was a smart man, always with a plan, but this was proving to be his most difficult situation.

He said, "We gotta convince him somehow that you're not pregnant."

"But I am—five weeks."

He stared at her and sighed. He was thinking. She could tell by the look in his eyes he didn't want to kill her. Maxine felt Bugsy loved her. If he didn't, she knew that she would've been dead the moment she stepped into the apartment.

He looked at her as if he had an idea. Maxine read his mind, saw the look in his eyes, and she immediately was against it.

"I'm not having an abortion, Bugsy. I can't. I know this is dangerous for the both of us, but this is my first pregnancy and I'm in love with you. I want to have your baby," she said as her eyes welled up with tears.

He didn't argue with her. It was his first baby too.

Maxine didn't have any family left and half her life was gone. She wanted this baby. In fact, she was willing to risk her life for her baby. Out of the blue, she started to feel these motherly instincts. She had been robbed of everything and a baby would change it all. If Bugsy loved her like he said he did, and then he would ride or die with her.

"I love you, Bugsy. I do. I want to have your son," she said.

He looked at her and said, "You think it's a boy?"

She nodded. "I think so. I can sense him growing."

Bugsy managed to smile. Maxine lifted her shirt to reveal her belly. It was still flat and unchanged, but that was going to change soon. She motioned for Bugsy to come place his hand on her stomach. It was still too early to feel any movement, but Bugsy placed the palm of his hand against her belly and what he felt was life inside of her.

Maxine looked at him. Bugsy was everything she wanted in a man, though he was much younger than her. She saw something in him that Scott used to be a very long time ago.

She said, "Let's tell him together then. I'm ready."

She all of a sudden found the courage in herself to confront Scott and everything else. Maxine had come this far in life and she planned on going further, but she needed Bugsy's help. She was a survivor by any means necessary. Bugsy and this pregnancy was her opportunity to not just survive, but to last in lavishness and have a secure future.

"That's a death sentence, Maxine. My father will kill us both."

"It doesn't have to be, baby. Think about it. Do you realize the power you have, Bugsy? These men out here, they respect you and they will follow you into hell. You're smart and you're loyal. Your parents are locked away and the chances of them seeing freedom again are slim. You're the one holding down this organization. You did the grunt work. You got your hands dirty for your family, and you have the connections, the power, the money, and the manpower to do whatever you want. Your father's withering away inside a jail cell using only his intimidation tactics to keep control over you. Do you want to be under his thumb forever?"

Maxine was planting the seed into his head. Now it was up to him to make it grow and bear fruit.

"We can become a family, baby. We can become everything that your parents weren't. We can run this city," she added on.

She was intimately close to him. She looked at him with ability showing in her eyes and skillfulness and encouragement in her words. This was a man who could run a Fortune 500 company with his intelligence and wit, and he emulated Michael Corleone of *The Godfather* with his mild mannerisms but lethal way of thinking.

"It's your time, baby. Take advantage of it," she said.

The look he had revealed to Maxine that he was pondering the idea. Go against his father, the man that taught him everything, who he loved and respected, and who raised him? However, times were changing, and Scott wasn't making wise choices, and Bugsy felt that he was doing all the grunt work. He was taking a lot more risks.

"It is my time, right?" he said.

She nodded and smiled. She kissed him passionately, and the night ended with them making love. With each deep penetration, Bugsy felt her twitch around his dick, the sensation beyond arousing. He felt the suction of her tight, wet tunnel and it was quickly milking an intense nut from him. When he came, he moaned and held Maxine closely in his arms. She was soft and assuring. She was carrying his child, and he wasn't about to let anything happen to her.

A brand new day was coming, and there was a changing of the guards on the horizon.

38

The guard announced that he had visitors—plural—but Scott was in no mood to see anyone. Since he found out about the pregnancy, Scott had been in such a foul and angry mood that he was ready to ignite and explode like TNT. His woman pregnant by some other nigga, it was a troublesome and disturbing thought and he couldn't shake it. He felt anger, but he felt hurt and pain. He sat inside a jail facing the federal government, and Maxine was out there spreading her legs and taking advantage of his situation.

She got pregnant by someone else, and there was no forgiving that.

It had been a week since the visit with Bugsy, and still no word about Maxine. So he figured that she was still alive. He worried that his son may have gone rogue and defied his orders. If so, Scott feared things were going to get really ugly.

"Who came to see me?" he asked the guard.

The guard shrugged. "Don't know, just peoples. Just doing my job."

"What ever happened to CO Mahan? I haven't seen him lately."

"He quit a few weeks ago," the guard said.

Scott had his doubts about the guard. He'd turned down money for the cell phone, a clear indication that something was off. He figured Mahan was a plant by the feds, but he hadn't taken the bait.

Scott stood up and the corrections officer marched him toward the visitation room. The moment he stepped foot inside, he developed a sour taste in his mouth when he saw Maxine and Bugsy seated together. Obviously the bitch was still alive, and his son had violated a direct order. *Why did Bugsy bring her with him? Why are they together?* he thought. The tension and anger he felt seeing Maxine in the same room with his son, breathing and living, was consuming. Scott knew that this would have never happened if he was on the streets.

While walking to the table, Scott wondered if Bugsy told her that he wanted her dead. Was he that stupid to tell her?

He sat across from them, and the atmosphere around them grew thickly tense. Scott glared at Maxine and felt the urge to rip her apart with his bare hands. But he kept his emotions in check because he was the boss—the head of a crime family. He couldn't keep having violent outbursts, and there were questions he wanted answers to.

The three sat at the table, and there was an awkward silence for a moment. Scott locked eyes with his son and noticed the uneasiness in them. It wasn't like his son to show uneasiness. But looking at Maxine, he saw an empowered woman. Did she think Bugsy could protect her?

"What the fuck is this?" Scott uttered with contempt. His eyes were transformed into a hard scowl, able to break concrete in half with his stare.

"We came to talk," said Bugsy.

"What is there to talk about? I gave you an order," he replied.

"I know, but we got something to tell you," Bugsy said.

Scott was under the impression that they were going to try and convince him that she wasn't pregnant. Or worse, try and convince him that the baby was his and she brought Bugsy with her to back up her claim. Did they believe that he was a fool?

"I am pregnant," Maxine finally spoke.

Scott clenched his teeth and felt the need to slam his fists against the table. He wanted to break the bitch's neck, but he sat rigid in his seat and restrained himself.

She continued with, "And your son, Bugsy, is the father."

For a moment, he thought that he had misheard her. "Come again? What the fuck did you just say?"

Bugsy chimed in with, "It's my baby she's carrying, Pop. We're in love and I just wanted to come and tell you face-to-face . . . man-to-man."

Father and son stared each other down, and surprisingly, Scott didn't react violently. But that was the scary part.

"You wanted to come tell me man-to-man, huh? You're a man now, nigga!" Scott said, finally exploding. "This bitch got you pussy whipped, Bugsy? You of all people!"

"I'm not trying to beef with you," Bugsy said.

"It's too late for that, nigga!" Scott retorted.

"I love you, Pop."

"Shut the fuck up!" Scott exclaimed. "You show your love by fuckin' my fiancée? And this deceitful bitch betrays me with my own son!"

Scott's blood felt like acid. His son fucked his bitch and got her pregnant. She was twice his age. And she was turning Bugsy against him. Maxine had the nerve to remain quiet and not look his way. This was a woman he had a long standing history with. *Is this her revenge? Did she plan this all along?* he pondered. And she implemented her plan when he was most vulnerable—when he was jammed up in fighting the federal government for his freedom.

"I don't wanna fight with you, Pop. We can work something out."

Scott didn't respond. The disappointment and anger on his face was manifested for Bugsy to see. Bugsy was his protégé—the one Scott loved above all the others. The betrayal was crushing. The more he saw them together, the harder it was for him to keep his composure, but he had promised the warden there'd be no more violent outbursts. He needed to speak to Bugsy alone.

"Maxine, excuse us. I need to talk to my son alone," he calmly said.

She didn't budge right away. Instead, she turned to Bugsy for his approval. It ignited more rage in Scott.

Bugsy nodded.

"I'll go use the bathroom then," she said.

Bugsy and Scott both watched Maxine disappear into the women's bathroom. When she was inside, Bugsy turned to look at his father. Now they could talk man-to-man.

He said to Scott, "Look, it just happened. This wasn't planned. I never meant to hurt anyone, especially you."

"How long has this been going on? When did it start?" Scott asked. He wanted to know if they were fucking around when he was home.

"It started with you, when you continuously sent me to check up on her to see if she was having an affair," Bugsy said. "She wasn't. We developed something. I can't explain it. She's alone and she missed you."

"Funny way of showing that to me," Scott blurted out.

"So where do we go from here, huh? Maxine's under my protection right now," he said boldly to his father.

"Oh really? I tell you where we stand. You're no longer my second-in-command—you fucked that up. And I want you to send Mason to come visit me. Until Meyer gets well enough to come visit me on his own and sit down for a meeting, Mason will become my number-two, not you."

Bugsy chuckled.

"You find this fuckin' funny, Bugsy?" Scott rumbled.

"That would be foolish of you, Pop," Bugsy replied.

"You think this a game, son? You dare test me?"

Bugsy locked eyes with his father. Now it was about who had the bigger dick. Bugsy was ready to show his father his war chest. There was no more uneasiness showing in his eyes.

He leaned closer against the table. "I'm not sending Mason to visit you and I'm not relinquishing my position as second-in-command. In fact, while you're locked up, I am the de-facto boss of this organization. You forget, I know everything and I did everything for you, Pop. I control the attorneys, and I was the one who handled all of your business dealings and managed the books and helped you legitimize. I brought this organization from the ground up, and the men, they all respect me! Look, the chances of your acquittal are slim, but if you so happen to get out, then we'll deal with each other then. But until that day, I'm the head nigga in charge."

Scott couldn't believe what he was hearing. His son had completely turned against him. He felt nuclear, burning rage crackling through his body like a short circuit. His eyes narrowed with anger at Bugsy, and a cruel sneer formed on his face. His eyes seared into his son as his hands trembled to react. He could feel a vein pulsing in his forehead.

"You want to take it there, Bugsy? You dare go against me and bite the hand that feeds you?"

"I already did," Bugsy remarked.

At that moment, Maxine reemerged from the bathroom and Bugsy stood up from his chair. Maxine stood by her man's side. The look on Scott's face could shrivel any man down to size and make them piss themselves, but Bugsy wasn't any man. He knew the power he possessed. Maxine fortified his courage to separate himself from the family and build his own empire. Scott wanted to murder the woman he loved, along with his first child. Bugsy had to protect them by any means necessary.

"We're done here, Pop. I came to visit you out of respect, but that's as far as it goes. Maxine lives, and we move on." He hated to come at his father so harshly, but he felt he didn't have a choice.

Scott could only glare at the couple. "I wish y'all the best of health," he mocked.

They left the visitation room knowing Scott was going to be a problem.

***

Scott walked into his cell ready to slam his fists through a brick wall. He would show Bugsy who had the bigger war chest, but he needed to make calls and connect with certain people. Fortunately, he had the right tool to work with. There was a cell phone hidden under his mattress. This one was given to him by a man he *did* trust. He knew the line was secure.

Having a photographic memory, Scott knew the cell phone numbers for all of his top lieutenants. One by one, he called his men only to realize that Bugsy was one step ahead of him. Bugsy had replaced everyone's cell phone before he came to visit. Scott would have done the same thing. It's what made Bugsy dangerous—they thought alike, but Bugsy proved that he could be a lot more crafty and cunning.

Scott desperately wanted to get in touch with Mason. Mason was someone he could trust to visit him and carry out the order to murder Maxine. He and Mason went back to Scott's earlier days, when he sold crack on the Brooklyn corners at thirteen years old. Mason was Whistler, before Whistler and Scott became best friends.

He was conflicted about whether to give the order to go after Bugsy, his firstborn. He was tempted to. His son needed to learn a harsh lesson about biting the hand that feeds him.

All that rage Scott felt was swirling inside of him like a tornado. He pivoted and slammed his fist against the cement wall. He needed to release his frustration. He needed to show to everyone that he wasn't weak inside the jail. He still had a couple of moves up his sleeve. Bugsy made his move, and Scott was making his. Bugsy didn't know everything and everyone. Scott had others who could link him with Mason and then Meyer. While he sat on his cot and the corrections officers patrolled the area, some aware of his actions and the cell phone, he made the call that would help his maneuver against his son.

Walker was a dirty cop that only Scott knew about. The man was in his mid-forties with enough time on the force to remember when

Scott was a young punk selling crack in Brooklyn during his adolescent years. The beat cop back then was now a corrupt captain over a Brooklyn precinct. Both men had watched each other grow significantly in their lines of work. And for the right price, Walker was always Scott's man. They formed somewhat of a friendship, and Scott kept Walker in his back pocket with greed and power. It was Scott who fed Walker numerous tips of rising drug dealers in the neighborhood to raid and bust and aided him with unsolved murders to help boost the cop's career. It was Scott who helped Walker hide his finances overseas and allied him to legitimate investments that the IRS or IA couldn't trace back to him.

Scott called the captain's secured line and immediately enticed him with cash for a favor.

"How can you help me when you're behind bars?" Walker asked.

"You doubt me?" Scott said.

"I never do, but your predicament puts me in danger. I shouldn't even be talking to you right now," he said.

"But you are, and you know I'm a man of my word."

"What is it that you need from me?" Walker asked hurriedly.

"I just need for you to help me get in contact with two people, one of them being my son in the hospital."

"I heard about him. I'm sorry."

"There's nothing to be sorry about. I just need a cell phone to his ear."

"And who's the other?"

"Mason."

"That fuckin' lunatic? He has two open murders in my precinct alone that they can't nail him on."

"I just need a word with him."

"This better not come back to haunt me," Walker warned.

"Has it ever? I kept you a secret from everyone because I know you're smart like me and we both have a lot to lose."

"Me more than you. And is this line secure?"

"It is," Scott said.

Walker exhaled noisily. "I'll have someone at the hospital tomorrow. Remember this cell phone number and then forget it when you use it."

"I will."

"Don't fuck me on this," said Walker.

"I won't."

Scott committed the number Walker gave him to memory. The phone would be given to Meyer. It was going to be a lot trickier to track Mason down. The man was a nomad, but Scott believed the captain would be able to find him.

***

The next afternoon, Scott called the cell phone number and Meyer answered. Hearing his son's voice, he felt overwhelmed with emotions. It was good to hear Meyer alive and doing well so far.

"Hey, son," said Scott nicely.

"Wh-what is that you want?" Meyer replied not-so-nicely.

"I want to talk. Are you strong enough to come visit me soon?"

"No. I'm still fucked up. I still have weeks of rehab left," he said.

Scott was disappointed by the news. "I need you, Meyer. I know we haven't been on good terms lately, but I'm willing to let bygones be bygones and move on to the future."

Meyer was listening, but he wasn't feeling anything his father had to say. "Future, huh?"

"Yes. And have you heard anything from Bugsy lately?"

"No, why you asking about him?"

"Listen, things are happening and pieces are moving around, and your brother and I aren't seeing eye-to-eye anymore."

"And that's my problem?"

"No, it's not."

"Look, you and I went our separate ways a long time ago, and whatever beef you got wit' Bugsy now, that ain't my business, Pop. And the next time you call me, call to see how the fuck I'm doin', not for what I can fuckin' do for you! So fuck you!"

The phone went dead. Scott frowned. His son was still holding a grudge against him. He sighed deeply.

Now he needed to get in contact with Mason. He knew Mason would do anything he asked. He had to play chess skillfully while contained in his jail cell. He was going to show Bugsy to never count a man truly down and out—to think he was drowning. No matter how deep his head was under the water, there was always a way to come up for air.

***

Meyer tossed the phone across the room. The nerve of his father calling him to ask for a favor and question him about Bugsy. Scott and Bugsy had a falling out and were clashing, and he was totally uninterested. All his life, Scott put Bugsy first and on a pedestal. If their honeymoon was over, he didn't give a fuck. Now his father wanted to run back to him and use him again. Meyer was in no condition to entertain anything his father had to say. He had been in the hospital for months, and his father didn't call him once to check on him. But today, he had a stranger come into his room to hand him a cell phone so he could talk to him. It went to show that Scott had reach and how selfish the nigga still was. He wanted to speak about Bugsy and ask questions, when Meyer had almost died.

Meyer had love for his family, especially his brother. Bugsy was his twin and he would do for him long before he did anything for Scott. Bugsy never missed a visit. He was there when he awakened from his coma. He was always at the hospital coaxing him to get better and make a full recovery. Bugsy never mentioned that he and Scott were at odds, and he wasn't going to bring it up. Meyer wasn't going to push him. His recovery was his number-one priority.

39

Scott walked into the private room at the jail and sat across from his well-dressed and high-priced lawyer, Arnold Meade. The lawyer looked like a million bucks while Scott looked like he was living on a slave plantation. The first things he noticed about Arnold was the diamond Rolex around his wrist and his tailored three-thousand-dollar suit. He had a Miami tan and slicked back hair and resembled Gordon Gekko from the *Wall Street* movie.

It made Scott envious. He missed the lavish life. He missed it all. He wanted to get back to his way of life, but they kept him caged like an animal—no bail, no bond, and his only way out was his looming court date. He needed to be acquitted of all charges—by any means necessary.

Arnold Meade's was one phone number Bugsy couldn't change. And Scott was ready to thrust his list of commands at him.

"Listen, I'm changing things around, and I don't want you to trust Bugsy," Scott said.

Arnold was taken aback. "But he's your son."

"I don't give a fuck who he is. I'm making moves and he's hindering me right now," Scott said.

Arnold didn't understand what was going on, but it wasn't his business to know at the moment. "Duly noted," he responded coolly.

"Also, I need for you to reach out to my top enforcer, Mason. You remember him?"

Arnold nodded. "I got him acquitted of a few charges over the years. He's a hard man to forget."

"I need for him to come visit me, right away. And I want you to keep tabs on Bugsy for me. I need to know his every move."

"But your trial date is approaching and my office needs to be preparing for your case. Depositions need to be worked on—"

"And that will be done, but I need this done right now," Scott commanded.

"Listen, I'm never in your business unless you need me to be, but this thing with Bugsy, I don't understand it. You trust him with everything. What changed?"

"Everything changed with him since he's been fucking my fiancée, or shall I say ex-fiancée."

Arnold had no response.

"And she's pregnant by him," he added.

Scott continued to pour out everything to him, and Arnold Meade listened intently. Arnold knew where all the bodies were buried. He had been under Scott's employ for decades, and he was an OG himself. He'd successfully defended members of the Gambino and Lucchese crime families. He was a tough talking New Yorker with a dogmatic persona and a no-nonsense reputation in the courtrooms and on the streets.

After hearing the story, Arnold sympathized with Scott, saying, "I'm sorry for everything."

Scott imploded. "I don't need your fuckin' sympathy; I need your fuckin' help! I want revenge."

Arnold sat there straight-faced from his client's reaction. He leaned forward in his chair, elbows against the table, hands clasped. He never took his eyes off of Scott.

"Look, Scott, I have to be honest with you. I can't help you with your demands," he said.

"What the fuck you mean, you can't help me?"

"Bugsy already came to me. We spoke."

"What?" Scott twisted up his face in anger and bewilderment.

"His instructions were simple—whatever you ask, not to comply."

"Are you out your fuckin' mind?! You're *my* fuckin' lawyer, not his!"

"I know, but he's the one who's paying for my services. At the moment, he's signing the checks, not you. So I have to accommodate his wishes."

What the fuck was going on? Scott wanted to leap across the table and strangle the life out of his attorney. "It's my fuckin' money that he's paying you with, you dumb fuck! I'm the fuckin' boss of this organization, not him!"

Arnold didn't jump or fold in fear from his reaction. He wasn't intimidated by Scott like many other lawyers would have been. "For legal reasons, I don't wanna know where the money's coming from. My only ethical duty is to successfully defend you in the courtroom, which I will do. I have a strong legal team presiding over your case as we speak. But for now, my orders come from Bugsy."

Scott scowled. "Arnold, I won't fuckin' forget this."

Arnold reached for his leather briefcase, stood up, smiled at Scott, and calmly replied with, "You'll thank me in court."

He exited the private room, leaving Scott in complete awe. Scott couldn't believe that he was being beaten by his own son. Bugsy was holding all the cards, but Scott felt he had one last ace up his sleeve, and that was Lucky.

Her muscles started to tighten, and her body shivered against the bed. "Oh shit . . . oh shit . . . don't stop, lick me right there, nigga! Right there—don't stop! I'm gonna come! Don't fuckin' stop!" Lucky cooed and moaned as she was on her way to an orgasm.

Lucky's nails clawed the back of the man's head as he ate her out. Her body needed it. Lucky was in her second trimester and she'd never been so horny. All of her hormones were surging through her at once and increasing her sex drive. It felt like her entire body was on fire with passion. The lucky man tonight was a young soldier in her organization who she found very attractive. His name was Packer and he was six-one with a chiseled physique and a gift for performing oral sex.

"I'm gonna fuckin' come!" she screamed out.

Her body quivered as he ate and ate. She closed her eyes, clutched the bed sheets, and held on for the ride of her life. Her legs straddled his upper physique and then the sudden sensation broke away from her like flood gates collapsing, and Packer didn't budge as she came in his mouth. He lapped up her juices like a treat and wiped his mouth. She was spent.

"You good?" he said.

"Oh, I'm good . . . very good," she said, smiling.

He smiled and removed himself from the submissive position. He was eye candy from head to toe, and that wasn't all. He was a cold-blooded killer and completely loyal to Lucky.

"I liked that," he said.

"I liked it too."

It took a moment for Lucky to prop herself up and collect herself. Her stomach was starting to protrude more and her body was going through extreme changes. She could feel her baby moving around inside of her. It was a bizarre feeling, but it was a wonderful feeling. Packer put his shirt back on and Lucky dismissed him from the room. She had her pleasures for the evening. It was time to get back to business.

The moment Packer walked out the room, her cell phone rang. She didn't recognize the number, but she answered it anyway.

"Hey, baby girl," she heard him say sweetly.

Lucky stood there in awe for a moment. Hearing her father's voice wasn't what she expected. It had been a long time.

"How are things going with you?" he said, speaking nicely.

"What the fuck do you want?"

"I want to talk."

"How did you get my number?"

"I still got my ways, you know that. Don't forget who I am," he said.

"Believe me, I want to," she replied.

"I'm hearing good things about you. You're coming up."

"Not because of you," she said.

Since the hospital, her attitude had changed. She was glad that he was alive, but their relationship ended a long time ago. She had never gone to visit him while he was locked up, and she was still salty about the abuse from him. Her tears had dried up, and life went on.

"I never apologized to you about that. I'm sorry. I should have never put my hands on you. I hate myself every single day for it. I was wrong."

She didn't respond to his apology.

"Can you come visit me?" he asked her.

"I'm busy."

"I missed you. You're the only daughter I have left. I need to see you."

"For what?"

"So we can sit down and talk."

"What is there to talk about? What is it that you want from me?"

"You're all I have left. Meyer and Bugsy turned their backs on me."

"You're being dramatic. Bugsy idolizes you," she returned.

He resented the implication. But she didn't know.

"This is important. It has to do with Maxine," he uttered.

Suddenly, he had her attention. But she wondered why he wasn't reaching out to Bugsy. She figured he already had and didn't get the result that he wanted. Therefore, she was the next best thing. The old Lucky would have jumped at the chance to go see him to get the gossip. What had Maxine done? The old Lucky would have wanted to be there for her dad—she was a daddy's girl, and a part of her missed that relationship, but she wasn't her old self and things done changed. She wasn't about to become anyone's pawn—not her mother's nor her father's.

"I just want to see you, baby girl. I want to see your face, and your smile, like at the hospital."

"I only came because I was worried about you. You're still my father. But that was a onetime thing. You've recovered from your injuries."

"But I still have a broken heart with you," he countered.

She sighed. That daddy's-little-girl feeling was deep and dormant inside her, but it wasn't coming out anytime soon.

"I need to talk to you. I need to see you," he repeated.

She'd never heard him sound so broken and depressed. Her father always represented strength and vigor. Hearing him almost beg her to visit was somewhat pleasing to her ears.

"I'll come see you," she said reluctantly.

"This Friday?"

"Sure."

"I love you, Lucky, and I can't wait to see you again."

Their call ended, and Lucky shook her head in disgust. She felt her father was a hypocrite. Where was the love when he was beating her ass? Where was the love when he chose Maxine over her and Layla? He'd treated her like she was nothing and placed Maxine on this pedestal and turned his back on his family a long time ago.

Fuck him!

S tep after step, without stumbling or falling to the ground, Meyer wanted to show off for his brother, Bugsy. He was walking without crutches or help from the medical staff. Months and months of physical therapy were finally paying off.

"You see that, nigga? I'll be back to my old self real soon."

Bugsy grinned. "Yeah, that's good."

Meyer was also eating regularly and gaining his weight back. He looked forward to visits from Bugsy. It's what encouraged him to progress in his rehabilitation. He wanted to matter again in the streets. He wanted to be respected and feared again. Every day in that hospital bed, he felt helpless and vulnerable, and it tore him apart.

"I'm gonna be better, watch and see," said Meyer excitedly.

Bugsy nodded, agreeing with his twin brother. He sat in the chair and watched Meyer walk slowly across the hospital room. He had a lot on his mind. He knew things were going to get ugly before they got better. Going against Scott was a power move, but it was a move he felt needed to be made. It was time for him to step up and release himself from the strings of his father. Lucky had done it and she was thriving. He couldn't allow his sister to outshine him. It was his turn to become independent.

"Did you get a call from Pop?" Bugsy asked.

Meyer stopped walking and took hold of the bar against the wall for a breather. "Yeah, he called. Y'all got beef?"

"Yeah."

"You wanna talk about it?" Meyer said.

Bugsy hesitated with his reply. Meyer was going through a lot, and Bugsy wasn't sure he should be pulled into this family drama.

"I got Maxine pregnant," he uttered.

Meyer's face showed perplexity. "What the fuck?"

"Yeah, she and I are together now."

The news almost made Meyer stumble and fall. He didn't expect to hear that at all. Bugsy and Maxine, how in the hell did that ever happen?

"Bugsy, what the fuck was you thinking? You serious?"

"Yeah."

"Oh shit . . . Wow, and you were Pop's golden boy." Meyer laughed.

"You find it funny?"

"Hey, don't snap on me. I got your back," said Meyer. "But why? Why did you go there with her?"

"It just happened," he replied.

"Damn, she must got some good pussy for you and Pop to be fighting over her," he remarked without consideration.

Bugsy didn't respond to the remark. Bugsy knew his father well, and he realized that even from behind bars, Scott would move heaven and earth to get at them. He and Maxine weren't safe. Although he'd considerably hindered his father's reach and authority, it wasn't going to be enough to prevent him from counterattacking. Scott always had a few extra moves up his sleeve.

"Don't worry, Bugsy. I'm getting better every day and I got your back. We go to war, then we go to war as a family because it's long overdue," Meyer said from the bottom of his heart.

Bugsy nodded. "One thing, though," he said, "Keep this information away from Lucky. I don't want her to know."

"I won't tell her a fuckin' thing."

Bugsy felt that his sister wouldn't take the news well and would send her goons after Maxine, which would start a civil war between them. She never liked Maxine, and this would definitely send her over the edge.

Meyer understood the severity of the situation and gave his twin his word and his complete support. It was imperative for him to get better. His siblings were going to need all the help they could get.

***

Friday after Friday, for weeks and weeks, Scott waited for Lucky's visit, and each time he was met with disappointment. When he was able to contact her and ask why, he was given excuse after excuse why she didn't visit him that day. She was a very busy woman. But Scott knew that it was payback for everything he'd done to her. He treated her like a princess before his mind got clouded with pussy. Of course she resented him, and it took a man to realize that. But Bugsy, he gave his son everything. He purposely lorded Bugsy over Meyer year in and year out. Bugsy was his trusted ally, his most favored child, and now Bugsy had turned on him. The animosity in Scott was so thick it was harder and harder to swallow.

He understood it. All of his children were against him. They hated him. But if it wasn't for him, then they wouldn't be in the position they were in today. It was time to deal with his reality. His offspring weren't going to be any support for him. He stopped calling Lucky, and he bided his time until the trial date. Scott sat for months with visits from only his lawyer or a representative from the office. Although he despised Arnold Meade for siding with Bugsy, he still needed the man's help. He wanted out of jail. He wanted his life back—his authority and power.

Scott wanted to stay bitter at everyone. If he beat the case and became a free man again, there was going to be hell to pay. He wasn't going to forget. Whoever went against him and defied him was going to regret doing so in the worst way. He still had some pawns on the chessboard and he was still a king—no matter what.

t was Lucky's third trimester and she was carrying small at seven and a
half months pregnant. She was still able to hide her baby bump from
the rest of the world, including Angel, but it was becoming difficult. The
summer months were her most trying months, wearing oversized clothing
to conceal the bulge. She had to move in cover. She made herself scarce to
her peoples, and only a handful of folks knew about her pregnancy. She
didn't do frequent trips to the OB/GYN. Instead, a private physician was
secretly escorted into her home for regular checkups and prenatal care for
the baby. Everything concerning her pregnancy was cloak-and-dagger.

Business was going great for Lucky, and she no longer needed
consignment from Angel. The money and product was flowing back and
forth like clockwork. Her men were loyal and ecstatic. They were making
money hand over fist. The Bronx was their playground and the city was
their stomping grounds. Lucky's organization was growing fast, but there
had been some bumps along the way. A few rival organizations refused
to bow down and allow a woman to take control of their territory, so
Lucky had to show them who was boss, and bloodshed ensued. Packer
was the main one to honor Lucky's name, and anyone who spoke against
her or tried to vilify her name, he was quick to blow their brains out. He
respected Lucky and he became her eyes and ears on the streets.

But life was good for Lucky. She had money and power. She had cut
all ties with her mother and she was on top of the world, and soon, she

was going to become a mother. She was having a girl—a daughter, her little queen to pamper and doll up. And no one was going to take her baby away from her. Lucky had grown an army to surround and protect her. Her men would die for her.

The autumn night was chilly, and Lucky wanted to dine out with a friend who was quickly becoming something else in her life. Packer was rising up in the ranks of her organization, but a romance was also building between them. Packer was in his early twenties and in great shape. He reminded her of a young Whistler. He was stimulating and spontaneous. He made Lucky feel safe and secure, and sex with him was mind-blowing. Most importantly, he vowed to be there for her unborn child. Lucky needed to hear that, and Packer went from being a soldier to her right-hand and top enforcer if needed. Though he was handsome with a dark goatee that framed his mouth, dark curly hair, and light skin, Packer had these dark, deep-set and cold looking eyes, and his fearlessness was a force to be reckoned with. He was Whistler and Meyer all rolled into one man.

Lucky wanted to celebrate tonight. Finally, Meyer was out of the hospital and he was fully rehabilitated.

She and Packer climbed out the backseat of a black Escalade and approached an elegant downtown restaurant on 20th Street called Gramercy Tavern. The place was embellished with a wood beamed ceiling and rustic chandeliers and fine art adorning the walls.

Upon entering the restaurant, they were greeted by the restaurant's maître-d and seated at a lovely table. Packer helped Lucky peel off her long beige pea coat and pulled out the chair for her. He was a gentleman. He sat opposite of Lucky at the decorated table dressed in a solid black long sleeve collared shirt and boot cut jeans. Every so often, he observed his surroundings, watching everyone and everything. He was steadily alert and had a pistol concealed in his ankle holster. One could never be too careful. There was an air of power about Packer that was magnetic.

Their night at the restaurant started off fine. They talked and laughed and dined on appetizers. They both refused to drink any alcohol, since Lucky was pregnant and Packer didn't drink. He wanted to always be alert and sober. In his world, one slip up could mean life or death. He felt his enemies didn't sleep, so he had to always be creative with his movement— no habits, no routines. Lucky saw him as more than an employee; he was an opportunity for her.

His family was from Puerto Rico, but he was born in the South Bronx. He'd been on his own since he was eight years old. His father was dead and his mother was on the streets. His older brother was a casualty of gang violence and his sister was a crackhead. Packer was the youngest and he was a survivor. He joined a gang at ten, started selling drugs when he was twelve, and committed his first murder when he was fifteen. Packer was a hardened criminal with ambition to climb through the anarchy of the streets and become an authority in the underworld. He had what it took to rise to the top, and Lucky saw it.

"I appreciate dis, Lucky. Ya takin' me out to a nice restaurant and shit. I never been to anything fancy like this. It's Chinese takeout and fast food all day for me," Packer said.

"You deserve it," she said.

"So, what you suggest I should order?" he said.

"Whatever you want."

"I don't know what da fuck dis shit is on the menu. Everything look fuckin' foreign to me," he said.

He was still rough around the edges, but in due time, he was going to be perfect, she felt.

"Well, I can tell you what's good. What you might like—" Lucky started, but then something quickly captured her attention.

Her eyes became fixed on the newest patron entering the restaurant. She appeared alone, despite being flanked by a bodyguard. Lucky watched her movement closely. She observed Maxine being ushered to her table by the maître-d and she watched the winter coat being removed from her body and the protruding belly.

"What the fuck! No this bitch ain't pregnant!"

"Who's pregnant?" Packer questioned.

Maxine sat down and noticed Lucky seated across the room. Both ladies scowled at each other. Lucky assumed that Maxine was at least eight or nine months pregnant—but she was only four months. She was growing as big as a house. Lucky assumed it was her father's baby. Lucky felt that Maxine should have been taken care of long ago, but that wasn't the case. She didn't want any half brother or sister from this bitch.

Packer turned around to see what Lucky was gazing at and saw the older pregnant woman seated on the other side of the place.

"Who dat bitch?" he asked her.

"Someone who should have been dead a long time ago," Lucky replied.

Maxine's presence had just ruined Lucky's appetite. She was ready to leave. Packer was right by her side. Lucky stood up and threw a C-Note on the table, her hard frown still trained on Maxine. Maxine looked at Lucky and smirked. She had the audacity to rub her protruding stomach.

"Yo, you want me go handle that bitch n' that nigga fo' you?"

She looked at him and was deeply impressed. "You would kill a pregnant woman for me?" she asked in a low tone.

"For you, I'll kill anybody," he replied.

He was definitely the one. But no, now wasn't the time to react. She simply gave Maxine the middle finger and she and Packer left the restaurant. But Lucky was so angry that she wanted to tear that baby out of Maxine's stomach herself and kick it down the street. How dare she? How dare her father get her pregnant?

She and Packer got back into the Escalade and the first thing she did was call Bugsy. The moment he answered his phone, she screamed,

"Why is that bitch pregnant with our father's baby? How is that fuckin' possible? Tell me it's not Scott's baby, Bugsy! What the fuck, they gave him a conjugal visit inside there? Tell me something, Bugsy. What the fuck is going on?"

"It's not his baby, Lucky," he said.

Lucky felt some relief to hear that. She started to calm down, but the feeling was short-lived.

"It's my baby," Bugsy told her.

Lucky nearly hit the roof of the vehicle. She couldn't believe what she'd just heard.

"What the fuck are you talkin' about, Bugsy?! Please tell me you wasn't that stupid! Please tell me you didn't fuck that nasty-ass bitch!"

"Yes, I did, and we're in a relationship now," he said coolly.

"Ohmygod—what the fuck! You were supposed to be the smart one! What the fuck is wrong wit' you, nigga? You just like our father, letting that bitch play you and use you, you fuckin' dumb fuck! Ohmygod! Oh my fucking god—"

The feeling hit Lucky hard and fast like a Mack truck and it took her breath away. She couldn't rant and scream any longer. Suddenly, she felt faint and she felt her water burst. She was going into premature labor.

"Ohmygod, I'm gonna have my baby," she cried out.

"Yo, take us to the nearest hospital, now!" Packer shouted at the driver.

The man put his foot to the pedal and accelerated quickly. Packer took Lucky's hand into his and he was doing his best to calm her down and coach her in the backseat. But he was more nervous than a long tailed cat in a room full of rocking chairs.

***

The next day, Lucky lay in the hospital bed exhausted after going through thirteen long hours of labor. She gave birth to a premature baby girl that weighed only 3 lbs. She named her daughter Lucchese Lily West, after famed mafioso Tommy Lucchese of the Lucchese crime family. Her infant daughter was so small, but she was perfect. Her pale skin and dark curly hair were telltale gifts from her father.

Giving birth was a lovely feeling, but Lucky knew she was still in hot water and she needed to correct the situation with Angel. She didn't want to spend the rest of her life hiding from him and looking over her shoulder. So, she had her peoples get in contact with Angel and tell him that she was already two months pregnant when they had sex and that she went full term with her pregnancy and gave birth yesterday.

Lucky hoped it wasn't a mistake. But if he came for her, she was going to be ready. She was going to protect Lucchese with all her might and bring the cartel hell if they tried to end her daughter's life.

***

Angel sat by the large pool sipping on his cocktail. He frowned at the news given to him by one of his men. He felt he'd been bamboozled by Lucky. He had his peoples constantly checking up on Lucky and they always reported that she wasn't pregnant at all—showed him glossy photographs of her, and it showed him that she wasn't carrying. That she had done what she was told and had the abortion. But now, she gave birth to a child. How could his people have missed that? Something just didn't feel right to him. Why not tell him sooner if she was already pregnant?

Angel downed the drink and stood up from the chair. Lucky was a slippery bitch he couldn't take for granted. Though he pretended to believe her story, the situation wasn't over. If she had played him after he gave her a direct order, then she and the child would both die by his hands.

He hated the cold weather, but he would be making a trip to New York City. It was time he saw Lucky face-to-face and saw that bastard baby with his own eyes.

H er trial date was looming, and there weren't going to be any plea deals or cop-outs. It was going to be a long federal trial in a federal courtroom with a federal judge and over a dozen jurors. Layla met continuously with her lawyer, Fitzgerald Spencer. They went over their game plan—moving through the discovery period, and there were depositions to strengthen, further evidence required, witnesses to weed out, and so on. It was tedious and tireless work for the defense—expensive too. Layla couldn't afford any fuck-ups or fumbling once the trial started. She'd hired the best and she expected the best, meaning a not-guilty outcome. But there was one credible witness that the U.S. Attorney had, and it was supposedly the nail in the coffin for the defendants.

Arnold and Fitzgerald combined forces and law offices to further strengthen their chances in court. Layla frowned at the idea of seeing Scott and sitting next to him in court, but she had to do what was best to receive an acquittal from the jurors.

But she wasn't going into her trial wearing a blindfold. During one of her meetings with her lawyer, she handed him a list of names.

Fitzgerald was confused.

"Who are these people?" he asked her.

"Your help to secure my freedom," she said.

He was dumbfounded by her response. The list included a police sergeant, a state prosecutor, and a mayor's aide.

"This is a federal case. Most of these people are local and state. How can these people help us?" he said.

"I'm sure you can find a way and be a lot more creative, Fitzgerald. This is my life—my fuckin' freedom we're talking about. I'm willing to do whatever it takes to get the fuck out of here. It's going on a year in this place and I need out," she proclaimed.

"I'll see what I can do. I'll get my guy on it."

"Please do," she replied.

***

A federal courtroom was a place where lives could drastically change. Scott took a seat near his codefendant, Layla West, with their respective lawyers flanking them. They were dressed nicely, Scott in a classy suit and Layla in a formal blouse and skirt. They both sat in the ostentatious courtroom looking straight-faced, but inside, their nerves were spinning wildly like a theme park ride. It was the United States vs. them.

U.S. Attorney Gloria Sheindlin was a fierce federal litigator with a 93% conviction rate. She sat on the opposite side of the courtroom sharply dressed in a dark blue suit exuding confidence. Fitzgerald and Arnold were well aware of Gloria's track record, and they were ready to do whatever it took to get their clients acquitted.

Gloria Sheindlin stood up and positioned herself in the center of the courtroom. To her right was a jury of twelve—men and women, black and white, Latino and Asian. The federal judge sat high on his bench, observing his domain and poised to keep order in the room.

Gloria's presence was influential and engaging. She knew the tricks of the trade to captivate the jurors' attention. Her opening statement was meant to damage the defendants' character right away. She called Scott and Layla "notorious drug kingpins" and "murderers" and "a threat to society." She was going to prove to the court that they should get life in prison. The defendants were forced to sit there and listen to a woman they didn't even know slander their names and vilify their characters.

After Gloria's lengthy opening statement, Fitzgerald Spencer stood up in the courtroom and gave a compelling opening statement. Arnold Meade followed with his opening statement. Day one of their trial was long and exhausting, but day two was going to bring about the U.S. Attorney's first witness.

The witness was escorted into the courtroom, and Layla and Scott were dumbfounded by who it was. It was *the* snitch, Whistler Hussain Jackson. But no one was more shocked than Layla. She had killed him. How could he still be living when she shot him twice? She leaned into her lawyer's ear with questions, but Fitz told her to be cool.

Whistler looked to be in horrible shape. He was missing one eye, compliments of Layla's .45. His unsightly face was making the female jurors uneasy. They immediately didn't like him. Layla and Scott despised him for their own reasons. He was a snitch and they wanted him to rot in hell.

The U.S. Attorney believed Whistler's testimony against the defendants would make her case concrete. But right away, it started to fall apart for the prosecution. Question after question, Whistler stammered his reply and he seemed unsure. He would take an incredible amount of time before he answered. It was annoying and irritating the jurors. Gloria tried to work her magic with the witness, but it was an uphill battle.

Meanwhile, Scott and Layla looked furiously at Whistler, the snitch and the pedophile. If Layla had the chance, she would kill him again.

"You were a major player in their crime organization. Right, Mr. Jackson?" the U.S. Attorney asked him.

"I-I . . . I was."

"Can you tell us your job with the West organization?"

Whistler spoke slowly and softly. He described himself as an enforcer, lieutenant, and a friend.

"Have you ever killed for them?" Gloria asked.

"Objection!" Arnold shouted out and gave his reasons.

"Overruled!" replied the judge. "Answer the question."

Whistler looked like he needed to think long and hard with his answer. Gloria tried to guide him into answering, but Fitz gave his objection. It was going to be a very long trial.

It was the third day in the courtroom, and Whistler was still on the stand. The U.S. Attorney was trying to make him a reliable witness for the jurors, but day three was shoddier than day two. The U.S. Attorney seemed to grow testy with him, and the judge was equally irritated. Both would have to ask him to try and answer the questions promptly. Whistler sat in front of everyone a shell of his former self. He wasn't what Scott and Layla remembered. *Is this a joke?* so many thought. Whistler would whine, scratch his head, and then dig in and around his exposed eye socket with a napkin, which made all of the jurors cringe. It was torturous for everyone. They had tuned out his testimony long ago.

"Who was the one that shot you?" the U.S. Attorney asked him. "Can you point them out in this courtroom?"

"Objection!" Arnold shouted out and gave his reasons.

And once again, the judge overruled.

It took Whistler a moment to answer. Layla didn't break her icy stare from him. She hated a snitch—even one that she tried to kill. She was seething every day she saw him in the courtroom. It was her blunder.

Three long days the U.S. Attorney had Whistler on the stand. She wanted to squeeze every bit of information out of him, and with his current condition it was laborious but necessary. She wanted her witness to paint Scott and Layla as a deadly and murderous couple—just like the mobsters they idolized. When the prosecution tried to introduce testimony about their children's names, the objection was sustained.

The U.S. Attorney for the Southern District of New York rested with her witness, and now it was Fitz and Arnold's turn to poke at Whistler and discredit him for what he was—a liar and a pedophile.

Fitzgerald started first. He had everything he needed to know about Whistler. He started with his background—his upbringing and his criminal past. Arnold went deeper into Whistler with pedophile accusations that made Gloria sing with objections after objections. The two defense attorneys were shaking up the memory of a snitch. And it took an additional four weeks for each council to redirect.

Scott was antsy. He wondered why Arnold was asking so many questions. He was tired of seeing Whistler in front of him, snitching. But Arnold's reply was that Whistler was a dream come true. He assumed that by the time the trial ended, the jury would be so annoyed with Whistler and dizzy from all his longwinded answers that they wouldn't trust anything he said.

Layla continued to sit stone-faced in the federal courtroom. The entire trial was tedious and exhausting. One day it was looking good for them, but then the U.S. Attorney would bring in an expert witness, another snitch, or a forensic specialist and the FBI, and it would start looking bad for them. It was a seesaw of emotions—a tug-of-war of guilty or not guilty.

It was a horrendous ordeal for Layla. She had to see Scott daily, her soon to be ex-husband and her codefendant—the ex love of her life. They were still married on paper, but their relationship had long been dissolved. If he went down, she went down. She felt already down from the pain and hurt he bestowed on her to be with Maxine. If she could kill him too and get away with it, she would have. But this was her life and her freedom on the line, so she didn't have a choice but to endure his presence.

However, what turned her stomach the most with upset and anger was occasionally seeing Lucky in the courtroom—seated in the back, looking aloof and distant from her own parents. The same bitch who'd left her high and dry. She heard through the grapevine that she was a grandmother now. Lucky gave birth to a beautiful, but premature baby girl. Layla didn't know if she would ever see her grandchild. Everything was starting to look bleak for her, but Fitz promised her that he had an ace up his sleeve. But he wasn't sitting in her position, looking at a life sentence. She and Scott had been charged with fifteen indictments, and the U.S. Attorney was hammering away to make sure they would be found guilty of every charge. She had no idea how this bizarre trial would end.

The U.S. Attorney stood once again in the center of the room and gave her closing statement, painting the defendants as murderous animals and menaces to society. She pleaded for a guilty verdict from the jurors and pushed for life incarceration.

Fitzgerald Spencer stood up to give his closing statement to the jurors. He painted his client as a married and educated businesswoman who made smart investments with her husband and who had no reason to run a criminal empire. He painted the U.S. Attorney's case as a fraudulent and tacky attempt to discredit and slander an African-American woman who was a pillar in her community. He spoke of Layla's kids, alive and deceased, a speech that made Layla somewhat tearful, and he even mentioned that she had become a grandmother recently. Fitzgerald poured it on heavily for the jurors to hear. Like Gloria, he was articulate and engaging to the jurors about his client.

Arnold Meade stood up, fixed his tie, and placed himself for everyone to see clearly. His voice boomed out with anger at the U.S. Attorney for trying his client in a criminal case, boasting that Scott was a man who pulled himself up by his bootstraps and became a self-made millionaire. He too characterized Scott West as a pillar in the community, a smart investor, and philanthropist who gave millions to charities and the less fortunate.

"Scott West has nothing to hide. We have proof of his income and his tax returns, but yet, the U.S. Attorney wants us to believe he's this murderous drug kingpin running a criminal empire who moonlights as a do-gooder on the weekends!" Arnold Meade exclaimed.

He poured it on thick and locked eyes with certain jurors, definitely capturing their attention. He moved strategically in front of the jury box as he proclaimed his client's innocence—his incorruptibility from the man he was born to be—a businessman. His closing statement was lengthy too, but it appeared effective. He finally sat down next to his client feeling optimistic of the end result.

Finally, the trial was over and the jury's deliberations would soon begin. For Layla, it felt strange having her life in the hands of twelve strangers who would decide her fate. The lawyers had done their job and she couldn't be any prouder of Fitzgerald's performance. He was an incredible lawyer, but she couldn't give him too much credit, because the verdict hadn't come in yet. The only thing they could do was wait.

The judge banged his gavel down and dismissed the courtroom. There were deep and emotional breaths from the lawyers and the jurors—even a few spectators. It was their time now, to decide the fate of Layla and Scott West. Who would they believe, the U.S. Attorney or the defense?

Scott and Layla stood up from the defendant's table and were approached by the court officers. It was that time again to be led into the back room where they were to be shackled and ushered back into lockup.

***

So far, the jury had been out for four days deliberating, and Scott and Layla had no idea what that meant. Were they leaning toward a guilty verdict? Fitzgerald and Arnold assured them that the longer the deliberation, the better—it meant that the jurors weren't so quick to convict them. But that answer still didn't bring their clients any relief.

Until the foreman read a not-guilty verdict, they couldn't relax.

Scott sat in his jail cell and started to read nearly three hundred pieces of unopened mail to pass the time. Since he had been incarcerated he would receive letters from reporters, online journalists, desperate women searching for the infamous kingpin to wife them, and other supporters and admirers. He had become a very popular guy.

To take his mind off the wait, he took the time to open and read each letter. One letter deep in the stack caught his attention. It read from: Bonnie, Clyde, Gotti West, with a Maryland post office box. Scott ripped open the letter and received the shock of his life.

44

Maxine walked around in the comfort of her Manhattan high-rise with a glass of water and some crackers. She was nine months pregnant and bigger than a house. It was a cold night outside, the temperature dropping to twenty degrees and windy. She sat in a cushioned chair and breathed out. Getting around the place was becoming difficult; she was waddling more than walking. She couldn't see her feet anymore, but she had everything she needed. Bugsy made sure of that. The baby's room was decorated with every imaginable toy and teddy bear, cushioned rocking chairs, a clear acrylic crib, and Disney wallpaper of numerous characters. She was ready to have her baby, and her wish was about to come.

On the coldest day of the year with snow in the forecast, her water finally broke as she was getting up to use the bathroom. This was it. She was going into labor, and Bugsy was right there to assist her. He was all smiles and anxious about the birth of his first child. He and his goons rushed Maxine to the hospital, exceeding the speed limit.

Bugsy wanted the best and he got the best for Maxine and his newborn son. They had a large private room with mahogany walls and cream sofas and silken throw pillows, along with ambient lighting for that radiant glow. There was even a posh kitchenette inside the room. A florist delivered enough flowers to Maxine's room to scent the entire hospital. Bugsy was a happy man and a proud father. Maxine was beat.

She had gone through eleven hours of labor, but she was unable to push out the baby after it'd crowned. She had to be rushed in for an emergency C-section, subsequently delivering a 10lb, 4oz baby boy, who they named Dillinger John West after the American gangster, John Dillinger. It was a family tradition that Maxine first mocked and laughed at, but Bugsy convinced her otherwise and she bought into it. She thanked God that she had a boy; she could only imagine the drama if it had been a girl.

"You did good, baby," Bugsy said, kissing Maxine on her lips.

She held her newborn son wrapped in his receiving blanket in her arms and she didn't want to let him go. He was the most precious thing in her life. He was an angel, sent from God. She hated that she waited so long to become a mother, but she was one now and she wanted to make every day count. Her newborn son was her everything.

Meyer came to visit his newborn nephew, but Lucky refused to see the baby though Bugsy had invited her to the hospital. Meyer was looking better and better each day. He put his feelings for Maxine aside and figured if Bugsy was happy, then he was happy. He was an uncle—twice. He gently held his new nephew in his arms.

He laughed, saying, "Dillinger, huh? I'm gonna teach you how to become a gangsta out there. Ain't nobody gonna want to fuck wit' you."

Maxine had some concerns with Meyer holding her son and talking gangster, but she kept quiet about it. She'd never seen Bugsy so happy. It looked like he was a different man. He was a father, and she already felt that their son was changing him. She wanted the feeling to last forever.

Meyer and Bugsy, together again—they looked unstoppable, like a superhero duo. They celebrated outside smoking cigars in the cold. Then Bugsy got the phone call. It was Arnold Meade.

"The jury came to a verdict," he told Bugsy.

This was it. Their parents would be either locked away for nearly life or become free again. The twins felt ambivalent about a verdict.

45

Layla sat in her jail cell thinking about the outcome of her trial. There was absolutely no way she would spend the rest of her life inside a prison. She didn't understand how Maxine could have done over twenty years and still come out sane. Or had she?

The thing that kept Layla going was the deep, deep hatred she now had for her daughter. Lucky had taken everything from her, and over what? Because she didn't want to reveal the location of her hidden money? Layla felt if Lucky was in her shoes, she would have made the same choice. But Lucky blamed her parents for everything and never took accountability for her own mistakes and flaws. They had spoiled Lucky and given her everything she ever wanted, and the spoiled child had turned into a spoiled adult. Lucky had a sense of entitlement that had come between a mother and daughter. Lucky left Layla high and dry when she needed her the most. Lucky had stopped visiting her months ago. She didn't even write or place any money into her commissary. Had it not been for Bugsy, she would have been forgotten.

There was an insane thought in Layla that made part of her hope that she got convicted because she knew if she ever got out that she would kill Lucky with her bare hands and have her buried somewhere. She had that much animosity toward her own daughter. She knew that she was a vengeful bitch. No way was Lucky going to live after everything she'd done to her—from stealing, disrespecting her, and abandonment. No fucking way!

And then there was Maxine. Layla hadn't forgotten about her.

She paced around her jail cell seething and worried at the same time. Word came to her that the jury had finally reached a verdict. She sat down on her cot and took a deep breath. She was only moments away from finding out her fate. But before she was to find out, she noticed a letter from Maxine was placed inside her cell. She wondered who'd put it there and why Maxine was reaching out to her. There was nothing that bitch could say to make Layla spare her.

She ripped it open and immediately a small picture dropped out. It was a photo of a newborn baby, and the letter was laced with love and forgiveness.

My dearest Layla, despite what you may think, I would like you to know that I would never want to see you in a cage. I've been there and that place changes you forever. It steals your humanity. I would like to finally say that I still love you. You were and still are my best friend. I hear that your trial isn't going well, the witness and all that. I empathize with you, sweetheart. And just as you were there for me during my incarceration, I would love to be there for you. You are, of course, the grandmother of my first child. Please meet Dillinger John West, my little bundle of joy. Bugsy and I are so proud of him. He's perfect! Once you're sentenced, please add me to your visiting list so we can catch up. BTW, you don't have a problem with Bugsy and I, do you? It just happened, just as you and Scott just happened, right? So let the past stay in the past as it is all love.

Love you forever, plus one day.

Maxine

Layla trembled in fury and screamed at the top of her lungs. How did she not know? The boldness of her. The bitch had gone to full term with her son's child and no one told her anything. It was like on cue that the letter showed up in her cell—right before she was to know her fate. Did Maxine know something she didn't? The nerve of her, gloating. On the surface, the letter read innocent and sweet, but Layla knew its true intentions—payback! She read between the lines and its subtle sarcasm was clear to her.

"I'm gonna kill that bitch!" she screamed so loudly that her voice seemed to echo for minutes. "I hate her! I fuckin' hate her!"

She started to trash her cell and continued to scream at the top of her lungs. Finally, several guards rushed into her cell to restrain her. They were baffled by her behavior. Usually inmates didn't react like this until *after* the verdict was heard. But Layla was beyond angry. She continued to rant and curse, and she even started to cry. How did her life take such a drastic turn?

When her anger finally subsided, the guard told her that it was time to return to court. She had about an hour before the verdict would be read and her fate would finally be known.

EPILOGUE

Scott and Layla sat in the federal courtroom stone-faced, both of them unsure of their future. The room was packed with spectators. Bugsy showed up with Maxine and his baby and Lucky was there with Packer. Meyer didn't even bother to show up. The jurors were all seated, quiet and looking straight-faced. It was hard to tell which way they'd gone—guilty or not guilty. It had been a long, arduous journey for them both. So many had turned their backs on them, but there was no bigger betrayal than that of their own children. Bugsy had gotten Maxine pregnant and hijacked his operation and men. Lucky damn near stole her mother's identity while subsequently leaving Layla with nothing—not even a roof over her head.

The judge looked at the foreman. "Has the jury reached a verdict?"

The jury foreman stood up and replied, "Yes, we have, Your Honor."

He was a round and plump man, bad pale skin with thinning hair and a wide nose. He was unattractive and looked to be a racist in Layla's eyes. Layla could feel her heart beating so wildly it felt like African drums were inside her chest. She had never been so nervous in her life.

"Will the defendants rise," ordered the judge.

Scott and Layla, along with their lawyers, stood to their feet. The room was tense and uneasy. There were so many charges against them, could they be found guilty of them all? Layla and Scott's attention were fixed on the jurors. These men and women controlled their fate. It was a sour thing to swallow, their destiny in the hands of twelve strangers.

Scott took a deep breath. He was ready for the outcome. Layla stood firm and on edge. How could she swallow a life sentence? She didn't know how she would react. But this was it, and all mouths dropped to the floor when the jury foreman started to read off the verdicts.

The judge asked him, "For defendant Layla West on attempted murder, how does the jury find?"

The jury foreman said the words, "Not guilty, Your Honor."

Layla was flabbergasted and so was the entire courtroom. But she had to contain her excitement. It wasn't over yet.

"For defendant Layla West on conspiracy to run a criminal empire, how does the jury plead?" said the judge.

"Not guilty, Your Honor!"

And it read on like that for all her charges. Layla couldn't help it. She hugged Fitzgerald so tight that she damn near squeezed the man in half. He was worth every penny. The courtroom erupted in excitement.

The same "Not guilty" verdict was rattled off for her codefendant, Scott West. Scott and Layla were acquitted on all charges, which was virtually unheard of when the federal government builds a case against someone. U.S. Attorney Gloria Sheindlin sat there dumbfounded by the outcome. Her mouth was wide open and she was in shock. In the heat of the moment, Scott and Layla even hugged. Once again, they were free.

Both Layla and Scott then turned to face their children with scowls on their faces. Layla glared at Lucky, and Scott glared at Bugsy. There were scores that needed to be settled, which was going to pit mother against daughter and father against son.

The world wasn't ready for what was to come.

GETTING LUCKY

FAMILY FEUDS

The stunning acquittals of Scott and Layla West resonate throughout the justice system, and the powerful cartels take notice.

The Wests were untouchable and their drug empire is still intact, but family ties begin to unravel.

New mom Lucky has a lot on her shoulders as she continues to deceive the head of the Juarez cartel. Partnering with her twin brothers, Lucky lines up the pieces on the chessboard, but she underestimates the king and queen.

THE SERIES BY

EXCERPT FROM
MAFIOSO - PART FIVE
GETTING LUCKY

S cott reached into his coat and removed a letter from the inner pocket. He handed it to Layla.

She stared at Scott with uncertainty. "What's this?"

"You need to read it. It's important. You were right."

A cop car flew by with its lights blaring. Scott fixed his eyes on it for a moment and then shifted his attention back to Layla. Her face was in the letter. She was reading it slowly. As she read, he could see the emotions forming in her eyes, the frown on her face, and the tears streaming down her cheeks. He remained silent. He wanted her to read it thoroughly, with no interruptions. They stood on the Harlem street corner, and though surrounded by noise and traffic, it felt like it was only the two of them. They had more privacy outdoors than inside.

Her eyes were flooded with blinding tears. When she finished reading the letter, Layla never felt so angry, furious, betrayed, and embarrassed. How could she have been so stupid? What kind of mother was she to leave her children vulnerable to be used as pawns in a twenty-year-old beef? Layla was visibly ill. Her hands got cold and clammy as her heart pounded so loud it felt like her eardrums would burst. *It's my fault,* she thought. *I paid this goon to kill my kids.*

Layla's eyes locked with Scott's and she uttered with contempt, "When do we kill this fuckin' bitch?"

Scott nodded. He understood her hurt and her pain. The letter revealed all that they needed to know—Maxine was the culprit behind everything. She was a mastermind, and they had greatly underestimated her.

"It's not that easy," he uttered.

Layla scrunched up her face. "Not that easy?"

"There's Bugsy and the baby," he said.

"And what they got to do wit' it?"

"First, we just beat federal indictments, and there's still attention on us. We're hot, and we're in the news. We react to this now, and it's gonna look bad on us," he said.

Layla seethed. She wanted Maxine dead—more than dead, she wanted the bitch to suffer, to be tortured until there was nothing left of her to torture, and then she wanted the bitch dismembered and her body parts scattered everywhere. Layla dried her tears, and now her heart was on fire with rage.

"She murdered our children, Scott! Our fuckin' babies!" Layla cried out.

"And she will pay, but we need to be patient."

Scott felt her rage. Since Bugsy and Maxine came to visit him while he was incarcerated and told him about their affair, he only thought of the day they would both die by his hands. But he couldn't rush to kill anyone—not yet, only when the time was right. And he needed Layla on board to help pull it off.

"I have a plan," said Scott.

Layla was listening. If Scott wanted her to agree to Bugsy, then he had to agree to Lucky. Walking back to where they came from, they discussed whether they should sanction the murders of Bugsy and Lucky like they were at a boardroom table. If so, they had to worry about Meyer, knowing how close he was to his siblings. Would he want to retaliate?

"If we do this, then we need to make the murders appear to come from an enemy. Tear a page from Maxine's playbook. We can't get our hands dirty. For now, we don't mumble a fuckin' thing to anyone—no one! We play things cool and enjoy being home for a moment," Scott proclaimed.

Layla was listening. She wanted him to keep talking. This was the Scott she fell in love with—smart, violent, and devious.

DON'T CALL IT A COMEBACK.